Incomparable Sweetness

His eyes were gray fire. With a groan, he lowered his head, taking her mouth with his. When he lowered her to the bed, Rachel tried to sit up, tried to say no, but his hands on her breasts woke sweet wildness within her, a burning urgency. . . .

Sensuous Longing

She helped him thrust her clothes aside, engulfed by the rising tide of savage need that swelled and surged, built to unbearable heights, then crested and broke in great waves of delight. She sobbed and laughed and clung to him, the frozen armor of her body shattered. . . .

Exquisite Surrender

She didn't know what would happen now, couldn't think of Harry, her marriage, anything. She only knew she had been dead and was alive again!

Books by Jeanne Williams

Bride of Thunder
A Lady Bought with Rifles
A Woman Clothed in Sun

Published by POCKET BOOKS

A Woman Clothed In Sun

JEANNE WILLIAMS

PUBLISHED BY POCKET BOOKS NEW YORK

POCKET BOOKS, a Simon & Schuster division of
GULF & WESTERN CORPORATION
1230 Avenue of the Americas, New York, N.Y. 10020

For Annette

*Beloved friend, who first took me to
Caddo Lake and introduced me to her
hometown of Jefferson*

Acknowledgments

To those who shared with me their love and knowledge of East Texas and the Big Bend, my debt is great. Annette Singleton Krenek, originally of Jefferson, but now of Bryan, Texas, first took me to her hometown and to Caddo, introducing me to many gracious people, of whom, because of special assistance and information, I would mention Mrs. James Hale and Mr. and Mrs. Marvin Singleton. Also, David Robertson, sponsor of the Jefferson Junior Historical Society, gave invaluable advice. To anyone who wants a glimpse of the Old South at its most charming and nostalgic, I recommend a trip to that most historic little town and its superb Excelsior Hotel.

The Big Bend, my favorite wild country, can't be separated from the friends who camped with me along the Rio Grande; June and John Wylie and Pete Williams, all of Austin, Texas.

Books that were particularly helpful were *A History of Jefferson* by Mrs. Arch McKay and Mrs. H. A. Spellings (no publisher or date, pamphlet); *Early Texas Homes* by Dorothy Bracken and Maurine Redway, Southern Methodist University Press, Dallas, Tex., 1956; *Baronial Forts of the Big Bend* by Leavitt Corning, Jr., Trinity University Press, San Antonio, Tex., 1967; *The Big Bend Country* by Virginia Madison, University of New Mexico Press, Albuquerque, N.M., 1955; *The Big Bend* by Ronnie C. Tyler, Superintendent of Documents, Government Printing Office, Washington, D.C., 1975; *Pioneer Surveyor, Frontier Lawyer: the Personal Narrative of O. W. Williams, 1877-1902,* University of Texas at El Paso Press, El Paso, Tex., 1966, edited by S. D. Myres.

And always and ever thanks to my daughter, Kristin, for tolerance and critical reading; Leila Madeheim for typing and catching slips; Claire Smith for being friend as well as agent; and Pat Soliman for graceful editing.

Jeanne Williams
Tucson, Arizona
February 23, 1977

I

The woods around Caddo Lake were always beautiful. In summer they were lush with blackberries and blueberries, orchids in mucky backwaters, jasmine, honeysuckle, a profusion of ferns, trees from yaupon and willow to maple, hickory and oak with a towering roof of magnolia, beech and pine. In autumn, black gum turned dark wine red while sweet gum flushed yellow and scarlet, glorious when sun glistened on morning frost. Dogwood took on red berries and leaves while cypress bore violet buds, very tiny, and dark red-brown balls. As winter deepened the woods cloaked themselves in Spanish moss to slumber until spring when fresh green burst out.

April was Rachel's favorite time and she always breathed in its mingled odors with abandoned pleasure. She had been born in April seventeen years ago, and it seemed to her the natural start of the year anyway, with dogwood still snowily in bloom and redbud glowing bright pink. Velvety white magnolia flowers shone against polished jade leaves and wild orchids, pink, red, white and yellow, enchanted shady depths. Blackberries bore white flowers where bees hummed in bliss. Even the forest floor was colored with bright toadstools. Mayhaws were ripening as the promise of summer blossomed everywhere, and neither heat nor scent were yet oppressive.

It was April when Etienne, while they were picking mayhaws, put one of the ripest reddest fruits in her mouth. Laughing, she closed her eyes to savor the sweet tangy juice, wondering why he didn't tease her, and looked up to find a strange, almost fierce expression on his face. His dark eyes glowed like those of an animal in the woods. His arms closed strongly about her, and they merged, the tingling in her blood responding irresistibly to the same longing in him.

Delightful weakness dizzied her as it had the evening she drank too much of her father's blackberry cordial. Etienne stroked her face and throat with strong slim fingers. She wanted his touch, his caressing, longed to feel it all over, and trembled when his hands lightly brushed her breasts and found the drawstring of her blouse. He gently smoothed and stroked until she pressed hungrily against him and he bowed his head to kiss and taste.

Sweeter than fresh-picked fruit, the blossoms around them, the sun-warmed grass where they lay down, where she marveled at his golden body, his lean young hardness. He *was* beautiful! The friend she'd known from childhood, her only friend, was suddenly a lover like those she'd read about and dreamed over. *His mouth is most sweet. He is altogether lovely. This is my beloved, and this is my friend . . .*

Solomon's Song echoed in her mind till thoughts drowned in wondrous delight. He made her feel like an opening flower, as if warm honey filled her, spreading into her loins, luring him. Something warm and tender, exquisitely sensitive, alive, touching her where no one ever had. She pressed for it, then gasped at the pain, but Etienne was beyond her now, past hearing.

She thought she would scream at the raw hurt as he lunged and quivered, but there was something awesome, breathtaking in his absorption, like a storm on the broad water that bent the cypresses and churned the waves to overwhelming force. She accepted him as she would a storm, enduring his wildness as a last cresting surge made him groan and convulse.

Deep within she felt a slow pulsing fountain, could almost *hear* it with the secret parts of her body. He collapsed on her, his lips against her throat, and was so still she grew fearful.

"Etienne?"

He didn't answer.

She gave him a shake. "Etienne! Are—are you all right?"

He raised himself on one elbow and gazed down at her, his face no longer that of a stranger but of her lifelong companion. She realized with a shock that his eyes were moist. Etienne never cried! And she, in imitation of him, seldom did, though she felt like it now.

"Are you hurt?" she demanded.

She had seen red wolves mating once, had one autumn come upon deer in a clearing, and the pairings of Etienne's hounds were frequent, so she understood the essence of what had happened. But perhaps it was different with men? Made them sick for a while, or sad? Then she wouldn't want it, even if the dull ache between her thighs would happen only this first time.

Cupping her face in his hands, he said huskily, "I hurt you, didn't I? Rachel, I'm sorry, I shouldn't—"

"It just hurts the first time, Etienne?" She had learned that from her reading, though she didn't understand why.

"Yes, I guess so—I mean—oh, sacré Dieu, my angel love! It's not just the hurt." He scowled, black brows drawing together above his straight nose, and she exulted in how handsome he was, with his cleft chin and coloring fresh as a girl's beneath his tan. "Has your father not explained anything?"

Rachel couldn't keep from trilling with laughter. Her father knew the Latin names for every flower and plant in this northeastern part of Texas that bordered on Louisiana, just as he knew the names of all the Roman Emperors and could recite most of Chaucer in rippling old English—those had been Rachel's lullabies, had soothed her childish nightmares and rare fevers, Papa's gentle hand and deep beautiful voice. But he knew almost nothing about women.

Five years ago she thought she was bleeding to death; only then had Bradford Delys roused from his plants and books long enough to tell her awkwardly that it was nature, that the flux would stop but come each month until—

"Will I have a baby now?" she asked her lover.

Etienne shook his head in dismay, but at least there was a softness to his smile and he didn't look quite so troubled.

"Not likely, little one. Not from this once. And it won't happen again till we are properly wedded. I shall speak to your father today."

Wedded?

Rachel lay very still. Thoughts, impressions, half-drawn conclusions came together, forming one deep-rooted resolve. It was so strong it never occurred to her to question it.

"I'm not going to marry, Etienne."

After a moment's astonishment, his frown took on a look of anger, and a note of hauteur chilled his tone. "Is it because I'm poor, or because I'm Cajun, or because old Matt Bourne never married my grandmother and my mother was born illegitimate in the house where you live?"

Would that festering wound never heal? One of Rachel's first memories was of a dark boy older than she coming out of the woods near Tristesse with his hounds. Rachel thought the hounds beautiful with their golden eyes and smiling tongues, and the boy had watched her gravely as she petted and crooned over them. He spoke to her in an odd kind of French. She answered him carefully, for French was not her best lesson, and she didn't want the splendid stranger to think her stupid. Papa had taught her to answer in whatever language she was addressed, Latin, French or English.

The boy had become more friendly then. He'd offered her chewy hardened sap from a sweet gum tree, and switching into English, he'd showed her a tiny plant with a tubular blue flower, poor-man's weather-glass, which opened in sunshine but closed when bad weather was coming. She had insisted he show Papa, who, as a botanist, was delighted to discover what he called *Anagallis arvensis*. This led to Etienne's staying to share vegetable soup, deliciously flavored with herbs.

After supper, Papa had read Mr. Longfellow's long poem about the Acadians, *Evangeline,* which told how one of the separated French Catholic lovers had been sent to Louisiana, as Etienne's forebears had also been. "Cajuns have a proud history," Papa told

Etienne. "They were loyal to faith and country and would not renounce either."

Next day Etienne brought several huge catfish to Tristesse, and the day after that a large plump gray squirrel felled by his slingshot, which he began to teach Rachel to use.

Fish and meat were thus added to the Delys table, and by the time she was nine Rachel was a canny fisher and an expert with the slingshot. She could even handle the pistol that was Etienne's pride, a heritage from his father, who'd drowned in a storm when Etienne was three. His mother had yielded to the ague that winter, and since then Etienne had lived with his grandmother's sister, his great aunt, miles back down the bayou through sloughs and brakes.

He thought of Tristesse as rightfully his, and early on told Rachel about his beautiful grandmother, Désirée, with whom old Matt Bourne had lived when he was young, when he first came to this country, which had been the Neutral Ground until 1821. Formed after the Louisiana Purchase when the United States and Spain could not agree on the boundary between Louisiana and what was now Texas, this land that stretched from the Sabine River to Arroyo Hondo was not open to settlers from either country. It had become the refuge of thieves, gamblers and outlaws, so dangerous to travelers that Spain and the United States had sent joint military expeditions against the brigands inhabiting the wild woods and swamps.

After the United States acquired the disputed territory, Matthew Bourne came out from Kentucky to establish a plantation, refusing the Mexican government's offer of a league of land to settlers, for he would not even nominally exchange his Presbyterian faith for the Catholic. Religious scruples did not, however, prevent his living with Désirée in the house his slaves built from virgin timber and bricks they'd molded and baked.

Matthew had met Désirée in New Orleans, abducted her from a much older protector, and allowed her to bring along her younger sister, Aurore. Though he loved her, marriage was out of the question, for mixed with her Cajun blood was an eighth portion of black.

She was pregnant when he began courting the daughter of a Nacogdoches family and started building another larger, finer home some miles from the lake which Désirée so loved. He married the Nacogdoches heiress and settled her at the house called Gloryoak, intending to support Désirée and continue to visit her at Tristesse.

She couldn't accept this. As soon as her child was born, she hanged herself from one of the hand-hewn beams in the basement. Matthew found her there. Furious with her, and torn with guilt and grief, he buried Désirée on a knoll above the house and found a wet nurse for his infant daughter, whom he could not bear to touch. As soon as the baby was weaned, its aunt, sixteen-year-old Aurore, told Bourne she was marrying and taking her small niece with her.

Bourne was probably relieved. He gave Aurore and her husband a comfortable sum, closed up Tristesse, and devoted himself to Gloryoak and his properly sanctioned family. Later he was thrown from his horse and died when his oldest son, Harry, was still a boy and his youngest, Tom, only a few weeks old.

It was Harry who had given Bradford Delys permission to live at abandoned Tristesse in return for tutoring his younger brothers. A kindly man who respected learning, Harry had let the Delyses stay long after his brothers were past lessons. Rachel had never met any of the Bournes, but she knew the middle son,

Matthew, was with the army in the west and Tom, the youngest, was a roisterer who plagued and perplexed his quiet brother-guardian.

Etienne, too, had never met his half-uncles. Aurore had told Matthew to leave her and his daughter, Amie, alone, and when Harry, taking up his considered duties, had penetrated into the swamp to see if his half-sister needed anything, Aurore, widowed but ferociously independent, had not let him on the stoop of her neat little house. It was possible the Bournes didn't even know of Etienne's existence, or that his mother, Amie, was dead.

He sat up now and regarded Rachel proudly, a few leaves lingering in his wavy black hair. "Answer, Rachel. Why won't you marry me?"

God help her, she'd hurt his pride! It would be difficult to soothe him now. Maybe if she tried to make him laugh—

Planting her finger between his eyebrows, kneading his scowl, she said gaily, "I could say both of us are too young and that would be true. But," she added laughing, "I wouldn't marry you, 'Tienne, if we had wrinkles and white hair."

He caught her teasing hand. "Because I have a drop of black blood? Is that what you mean?"

"Certainly not that! If someone's worthy of love, they're worthy of marriage."

"But you just said—"

She laid her finger on his lips. "That's for people who marry. I shall never marry anyone."

If at first he'd been baffled and hurt, now he was dumbfounded. He started to speak several times. "But of course you will," he blurted. "All women do, at least the pretty ones."

"I won't."

With a sigh of self-reproach he gathered her in his

arms and stroked her as he would soothe a nervous animal. "My love, was it so cruel for you? I should have been gentler. Name of God, I shouldn't have had you at all till a priest blessed us!"

She pulled away, impatiently trying to make him understand how she felt. He listened, restlessly humoring her, as she shared her observations about the lot of a woman who became a man's and had his children, the seeds of other things that might be stifled by being a wife and mother. Etienne's grandmother, Désirée. Her own mother dying in childbirth.

"What would you think of a man," she probed impishly, "who listed his occupations as husband and father?"

"But that's different!" Etienne burst out. "A woman *must* look after babies and young children."

"I know. So for years she has one baby after another, making her heavy and awkward, and by the time they're old enough to do without her, it's too late for her to do much but help raise her grandchildren."

"I can't see what's wrong with that."

"Mule! Nothing, if that's what she wants. But I don't want it!"

His eyes widened with horror. "You mean to be a nun?"

"No, 'Tienne!" Why was he so determined not to understand? She brought his hand to her breast and smiled. "We will love each other, and each time it will be better, but I *won't* marry you and have a baby."

He looked as if the world had turned over on him. "You—you're not supposed to talk like this, Rachel! That's the way men think. Women want to marry. And have babies."

"I don't." She leaned forward and kissed him. "Don't growl. Touch me. Make me feel nice. And I'll —do you like that?"

His answer was to hold her closer. For a long time they discovered and admired and pleasured each other, but he didn't enter her again.

"I must talk to your father," he said stubbornly. "I want to marry you, *cherie,* to take care of you. You're not like—"

He stopped. She felt a swift stab of jealousy. "Don't go to other girls," she commanded. "Come to me."

"You're crazy, Rachel!" Gripping her shoulders, he gave her a shake. "If you had a baby—"

"There must be some way not to."

"Yes. Keeping away from men."

"No. There must be some pattern, like monthly courses. I'll ask Papa."

Etienne choked. "Even if he knew, do you think he'd tell you? And suppose he thought I'd seduced you and killed me before I could explain you're the one who won't be honorably married?"

"Papa kill anyone?" she laughed. "You know I do the fishing and kill a squirrel sometimes or we'd have no meat except what you bring. Anyway, I shall tell Papa exactly how I feel. He'll understand."

"That's more than I do." Etienne watched her sullenly as she slipped into her clothes. "If a woman—a decent woman—doesn't intend to marry, she must remain a virgin."

"Who says?"

"Why—why, the Church, God, everybody! And so will your father. You'll see."

"Yes, so I shall." She straightened her shoulders and lifted her chin determinedly. "Will you have supper with us, Etienne?"

"Not if you're going to talk about this!" At her laughter he caught her wrists and said grimly, "Your father will tell you how it is in the world, and what you should do, which is marry me. When he's made that clear, I'll gladly speak with him."

"Don't worry," she said, keeping her face straight with great effort. "I'll tell him you were intent on righteousness, duty and a large family but I objected. He won't blame you."

"No, I don't think he will," agreed Etienne. "After all, he knows you. He must accept some responsibility for letting you grow up with such mad notions! All that Latin and Greek!"

"French, too," she added mischievously. "The French are supposed to be the greatest lovers of all, aren't they?"

His jaw set. "You'll change your mind," he said. He wouldn't kiss her again, but pulled her to her feet and walked her to where Tristesse showed white through trailing vines and Spanish moss. "Your father will tell you what you must do," he said. "I'll come tomorrow and we'll make plans."

She gave him a look of vexed amusement and crossed the thick grass to the old house. Tristesse had a mellow graciousness that made Rachel think the happiness of Matthew and Désirée had outweighed that last terrible act. But there was sadness in the place, too, in its shabbiness, the need for whitewash and repair. During the time it had sat empty, all the movable furnishings and housekeeping goods had been pilfered so the rooms Rachel and her father used were furnished with crude benches and small, rough tables. The draperies and rugs had been carted off, too, but that made the floors easier to sweep and scrub and let in more light. Most of the rooms were never used. Rachel and her father each had a bedroom, and the dining room was where he had his desk and books and where she read or mended or sewed, though she spent much of her time in the big kitchen. There was a rocking chair by the hearth where her father often sat and read to her while she cooked or baked, and it was the warmest room, so during the coldest months they often sat there instead of in the dining room. Every room had a fireplace, but Papa had never learned to handle an axe or saw and Rachel didn't like to overburden Etienne with keeping the woodpile stacked high.

The wilderness had grown up to the house, softening the peeling whitewash with ivy and honeysuckle and jasmine. Holly and yaupon thrust up beneath maples and oaks in a green leafy march on the clearing which had already overwhelmed the stables and outbuildings. The only place where Rachel contended for the soil was the garden, fenced off from old Bess, their mare, and the cow, Mollie. Tomatoes, cabbage, lettuce, green beans, carrots, okra, sweet potatoes, onions and peas grew in the small patch. There were hills of cucumbers, squash and watermelons. They were already having lettuce, and in a few more weeks there'd be new potatoes the size of marbles to cream with tiny peas. In the summer they ate mostly from the garden, supplementing their diet with fish from the lake. The woods yielded a fall harvest of persimmons and hickory nuts, and berries and mayhaws in the spring and summer.

Papa's one practical talent was making excellent wine from dandelions, blackberries, blueberries and tangy wild grapes. He traded this to Tante Aurore for ham and side meat. Since Tante kept pigs and chickens, she had enough fat to make soap. Every spring, during the waning moon so that the mixture wouldn't boil over so rapidly, Rachel spent the day with her, carrying water to the ash-filled V-shaped hopper through which water leaked to drip strong alkali liquid into the wood trough below. When Tante could float an egg on the surface of the brown fluid, it was strong enough to pour over the grease and boil in the big black iron kettle till it was stringy. This soft soap was hardened into cakes by adding salt and pouring the mass into wooden molds. Rachel added dry rose petals or rosemary or lemon balm to the boiling mass to make a sweet scent.

Tante was a dour wizened little woman who focused her affections on successive generations of calico cats. Etienne was used to her, but they were together by accident, not by love. Rachel sometimes wondered what people outside were like.

Two or three times a year she rode pillion behind Papa to the town of Jefferson, thirty miles away, and they bought salt, thread, needles, an occasional pair of shoes, the few things they needed that couldn't be homemade or improvised and a book or two for Papa. His periodicals and journals arrived sporadically in town, and he picked these up on his tutoring excursions as the trips were not, for him, the events they were for Rachel. She would be nervous about the curious, disapproving glances of women they saw, and even more disturbed by the way some men watched her, a sort of greed in their eyes that made her think of one of Tante's cats stalking a bird. She was always glad to get home and to be back in her own world, the woods and lake and bayous, Papa and Etienne.

But Etienne was changing. And perhaps she was, too, for when she started to ask Papa about not having babies, blood rushed to her face, her tongue went clumsy, and she ended up asking if he wanted a cup of lemon verbena tea.

Etienne loved her through April and May and early June, through dogwood and redwood, bluebonnet, paintbrush, the time of lilies, swamp mallow primroses and mistflowers. Fruit was setting, the air hummed with bees, birds fed their gaping young, and the fullness of life and the season was everywhere. But Etienne wasn't happy. He would try not to take her in his arms, staying away for days or a week, but when he came, if they were alone, the sweet wild hunger between them could not be subdued.

"I'm going to speak to your father," he said one afternoon. His long dark eyelashes lay on his smooth cheek; he looked so young and beautiful in his exhaustion that it stabbed Rachel.

"Please, Etienne," she coaxed, stroking back his tangled hair. "Be happy—"

"Happy?" He raised himself fiercely on one shoulder, watching her with such anger that she shrank from him. "Are you happy?" he demanded, gripping her wrists.

"Y—yes, when you're not—not like this. Oh, Etienne, can't we just love each other and go on as we are?"

"No, I'm not staying here."

She stared at him in shock. Oh, he had sometimes mentioned going to New Orleans but she had thought it was passing restlessness. He was part of the bayou. She couldn't imagine him anywhere else, couldn't imagine loving him anywhere else, out in the world of people where eyes would fix on them as did those of the people in town, prying, questioning, surmising. Even if they *were* married she'd hate having strangers know they made love, perhaps imagining the way it was. She felt soiled at the very thought.

"Don't look like that!" he said impatiently when she did not respond. "I'm going away. I've told you so. I wouldn't have stayed this long if it hadn't been for you."

If it hadn't been for you.

Those fatal, blaming words threaded through most human loves, attempting to forge bonds almost as threatening as those of marriage. Rachel controlled denials and accusations, keeping her spirit smooth and still to elude the chains that might catch and hold onto an angry phrase, an edge of guilt.

"Maybe you'll come back," she said. "In a year or two. And I'll be here for you, Etienne."

His jaw hardened. "It'll take more than a few years to do what I mean to. I'm going to be rich and show those high-nosed uncles of mine. I won't come back till I can buy Tristesse and make it grander than Gloryoak." When she said nothing he gave her a shake. "You think I can't do it. That's why you won't marry me! You think I'm just swamp Cajun and won't amount to anything."

"I never thought about any of that, Etienne. I'm sure you can do whatever you want if you put your mind to it."

"You'd marry me if I owned Gloryoak."

"No, I wouldn't!" Her temper was rising in spite of her resolve. "I don't want to marry at all, but I certainly wouldn't marry a rich man! He'd think he owned me! So if you mean to be wealthy, you really do need a different woman!"

She tried to rise, but he swept her against him. "I want you, Rachel. You're part of me. So you have to come."

"You're part of me," she said, trying to smile. "So you have to stay."

His mouth was cruel. For the first time, he forced her down, took her without the eager response. When he convulsed and groaned, leaving her body, she disengaged herself from his lax arms, a coldness in her like frost as she got to her feet, brushing the leaves and twigs from her hair and garments.

His eyes opened. He lay as if wounded, somberly watching her. He sighed as she turned to go. "I'm sorry, little one. But when you won't understand, it's as if my hand refused to do what I willed."

"I'm not your hand, 'Tienne." Though he had overpowered her, she felt more sorrow for him now than anger, but the strange chill kept her from touching him. " 'If thy right hand offend thee, cut it off and cast it from thee,' " she quoted. "And if you go away, that's what you must do with me."

They had never quarreled before. It made Rachel miserable. She was wretched, too, because the cold feeling persisted, a sort of icy shield, and she hated to feel that way toward Etienne. Early next morning she took her pirogue between the twin cypresses that guarded the slough with its shaky pier. An anhinga sunned its turkeylike feathers as it perched on an upthrust cypress knee, a Lord-God bird drummed on a dead tree, and she caught a glimpse of its red crest and black wings. A blue heron speared a fish and, from a low-lying bough, a whole row of turtles dropped into the water at her approach. But this was not one of those mornings when she would drift for hours, watching her fellow creatures of the lake.

She had never taken a bird for food, not even a duck, and she suspected the time was coming when Papa would have to do without the squirrels and rabbits she got with her slingshot. She found it increasingly difficult to ignore the change of a fleet furry body to a lump of stewing flesh, to know she had caused bright eyes to glaze against the leaves and sky, ended the rapid marvel of a beating heart. Poor Papa! It was going to be fish for him, though at least there was Tante's ham and sidemeat.

What would Tante think of her nephew's ambition?

Would she miss him? Rachel tried to picture life without her companion, found it as impossible as summoning up a vision of life in a city, or life anywhere else. She was sure Etienne meant what he said. He would be going.

Rachel rowed for the broad water, the vast untroubled expanse of the lake where only an occasional cypress island hinted this was not a sea. She watched the luminous sunshine on the water, took in her oar and drifted, eased by the current toward what was called the Oxbow, till she was calm and unified within herself again, ready to send the pirogue back through the twin cypresses.

How could Etienne want to leave? What would the city and wealth give him to match this? Even if he went, surely it wouldn't take him long to discover the ground of his being was here.

Papa wandered in while she was making corn bread and mixed greens for lunch. He expounded on the oil refinery being built at Titusville, Pennsylvania, where the first American oil wells had been drilled the year before in 1859, speculating on a time when petroleum would be used to power machinery instead of simply replacing whale oil for lighting.

"You smile at my fancies." Bradford Delys' fine gray eyes were framed in crow's-feet that came from laughter as he glanced keenly at his daughter. She thought fondly that he was very like Chaucer's clerk who would rather have by his bed books of Aristotle than the richest of robes.

"As Darwin says," Bradford continued, "man is the descendant of a hairy quadruped, furnished with a tail and pointed ears, probably arboreal in its habits, but he is a good deal more. He has a hand adapted to making and using tools. Through language, he can share and pass on knowledge. It's a miracle, my child!

Those who live now profit from discoveries made in the caves. We can know Chaucer and Shakespeare, Sappho and Plato and Homer, have them on the shelf along with the latest work of Dickens, Tennyson, Emerson, Thackeray, the Brontës and Sand. Man will run engines with petroleum, and one day he will harness the power of the sun." With a comic look of consternation, he leaped to his feet. "Meanwhile, the wood box is empty!"

He returned with an armload of wood and dusted off his frayed black coat.

"My dear," he said, angling his balding head to one side as he did when perplexed. "I was visited this morning by young Etienne, who has asked me to intercede for him. He says you have repeatedly refused his offer of marriage."

"He did?" Rachel was indignant. "Well, that's true."

Her father continued to watch her. "But I thought you were exceedingly fond of him, Rachel? You've been inseparable since you were children. It seems you've inspired him to want to better himself."

"Is that what he calls it?" Rachel asked grimly.

Bradford sighed. "I'm still thinking of you as a child, I'm afraid. Etienne made me realize how selfish I've been. You have my blessing, Rachel."

"But I don't want it!" *Why* would no one believe she didn't need a husband? Was she mad or were they?

Her father blinked. "You don't love him? He led me to believe that you did."

"Of course I love him, Papa. But—" she broke off, exasperated. How could she make him understand? "Do you remember the huntress in Chaucer, where she speaks to Diana?

'I am, thou woost, yet of thy companye,
A mayde, and love hunting and venerye,
And for to walken in the wodes wilde,
And noght to been a wyf, and be with childe.'

"That's it, Papa! I want to walk in the woods, free
and strong. I don't want to keep house all day and
have babies."

"But my dear! You're fated to be a woman."

"A woman doesn't have to marry."

Bradford watched her with furrowed brows.

"You've always been my delight, sharing my books
and thoughts. Rachel, I shall be wretched if I've made
you unsuited for a happy life in your own home."

"Papa, I'm happy as I am."

"Maybe you need to meet someone different. Like
Harry Bourne, who's a gentleman and fond of books
for all he manages Gloryoak. Tom, the young one, is
wild, but my favorite was Matt. If you knew him—"

"Well, he's off with the Army, and even if he
weren't, he wouldn't marry anyone who couldn't flirt
her fan and shine at a ball."

"Matthew's not like that. You have no brothers, no
family. Who will look after you when I die?"

"You'll live for years, Papa! But I shall die of hunger if we don't eat. Would you pour the buttermilk
while I get the corn bread?"

Etienne wasn't so easily diverted. When she refused
again to marry him and go to New Orleans, they had
a furious quarrel.

Her father fell sick the night following their dis-
cussion, shaking with fever and chills. The teas and
remedies Rachel used didn't help, but she was afraid
to leave him to go for a doctor. When Etienne came to
tell her good-bye, she begged him to ride to Jefferson.
That night her father died in her arms, thinking she

was her mother, hours before Etienne hurried back
with Dr. Martin, a plump frizzy-haired English-
educated physician who said he couldn't have helped
her father anyway, and declined payment. He offered
to send out the Presbyterian minister from town, but
Rachel knew Bradford would have considered that an
intrusion.

She and Etienne buried her father on the slope beside her mother and Désirée, the rich black earth a
raw patch that would soon grow grass over like the
mounds next to it, which were overgrown with red
roses. Rachel managed to trail some of the ramblers
over the fresh grave. It was placing the sweetness of
her mother about her father. Only when that was done
could she weep.

Etienne left her by the graves. After sobbing out
her grief, Rachel slept in exhaustion, for she had only
napped during the five nights and four days of Bradford's illness.

She awoke in her own bed and when she sat up,
wondering for a moment why she was still in her dress,
Etienne got up from the window seat and brought her
bread and milk, feeding her and holding the cup to
her lips.

"You're very tired, *cherie*. When you've eaten, you
should bathe, put on your nightdress and sleep again."

"But Etienne, you were leaving!"

He stroked her hair and kissed her eyes. "New Orleans will wait. When you're rested and not quite so
sad, we shall talk."

But no peace came of their talking, though he
waited several days till Rachel was physically restored
before he began to urge her to come with him.

"You can't live here alone," he argued one morning
after breakfast. "And Uncle Harry's bound to ride out

sometime to discuss your tenancy. Will you pay him as Désirée paid his father?"

"From what Papa said about Mr. Harry Bourne, I doubt he'd dream of such a thing," Rachel said in a cold tone that she hoped concealed how much the gibe had hurt. "I—I'm sorry to have kept you from your journey, Etienne. Please don't let me delay you further."

The veins in his temples swelled, and the curve of his nostrils showed pale. "You must come with me, Rachel! Damn you, I can't leave you here alone!"

He pulled her to him, kissed her on the mouth for the first time since her father's death, all gentleness and restraint gone as he tore the gown from her shoulders. Rachel struggled with this strange and terrifying Etienne. She froze along with him at a drawling voice from the door.

"Say, Cajun, if it'll ease your mind before you travel, we can promise this sweet little lady won't be alone. That right, boys?"

II

Gasping, trying to cover herself, Rachel stared from a husky masked yellow-haired young man in the door to a lean dark one behind him and a third whose red beard stuck out from beneath a black cloth mask. He laughed, and even at that distance, she smelled his wine-sour breath.

"Don't let us keep you from your journey, friend!" He lurched forward, grinning at Rachel. " 'Course if you'd like to share this filly once we tame her down, we ain't pigs. You can have her last."

Etienne lunged forward. The redbeard stuck out his foot. As Etienne tripped, the stocky man hit him on the side of the head with a pistol. Etienne cried out, fell limp on the floor. Rachel bent over him, but the lean man dragged her backward while the redbeard grasped her ankles. She wrenched her body with all her might, and sank her teeth into the blond man's hand as he forced her down.

She tasted blood. He swore. A blow to the head dazed her. She dimly felt the brutal suddenness of his thrusting, but her mind had gone hazy. It wasn't true. It wasn't happening . . .

Then a weight rolled off her, the pinioning hands were gone and someone said, "Hey, Tom, this Cajun's dead!"

"And the girl looks close to it. Let's go. I don't like this!"

"Ain't had my turn."

"We'll find some live meat. Come on. Sure didn't think I hit that fellow so hard."

"Reckon we should finish the girl? She could describe us some even if we are wearing masks."

"She don't look like she'll be describing anything, but if she does, who'll care? Let's get out of here!"

Who'll care? Who'll care? echoed in Rachel's confused mind as boots clumped from the house.

Etienne . . . dead? Head throbbing as she raised herself, Rachel went to Etienne. There was not much blood from the contusion at the back of his head, but there was no flutter of breathing. He lay terribly still. Pressing her ear to his heart, she heard nothing. She touched his hand. It hung limp, the fingers that had loved and comforted her as lifeless as her father's had been.

" 'Tienne! 'Tienne!" she breathed, cradling him against her, oblivious to her own aching violated body. "Please, 'Tienne—"

He could not hear. He could not speak. He would never laugh or love or dream again, never outgrow or fulfill his need to make the Bournes aware and proud of him.

"Who'll care?" The callous words reverberated in her head. She'd make somebody care! She'd carry the body to town and force the sheriff to hunt for the killers. She'd even ride to Gloryoak, if she had to, and ask Harry Bourne to avenge his nephew's death. *He'd* care that a young man was killed for trying to protect a woman.

She washed quickly, biting her lip as she cleansed herself of the blond man's savagery, welcoming the pain as a sort of cauterization.

Old Bess, as usual, was grazing near the house. Rachel saddled her and brought her to the back stairs, as near as possible to the kitchen. At first she tried to hoist Etienne on her back but though he was lean as a young hound, he was tall and his weight was more than she could manage. Getting a quilt, she rolled him on to it, pulled him through the kitchen and porch and onto the steps. At first she tried to handle him gently but in the end she had to drag and haul to get him across the saddle. Bess, at least, showed none of a horse's reputed fear of a dead body, but stood patiently while Rachel settled Etienne face down across the saddle. Mounting so the body rested over her knees, Rachel started for town.

It was drowsy early afternoon when she rode down Austin Street past several saloons and Freeman Hall which had served as a courthouse since Marion County was formed that year. She used the hickory switch she had broken off to keep Bess moving. There were few people about, but by the time she stopped in front of the jail at the end of Austin Street, a small whispering crowd had gathered.

"What's happened, ma'am?" drawled a rangy black-mustached man who appeared in the jailhouse door and wore a sheriff's badge on his vest.

She told him, describing the murderers but not admitting that one had ravished her. The sheriff came to examine Etienne, grunted as he glanced up from scrutinizing the wound.

"Well, he's dead, all right, and it looks like that blow on the head did it. But if you didn't know the men or have any witnesses, there's not much to go on, Miss—who'd you say you are?"

"I'm Rachel Delys."

"Oh. The tutor's daughter. Died last week, didn't he?"

"Yes."

The sheriff's black eyes touched her with more interest. "I'm mighty sorry, and sorry your—friend here is dead. Want I should get the undertaker for you?"

"No! I want you to find the killers and I want to see them tried!"

The growing knot of spectators was pressing closer. "Now, folks, go along with your business and let me take care of mine," the sheriff urged. "Step back there, please!"

As the bystanders retreated, the sheriff spoke in a softly confidential tone. "You're a mighty fetching woman, Miss Delys. Easy to see how young sprouts could fall out over you, and accidents do happen."

Rachel couldn't believe her ears. "They entered my home without knocking and were—impudent to me though they'd never seen me before! There's no way you can make this into a light-hearted frolic that turned deadly, sheriff. Those three were drunk and set on trouble!"

"That's your side of it, Miss Delys." His stare raked her in an appraising way that brought blood to her face. "But there's no names, and I'm tellin' you, as if you was my own daughter, to stop and think this through. Even if I chase down three men answering your description, it's going to be your word against theirs. Lots of ugliness. Won't do your reputation no good." He rested his hand on the back of the saddle, his hairy arm brushing against her. "I'd like to help you, seein' as how you're alone. Let me get the undertaker, and then I'll see you home."

He could say that, standing only a few feet away from Etienne's drooping body. And his eyes, his manner, spoke more than words. Blinding white fury exploded in her. She slashed the green hickory switch fiercely across his smile.

"Why, you damn vixen!" A weal stood out along his cheek. He grasped her wrist, set his other arm about her waist, wrenching her from the saddle. Etienne's corpse spilled to the street. Rachel screamed at that, blindly fighting strange grappling male hands for the second time that day.

"Carey! What is this?"

The deep cultured voice made the sheriff's hands fall as if he'd been scalded. Shuddering, Rachel gripped the saddle horn and looked into thoughtful hazel eyes in a face that bore small humor lines, though it was now grim and hard-jawed. But what she blessed him for, and what was characteristic of Harry Bourne, was that he knelt in the dust to lift the body of a man he didn't know.

"Selah!" he called.

The tall black seemed to understand what was wanted. He took Etienne effortlessly in his arms and held him while his master bowed to Rachel.

"Will you tell me, madam, how I may be of service?"

His courtesy unnerved her as harshness could not. She tried to speak but words stuck in her throat; she gazed at her rescuer, shaking her head, hoping he wouldn't think she was demented.

Coming to stand by her, he turned to confront the sheriff, who loudly protested, "You must have seen her hit me with that switch, Mr. Bourne. I don't bear her no ill will, broke up as she is about that young feller, but there's no use stormin' at me with a wild story and no names—"

"I'll see you presently, sheriff," cut in the stranger. He offered his hand to Rachel. "May I take you into the inn for some refreshment, ma'am? I assure you that your requirements will be taken care of as speedily as you can apprise me of them."

"Etienne—"

"Your friend is safe with my man. Come, my dear. After your cup of coffee, we'll do everything necessary." He helped her dismount, steadying her in her weariness. She realized as he took her arm in a firm, protective way that Bradford had been a scholar and Etienne a boy, but this was a man. A gentle man.

He grew even gentler when he learned she was the daughter of his brothers' old tutor. "Dr. Martin told me about Bradford's early death," Harry Bourne said as they sat over coffee and small buttered muffins which he spread with marmalade and encouraged her to taste. "I meant to ride out in a week or two and see if you wished to remain, for I knew he had a child." Frankly admiring brown-green eyes studied her. "If I'd understood you were quite alone, Miss Rachel, I would have come at once. It's out of the question, as today's shocking events prove, for a beautiful young woman to live by herself in the bayous."

She hadn't told him, either, that she'd been raped. Pride and a sense of self-protection had kept her from telling Sheriff Carey, but different feelings kept her from revealing it to this quiet, kind man with his old-fashioned gallantry. He would pity her, she was sure, and treat her with unfailing consideration, but she herself would feel ashamed, as if in some way she were to blame for what had happened.

Was she, in fact, to blame? Her earthy common sense recoiled at the notion. Those men were bent on mischief. If her father had been with her, he might have been killed in Etienne's place. Coming in upon Etienne's forceful courtship of her would not have provoked such behavior in decent men. What had happened was the doing of trespassers, rapists, thugs.

She couldn't really, even in her grief, feel guilt for refusing to go to New Orleans with Etienne. A person's choice about his own life couldn't be made by trying to please others. Etienne had the right to ambition and the city, and she had the right to a simple life on the lake.

Those three roistering men had ruined those natural dignities. She didn't want to tell Harry Bourne the extent of that devastation because as long as she didn't put it into words, as long as no one else knew, it seemed less true. It was Rachel's first experience of the power of what other people thought about her, a humbling and humiliating one. Why should she care what Sheriff Carey thought when she had laughed at Etienne's opinions?

"You've described the intruders to the sheriff," Harry said. "I'll talk to him so you needn't distress yourself with repeating the story. But should your young man be buried in town or has he a family that would desire otherwise?"

How strange, how tragic, to tell this man who would surely have aided and befriended his bitter nephew that Etienne was the grandson of Harry's own father, the grandson of lovely Désirée.

"So he wanted to succeed out in the wide world," Harry pondered after his first startled exclamations and questions. "And I never even knew he existed! I rode over to locate my half-sister after Father died, see what I could do for her. But she was dead and her aunt, a formidable woman as I recall, didn't even ask me inside. She certainly never mentioned the baby boy."

"Now he's dead, too," said Rachel. "Younger than Désirée or his mother."

Harry sighed. "I must take him to his aunt, I suppose, but if she's willing, he can be buried in the family cemetery."

An ironic way to be acknowledged. Without a tear, Tante Aurore gave her consent, though she would not attend the funeral or accept anything from Harry.

"Etienne didn't belong here anymore," she said with a hard stare at Rachel. "He was set on being rich and having a great name. It should content him best to share dust with that wicked man who ruined and betrayed my sister."

Harry whitened about the lips, but he controlled himself. "Your nephew will be buried with all dignity," he told the stern old woman. "And I beseech you, madam, to call on me if ever I can serve you in any manner."

She gave him an implacable look and vanished inside her weathered gray cottage, so completely surrounded by vines and trees festooned with feathery Spanish moss it was easy to imagine that the wilderness, when Aurore died, would engulf the cottage to give private burial to this woman whose feelings, if she had any, were as hidden and difficult as the swamp's.

Etienne was buried in the Bourne lot, with old Matthew and his legal wife, a few stillborn babies, and several well-loved servants. Rachel felt isolated from it all, removed from this Etienne who had longed for wealth and respectability. The Etienne she loved had been part of her growing up, the wild mysterious beauty of lake and woods. She had lost that boy to the emerging man.

Boy or man, she wanted his death avenged. Harry had broadsheets printed offering a reward for information about the killers, but there had been no response. When Harry took Rachel to town, she watched every youngish man they saw for some hint of gait or gesture that might give him away. She strained to listen to their voices, but she was beginning to think the three were wandering rogues from far away.

After a week passed with no clues, Harry had the sheriff send handbills to every town and settlement in northeast Texas and western Louisiana. He counselled Rachel to be patient, that sooner or later such riffraff would boast of the murder to someone who would turn them in for money. As days passed, Rachel grew to accept that the criminals might not quickly, if ever, be brought to trial. In the meantime, she must decide where to live. Bradford had left his books and a few dollars. Bess and the cow would fetch a small sum. But then what?

Panic clutched at Rachel as she faced her situation, penniless, without family or friends except for Harry, upon whom she could not continue to impose. She had no service to offer him in exchange for rent at Tristesse, but she might find a small hut or get one built in exchange for the cow and horse. She could raise most of her food and get the rest from the lake and woods, and she might sell enough hickory nuts and mayhaws and berries for the few things she'd have to get in town.

But it wouldn't be the same. Not ever.

Etienne would laugh and love with her no more. Father would not look up from his books to read a paragraph, snort with disgust or nod with approval,

and ask what she thought. Most chilling of all, now
that she knew how men could force themselves into
her home and into her body, she would never "walken
in the wodes wilde" with the same gay confidence.
She was not the same. She never could be again. This
time she was afraid to live alone in the back country,
even if she'd had the means.

If only Papa had left her enough to live on for a
while! This lamentation ceased with the dazzling recognition that he had supplied her with something far
better than money. He'd given her an exceptional
education! She, like he, could teach, perhaps in a
school, perhaps at some remote plantation with several
children. Much encouraged by this realization, she rose
from the velvet chaise at the foot of the great four-
poster, where she had been reading and brooding and
went in search of Harry.

Life at Gloryoak was tranquil and well-ordered under the firm hand of Tante Estelle, nurse to all the boys
and now housekeeper, the tiny, golden-skinned woman
whose hair was still coal black. Now in her middle
years, her still seductive figure and slanting tawny eyes
made it seem likely that she'd been more than a
servant to old Matthew, but however that had been
there was great affection between her and Harry. She
had been wonderfully kind to Rachel, doing everything
possible for her comfort, though accepting that she
needed solitude. She'd made it clear that Rachel was
welcome in her sitting room just off the kitchen, where
she planned menus, did accounts, mended Harry's
clothes and sometimes played a graceful rosewood
harp with a mermaid pedestal which Matt and Harry
had given her for Christmas some years ago.

If she loved Harry, she plainly adored Matt. On the
occasions when Rachel joined her for tea, Tante Estelle spoke of Matt wistfully and invariably produced

some letter of his. One of those letters told how an Apache chief, Cochise, had saved him from renegade Indians, and Rachel felt momentarily restless and bored with the tranquility of Gloryoak.

No one seemed to know where Tom, the youngest brother was. From Tante Estelle's expression and the few remarks Harry had let slip, Rachel guessed that Tom was headstrong and addicted to pleasures not easily found in Jefferson. He had studied for a while in Virginia but had last been heard from in New Orleans.

Now, as Rachel inquired for Harry, Tante Estelle said she thought he was in the library. "You look happy, Miss Rachel." Warmly interested honey-colored eyes searched her face. "Go right along to Master Harry while you've got that sparkle. It'll do him a world of good. He's been worried over you."

"I hope I haven't been a burden, Tante Estelle." Rachel looked anxiously at the white-aproned tiny-waisted woman who reached only to her nose. "I wouldn't have stayed so long except . . ."

"Nonsense, child, we need somebody young and pretty around this big old house. And now you've got a smile again—well, you go right along to Master Harry!"

Harry was at his desk in the big room that also served as his office. He rose quickly as she came in, and his eyes lit up at sight of her.

"Why, Miss Rachel!" He came around to take her hands. "You look like a sunrise. And just when I was about to ask Dr. Martin to call on you!"

"I'm sorry to have worried you, sir. You've been very kind. And part of my trouble has been not being able to think of how I could make a living. But I can teach!" At Harry's amazed look, she plunged on. "Papa taught me well, sir. And if you could recommend me to a female institution or perhaps some remote plantation where there are children—"

His long sensitive fingers tightened on hers. The gladness left his face. "Why, Miss Rachel, aren't you comfortable with us?"

"I can never thank you and Tante Estelle enough." Bewildered, for she had certainly not wished to hurt him or seem ungrateful, Rachel floundered helplessly, increasingly aware of his closeness, the strength of his grasp. "But I can't take advantage of your generosity much longer. I thought if you could help me find a place . . ."

"A place!" The words seemed wrung from him. His gaze burned suddenly, frightening her. "Rachel, my dear, have you no idea of the place I long to make for you?"

She stared at him mutely, the eager vulnerability of his usually controlled expression making her understand. Shrinking, feeling trapped and guilty, she hoped he would not go on, but his words came now as if a dam of restraint had burst.

"I love you, Rachel. I've loved you since I saw you in the road, so frightened yet so brave. I knew and esteemed your father, and in you I recognize his qualities of thought and perception. It's early to speak, and I'd think shame of taking advantage of your presence in my home, but when you talk of leaving, you give me no choice. Be my wife, Rachel. Do me that honor."

"Sir, I—I cannot."

He flinched. She echoed the pain in her own flesh. Why did she have to wound this man who had been so wonderfully good to her,

"Why?" he asked after a long moment. "Do you find me distasteful? Too old?"

"Oh, no! If I thought of marriage at all, sir, I can imagine no one with whom I'd more willingly assume that state. But I decided long ago I wasn't suited for that condition."

He relaxed, his smile indulgent. "That's whimsy bred of too much reading, growing up with no female influence, child. You really are, you know, something of a young Amazon! But you must realize that a young woman cannot live alone, and you have no family. The powers of reasoning you inherited from your father will soon bring you to put aside your fancies."

If she'd rejected marriage before, how much more now, since the brutal attack, she detested and feared giving power over her body and life to a man. "No," she said, shaking her head, trying to withdraw her hands. "It's no fancy, Mr. Bourne. If I was of that mind as a child, I am doubly so as a woman."

She gazed up at him, strengthened by resentment of his patronizing attitude. What could he know of being held down, forcibly entered? And if he knew that she'd been raped, his enthusiasm for marriage would doubtless ebb immediately.

"You loved that young man?" Harry asked slowly.

"Yes. Always. Etienne was—he was part of the woods to me, the lake, the bayous."

"But he was going away."

"Yes. And he was angry because I wouldn't marry him."

Harry gave a philosophic sigh. "It gives me hope that you rejected the proposal of someone you loved. At least it proves the notion of marriage is what dismays you, not me as a husband. Shall we let the matter drop for a time?"

"Please, sir, I hope you'll let it drop forever."

"You intend to mourn that boy?"

Stung at that, she tried to free herself. A sound came from Harry's throat. Drawing her to him, he kissed her mouth till she forgot he was Harry, knew only forcing hands gripping her. She writhed in panic, sobbing, gasping, coming back to her senses to find the kiss ended and Harry watching her with horrified shame.

"Forgive me," he muttered. "I have no excuse. I wish you had a brother or father to give me the horse-whipping I deserve for handling you like that."

Her mouth and wrists were bruised but she ached more at his self-contempt. "Please!" she begged. "What I said must seem most ungrateful. I should have spoken with more care."

"Damn it, no!" He thrust his hands behind him. His voice was husky with self-disgust. "That completes my humiliation, Rachel, that you blame yourself for my aggressiveness! Let me offer some amends by providing you with a home."

"I can't impose."

"You call an imposition what is my joy. Stay, Rachel. I swear I'll never touch you again unless you wish it, though that's like saying I'll never drink again or breathe."

Why couldn't she love him? With her old life shattered, with her dread of being preyed upon, wouldn't the splendor of Gloryoak and his protection be better than anything she could hope for?

Even as she pondered that with some detached part of her mind, she knew he'd expect a virgin. She could not cheat him. And beyond that, in spite of the ecstasy and delight she had known with Etienne, her feelings toward sex now were overlaid with revulsion and dread. Hadn't Etienne, just before the three broke in on them, manhandled her? Lust could drive even Harry out of his usual kindness. What had been a natural pleasure once, an innocent and healthy flowering, was tainted now by the terror and outrage of being used, of being violated in spirit and body.

Some of this must have shown in her expression, for Harry took her hands and brought them to his face. "Trust me, Rachel."

But she could comprehend some of the frustration and physical urgency her presence would cause. And he had been so good to her. She wished she were able to give him what he desired. But she also knew, in every fiber of her body, if he raised his mouth from her hands to her lips, if his voice thickened with passion and he brought himself hard and seeking against her, she'd think back to the tearing of her clothes and body and fight like a cornered wild animal.

"I trust you, Mr. Bourne, but it's not fair for me to remain at Gloryoak when I can't offer any hope for what you generously offer."

He laughed, let his long fingers lightly touch her cheek. "While there's life, there's hope. You're very much alive, my dear, though you need time to recover from what you've been through." When she started to object, he assumed the air of assurance typical of a man of his wealth and position. "I was your father's friend. For the sake of that friendship, stay on at Gloryoak until a suitable alternative develops."

"You'll inquire about positions?"

His eyes danced. "Be sure that I'll be on the watch for back-country planters with huge families to educate or a genteel female academy that doesn't starve its staff. Meanwhile, you could keep in practice by refreshing my Latin and literature. Chaucer was one of your father's favorites, as I recall." He smiled charmingly. "I can promise you'll find me a most receptive pupil."

"You're not just trying to make me feel useful?"

"Rachel, you adorable little puritan! You'll be useful! But I freely confess these elevating studies will be a way to put you at ease about spending time with me, a good deal of time." His eyes twinkled so infectiously she had to laugh, and they went to luncheon in such a mood of gay companionship it was easy to forget those frightening seconds when he'd ceased to be her patient friend and protector.

In the days that followed, Harry seemed to have forgotten, too, though they spent most waking hours together. After a breakfast of ham, grits, eggs, beaten biscuit and muffins with marmalade and butter, they rode, usually to one part or another of the plantation. Gloryoak grew mostly cotton, but there were vast forests of magnolia, pine, oak, cypress, black walnut and hickory which Harry allowed to be felled only with careful selection.

"I fear God too much to end the life of a tree that's been here for hundreds of years," he told Rachel. "If I had come first, Gloryoak would not be so rich or have so many fields, for I'd never have cleared them. In a way, the ruthlessness of a father can make possible self-righteousness and tender conscience in a son."

She stroked the neck of Lady, the handsome bay mare he had selected for her as both spirited and sweet-tempered. "You'd have had a tender conscience, Harry, whenever or wherever you were born." It had become a game of theirs to toss out quotes for the other to identify. " 'He is gentil that doth gentil dedis.' "

"Chaucer?" guessed Harry as they left woodlands for luxuriant fields of sorghum and corn. Gloryoak had its own sorghum mill and sold what its people didn't use. Except for coffee, tea and spices, virtually all the plantation's food was grown on its rich black loam. Apart from style of serving and preparation, in fact, there was little difference in the food on the Bourne Meissen and the earthenware of the slave quarters past which Harry and Rachel would shortly be riding. "Since you've come, I've remembered much your father taught me," Harry went on. "Without him, I might have had quite different ideas. I had but a glimpse of Virgil," he continued in Latin. "But 'Note too that a faithful study of the liberal arts humanizes character and permits it not to be cruel.' "

"Ovid," smiled Rachel, but grew quiet as she saw small dark children playing around the cabins under the eyes of a few old granny women. "I'm glad you're letting your people buy their freedom, Harry."

"I freed my father's long-time personal servants at his death," said Harry. "I wish I'd freed them all, but these days, with tempers running high over abolition, the most I dare is to give credits beyond food and clothing till a reasonable sum is reached. Most of my hands stay on and draw wages."

Rachel contemplated the children. Those more than seven or eight were working, but there must have been a dozen under that age. "If they're all going to be free, shouldn't they know how to read and write and do simple arithmetic?" she asked.

Harry threw back his head and laughed. "I might as well be hated for making blacks uppity as for freeing them," he said. "By all means, give it a try. And I hope it will content you, madam, to thus earn your place at Gloryoak."

Harry supplied slates, chalk, pencils and foolscap as well as giving Rachel freedom to use books from his library. On a long bottom shelf she had found well-worn children's books, including texts her father must have taught from; spellers, geographies, grammars, written and mental arithmetics and one dog-eared book each on physiology, rhetoric and orthography. She glanced through and discarded everything but the geography and a history of Egypt.

School began in the grape arbor, where a globe hanging near Rachel's chair sometimes swayed in the breeze that rustled the trees around them. Eight boys and girls in spotless, well-worn clothes perched on two benches clutching their slates. Glances that were variously curious, sullen, excited or resigned focused on Rachel.

Was this a mad idea? Would a little learning simply make their lives harder, for even if they became free, many people would still consider them a kind of animal, and uneducated whites would particularly resent a black who could read, write and do sums. They wouldn't be so easy to cheat, for one thing. Rachel seemed to hear her father saying, as he often had, that this was the most common argument against liberty and education, that people were happier without them, but that this nation had been based on the faith that human beings were born equal with certain natural rights. The irony that Jefferson, himself a slaveholder, had framed those lofty words didn't destroy the hope.

"How many of you know the song about Moses and Pharaoh?" she asked. They all did, for meeting was held every Sunday in the small whitewashed church near the commissary, and the singing was loud and lusty. Rachel smiled at the show of hands. "Let's all sing it. Then we're going to find out about the country where Moses grew up."

> When Moses was in Egypt's land—
>   Let my people go!
> Go tell ole Pharaoh, let my people go . . .

They were all swaying by the end of the powerful verses. Rachel's skin prickled. What a song for slaves to know! How could they sing it without wondering when they were going to be free?

Father had believed it must be soon, especially after John Brown's attack last October on Harper's Ferry in Virginia. He'd been hanged in December for treason and criminal conspiracy. Father considered him deranged because of the terrorism he'd fostered in bloodily divided Kansas, but insanity was rampant in national and state legislatures, with South Carolina and Mississippi already voting appropriations for military forces.

"Let my people go . . ."

With the song reverberating on the soft, blossom-scented air, Rachel turned to the globe. "The Bible tells about the rivers of Eden. One of them, the Euphrates, flows into the Persian Gulf here, but it once passed the great city of Ur, where Abraham lived."

"Father Abraham?" called a little girl whose many pigtails were adorned with yellow ribbons.

"Father Abraham," said Rachel. "Now, you know he traveled to the land of Canaan, which is right over here along the Mediterranean. And you know his grandson Jacob had a beloved son Joseph who was sold into Egypt by his jealous brothers. Joseph became a friend and advisor of Pharaoh and his brothers and their families came to live in Egypt, but after many years there were so many Israelites that the Egyptians were afraid of being outnumbered and decided to control them by making them slaves. They worked on the pyramids, the tombs of kings, and raised other buildings from bricks they made of mud and straw. Tomorrow we can make bricks till we have enough to put together a pyramid. Now let's think for a while about Egypt. It was a dry desert country, but it was watered by this big long river, the Nile . . ."

III

The brick-making was done with serious glee, and after rows of one-by-two-inch rectangles were drying in the sun, Rachel drew hieroglyphs of birds, a serpent, a hand, foot and boat, explaining that the Egyptians first drew pictures of things, then developed signs for actions and ideas, and that they had an alphabet of twenty-four consonants.

"They believed writing was a gift of God," she explained, deciding not to complicate matters with Thoth or the deciphering of the Rosetta Stone, which had so enchanted her father. "And the Israelites believed the alphabet was written with a flaming pen around the crown of God," Rachel went on. "So you can understand that learning your alphabet is a wonderful thing. What is in books or on paper will not be a secret to you, and you can keep a record of important things."

Those benefits didn't seem to impress the youngsters, but they zealously copied hieroglyphs on the bits of mud they had patted out and each scratched his or her own name, which Rachel printed first, at the bottom of the glyph.

Next day, when the bricks were dry, they constructed a pyramid and began to learn to count, add and subtract, by piling on more bricks or taking them away. After a while, Rachel made the alphabet with straight lines and circles and printed the words they wanted to copy on their slates. "School" let out at noon, so she finished by gathering the children about her to admire the illustrations in *Aesop's Fables* while she read several of the ancient tales and explained that the stories had been made up or collected long ago by a slave in Greece but could now be enjoyed by people all over the world.

"I still think that was a plumb ign'rant dog who dropped his bone in the water," said bright-eyed Elijah with a squirm.

"Huh!" snorted his sister Lilia, she of the braids and ribbons, "You a fine one to talk! Always thinkin' everyone else got more molasses than you or a bigger hunk of pork!"

Harry strolled up, spoke to most of the children by name and admired the pyramid and glyphs. "I always thought myself lucky in my tutor," he chuckled as he escorted Rachel to the house, carrying her books. "But you'd have made me a scholar, for I'd have studied to exhaustion just to get a smile from you. How in the world did you get those youngsters interested in the pyramids?

"Rivers of Eden," he mused when she'd finished explaining. "Father Abraham. Moses and Pharaoh and sacred writing. What a lot you have stored in that pretty head of yours along with the wit and sympathy to pass it on to these children!"

"Don't tease me, Mr. Bourne, or try to make me feel I'm really paying my keep."

She heard him catch his breath. He caught her arm and swung her about to face him. Since she stood two steps above him she had to look straight into his eyes, green shining with gold. "Pay your keep?" he growled. "Oh, my love, my sweetheart, if you knew—"

"Sir, you promised!"

He bit his lip, glancing away as if the sight of her might undermine his resolve. "I promised," he said. "But it's not breaking my word to say that more and more I stand in awe of you. And we play a game of quotes, don't we? So here is one." Watching her now, he spoke softly, his tone a caress that sent waves of melting sweetness through her, though she stiffened against this treachery. " 'And these were the dishes wherein to me, hunger-starven for thee, they served up the sun and moon.' "

His mouth was close to hers. He had a clean man's smell of shaving lotion, soap, leather and tobacco. It would feel so good to be held in strong arms, cradled against him. But—but that wouldn't be all he'd want and need. She couldn't, must not, take comfort in his strength and warmth when she wouldn't give him what naturally followed.

"I—I don't know that one," she said, turning.

"Augustine's *Confessions*. He tasted all the joys and sins and then became a saint." Harry mocked her gently. "Do you wish to be a saint first, Rachel, before you know what you're renouncing?"

What would he think if he knew Etienne had been her lover? "I shall never be a saint," she tossed over her shoulder. "Are you pleased with those turning plows you bought from Mr. Kelly?"

It developed that he was, and that was their topic

through luncheon, that and the way Jefferson was flourishing from the steamboat trade.

The days went smoothly with little variation except for Sundays, when there was no work or school. Harry had offered to drive Rachel to church but she declined, nor would she accompany him when he went to town on business.

She still dreamed about riding with Etienne's body before her and being treated so callously by the sheriff.

One noon she was astounded to enter her airy chamber and find two gowns spread carefully upon the ruffled counterpane, one of yellow dimity, the other white muslin with blue sash and embroidered roses at neck and hem. Rachel had never seen such pretty things, swallowed as she knew she must refuse them. But she couldn't resist touching them, holding them up before her as she turned to the tall mirror held by laughing bronze nymphs.

The muslin looked especially good with her sun-browned skin and dark hair and eyes. She touched the blue sash yearningly before, with a sigh, she put the dress from her, tidied herself and went to the veranda where, in the shade of the great oak for which the plantation was named, a tempting lunch awaited— ham croquettes, golden corn fritters and huge strawberries in a crystal bowl.

Though Harry rose at once to seat her she didn't take the chair and instead gazed at him in distressed appeal. "The gowns are beautiful, sir, but you know I can't take them!"

"I thought you'd agreed I was to be Harry," he reminded, firmly easing her to the chair and moving it properly forward. "What's this about gowns? I confess you have me at a loss."

"You—you didn't get them?"

"Indeed not, though I approve the gumption of whoever did since you say the gowns are pretty. I'll admit I've wished to see you decked out, but my rueful knowledge of your stiff-neckedness kept me from daring to suggest a small loan."

"But if you didn't—oh, it has to be Tante Estelle!"

Harry chewed tranquilly on a bit of croquette. "Quite likely. And you may command me, Rachel dearest, but you'll waste your breath on Tante. If she thinks you need gowns, then gowns you shall have." He hunched his shoulders defensively. "Don't drag me into it, please."

Rachel looked at him suspiciously, but he began inquiring about the progress of the school, and she was soon absorbed in telling him that Elijah already knew his alphabet, Carrie could count to a hundred, and all eight students could write their names.

After luncheon, Rachel sought Tante Estelle in her private parlor and asked about the dresses. She got an anxious stare in response.

"Oh my gracious! Don't you like them, then, Miss Rachel?"

"I love them! But—well, if Mr. Harry gave you the money to buy them, I still can't take them. And if he didn't, they're much too costly to accept as a gift, though however it happened, I can't tell you how kind you are, how much I appreciate it."

"Appreciate?" scorned Tante darkly. "Don't sound much like it! Two perfectly lovely gowns just needing bad to be showed off and pleasure folks, but our young lady, she's too proud to do that! No matter she worries Master Harry and throws my trouble in my face. None of that matter! She got to be independent and traipse around in worn-out duds that if we had company they'd think Mr. Harry was a miser who grudged you a hunk of bread and sowbelly!"

"Tante!"

"Isn't that it?" demanded the tiny woman merci-lessly, slanting eyes lit for battle. "You studyin' your pride, not how other folks feel." She went on grimly, with great satisfaction. "It so happen that nary a penny of either mine or Mr. Harry's went into those dresses and there's more where they came from so what you got to say to that?"

"I—I don't understand."

"Good! May be hope for you yet if you can admit that," Tante sniffed. "That material had been fetched, with all the trimmings, to make Miss Eleanor's sum-mer things the year she died. She was still mighty young and pretty and in between the children, she had an elegant little waist. There's material for three more everyday dresses and one party gown packed away in the big cedar chest. No use of it staying there another twenty years till it rots."

"But all that sewing, Tante! You must have been working every spare minute."

Tante thrust out her jaw but her voice had a muf-fled quality that stung Rachel into self-reproach. "I pleasured in doing it, child, thinking how nice you'd look, how happy you'd be. Besides, the grannies of those children you're teaching wanted to help with the stitching. I didn't do much."

Completely undone, Rachel knelt and threw her arms around the older woman. "Oh, Tante, you can't imagine how beautiful the dresses are to me, both of them! I never dreamed of having anything so lovely. But I didn't see how I could be more expense to Mr. Harry."

"Well, there wasn't a copper out of his pocket. Go try a gown, honey, and let's see how I guessed your fit." Tante grinned. "There's still all that material to make up."

The dresses fitted exactly, for Tante had an uncanny eye for measurements, and within two weeks, with Rachel helping and her pupils' grandmothers making seams and hems, three more gowns hung in the rosewood armoire, a silvery green muslin, a blue stripe set off by white ruffles and a crisp brown gingham. The sheer voile and lace for the party dress was filmy ecru, and this Tante would not allow anyone but herself to touch.

"No hurry on it," she said. "But when it's time for a party I mean for you to have the most scrumptious gown there."

The end of July came, and with it the humidity and the overpowering richness of summer blooms. Rachel had been over six weeks at Gloryoak, and though she missed the lake and deep woodlands, though this was not the life she would have chosen, she felt safe and often happy with Harry and Tante Estelle, and teaching the children was a constant revelation and challenge. She knew she should prod Harry to find her a school or position but shrank from the prospect of beginning a new life among total strangers.

Though Harry had kept his word and hadn't spoken directly of love, his gaze sometimes rested on her with such longing that Rachel felt herself weakening. But apart from her own fear of marriage, she couldn't give him what he expected and deserved. She would have to leave. Only not yet.

Then Tom, the youngest Bourne, came home, riding up to Gloryoak one twilight with his servant who took the horses on to the stables. Spraddling like someone who'd ridden a long way, the blond young man came up the steps to the veranda, stopping by one of the great cypress pillars to cock his head at Harry and Rachel.

"Behold the prodigal, elder brother!" He peered at

Rachel. Even in the dim light, his eyes showed blue as untroubled summer sky. "Why, Harry, you sly dog! Can it be you've married this enchanting lady while I was too far away to give you competition?"

"Rachel, may I present my brother Thomas?" said Harry. His manner carried reproof. "Tom, Miss Delys is our very honored guest. You will remember her father, your tutor, who passed away several months ago."

The young man's rather stocky well-built frame seemed to stiffen before he came over to Rachel. Bowing very low, he took her hand and kissed it.

"Indeed, Gloryoak is honored by such beauty."

Rachel scarcely heard the veiled mockery in his tone, sat frozen, mind whirling while Tom called for a drink and the brothers exchanged news. The moment Tom touched her, she had known, her flesh had crept at the remembered brutality of those fingers.

He had been the leader of the masked men. He had raped her and killed Etienne. She should scream it out.

And thus repay Harry?

But it was intolerable, unbearable, that the devil should live, swagger past Etienne's grave. She must avenge her love. But how? She knew some poisons but rejected that method along with tampering with his saddle cinch and similar underhanded tricks.

If she were a man, she could duel with him. If? Why not anyway?

Harry wouldn't allow it if he knew. There must be no way for Tom to evade or refuse. If some confused sense of honor prevented his shooting at a woman though he'd had no qualms about rape, that was his bad luck.

Tante, alerted by Selah, who had brought Tom's drink, flurried out now to embrace and pet the youngest Bourne. Another good person who mustn't know of what he was capable. Rachel steeled herself against the pain Harry and Tante Estelle would feel if she succeeded in killing Tom, leaving the body to be discovered, dead by an unknown hand. Such a tragedy could be mourned and endured, but if Harry knew what his brother had done, he might kill him himself, or suffer deep shame.

It was so strange to sit on the veranda beneath the great glory oak and plan to ride after the young man opposite one day soon, invite him into the woods— he'd come, she was sure of that—and then tell him to fight or be shot. There were two sets of handsome dueling pistols in the library, kept in velvet-lined caskets. It shouldn't be difficult to take a pistol, use, clean and put it back before it was missed. And she must do it soon, before fury at Tom's cool assurance, his hypocritical gallantry, drove her into some outburst.

"Lovely ladies shouldn't have thoughts dismal enough to make them frown," Tom was chiding. "Penny for them, Miss Delys?"

"Why, sir," she said, managing a smile though her teeth hurt her lips. "They're worth your life."

"Too high," he laughed. "I must rest content with my drink."

And I with two aims, Rachel thought. *To kill you, handsome young man, as you killed Etienne. And to protect these good people from knowing why you died.*

Though he was overtly flattering at breakfast and luncheon the next day, Tom ripped the veil of pretense that afternoon when he found Rachel alone in the library, where she had gone to examine the pistols. As the door creaked, she moved quickly away from the walnut cabinet where they were kept and was studying the dictionary when Tom came over to her.

"So here you are snug at Gloryoak," he said. "And when you're suitably consoled for the loss of your Cajun sweetheart, no doubt you'll make a very good thing of my noble brother's mooning."

His eyes were so innocently bland she could scarcely credit what he'd said. Burning with hatred, she forged her words slowly. "You aren't pretending, then, that you didn't break in, kill Etienne and—"

"Pursue fair game?" he supplied. "And you're still fair game, Rachel, for you took care not to tell Harry everything that happened. He's besotted, but not to the point of overlooking your rollicks with that Cajun."

"I've refused to marry your brother."

"Extremely clever of you, my dear. You've whetted him to fever pitch. When you at last succumb to his ardor, he'll feel he's won a prize."

"You filthy cur!"

"Perhaps, but I can sniff a hot bitch when I find her. We can deal well together, my pretty, if you'll be obliging. In return, I won't tell Harry about you." Tom laughed uproariously. "Sober old Harry, head over heels and set on marrying you, as he told me at boring length last night. Think of him dazzled by a hussy out of the swamps when he's been chased by every belle in three counties!"

"Tell Harry what you please. I'll not marry him."

Tom's eyes narrowed. "Don't try to gull me," he said coarsely, rounding the table, catching her wrist. "You need some lessons, but with them you'll prove, I'm bound, the juiciest trollop between here and New Orleans."

Dragging her close, he drove his body against her, savaged her mouth with his, probed with his tongue till she choked with revulsion. Her arms were clamped against his chest and her useless struggles to wrest free only made him laugh and thrust his hand into her bodice, roughly stroking her breasts.

Panic drowned her consciousness; she didn't know what was happening till suddenly she was free, thrown off balance by Tom's being hurtled to one side. He fell under Harry's sledging blow, crouched there, moving his head dazedly.

"Are you mad?" Harry panted.

Tom lunged up, putting the table between them. Blood trickled from his mouth, and he spat out a piece of tooth on the Aubusson carpet. "Not as mad as you, dear brother. I've the wit to know a whore."

Harry flushed crimson, then went white. "I'd kill you for that," he said, "if I hadn't been your guardian since Father died and must therefore hold myself somewhat accountable for your behavior. You'll apologize to Miss Delys, pack immediately, and stay away from Gloryoak till amended behavior shows you fit company for decent people."

"Decent!" Tom jeered. "God, she's fooled you! If you'd seen her with that Cajun—"

Harry recoiled. Tom broke off, realizing too late the admission in his words.

"*You* were one of the masked men," charged Harry. "You—you helped kill that young man, our own blood nephew!"

"If you claim kin to all Old Matthew's whoring offshoots, we'd be kin to half the high yellows around here," drawled Tom. At the disbelieving anger in his brother's face, he added hastily, "I didn't mean to kill the fellow, Harry! But he attacked me. I had to defend myself!"

"When you had broken into the Delyses' home?"

"We just stopped for a drink and a bite of dinner."

"In masks?" Harry shook his head. "It won't serve, Tom. You'll have to stand trial."

"Damned if I will!" cried Tom. "It was an accident! And if that slut hadn't been hugging her Cajun with her tits spilling out—"

Harry sprang around the table, knocked Tom across the room. Tom scrambled up, and as Harry followed, Tom snatched a marble bookend from a stand and crashed it against his brother's head. Harry went down with a groan. Engulfed in what seemed like a nightmare repetition of Etienne's murder, Rachel screamed and ran forward, raising Harry's limp form.

"Tante!" she wailed. "Selah!"

Tom had already vanished.

When Selah heard what had happened, his face grew terrible, and he ran from the room without any orders. Rachel held Harry while Tante brought wet towels to hold against the swelling blood-edged weal above Harry's temple.

"My God, my God," the brothers' nurse moaned. "Now, why'd the boy do a thing like this? Mr. Harry! Mr. Harry, honey, can't you say something?"

One of the maids ran in with a glass of brandy. Propping Harry up, Tante and Rachel got a small swallow down him. "Tell one of the men to ride hard for the doctor," Tante commanded the gaping maid. " 'Case Selah hasn't."

Rachel was sure Harry's devoted body servant had gone after Tom but didn't say so. Whether Tom escaped or not seemed unimportant beside Harry's well-being. His heart was beating, wasn't it? But she could hardly breathe herself until his eyelids flickered.

He stared at her and Tante in a baffled way for an instant. Then his jaw snapped shut and he tried to jump up, wavered and let the women support him for a moment before he gritted his teeth and demanded, "Where is he?"

"Run off," keened Tante, weeping. "Plumb run off! Mr. Harry, what in the world was you two arguin' about to get in such a passion? You never hit either of your brothers your whole life long, though Lord knows they sometimes both of 'em deserved it! What got into you?"

Through this mournful plaint, Harry had been visibly pulling himself together. Now he freed himself of both women, though even in his stunned outrage he looked compassionately at Tante.

"Tom's killed a man, Tante. I've got to try to find him."

"Lord have mercy!" Tante caught at Harry but he slipped through her clutching fingers and hurried out. In a moment the alarm bell began to toll from the veranda. Tante turned blindly to Rachel.

"What happened, child?"

Rachel explained as briefly as she could. Tante sat down with her face in her hands. "Tom was always getting into scrapes," she grieved, "but I always prayed he'd never do anything really bad. So he's killed your poor young man! And his brother's after him like hounds 'cause Mr. Harry's a stern one for the law." Tante lifted stricken eyes to Rachel. "Tom and the others broke in on you and Mr. Etienne, but what'd they do after—after Tom knocked him down? Honey, you tell me! What'd they do?"

Rachel stood moving her head back and forth. She couldn't say it. But Tante knew. With a moan she gathered Rachel in her arms and held her like a baby.

Harry and the searching force he had organized had not returned. Tante sent one of the boys to tell Dr. Martin that his patient was presumably all right and then she'd insisted on Rachel's drinking mint tea and bundled her into bed. Rachel submitted because she meant to steal away from Gloryoak before Harry returned. She had brought misfortune and shame to the man she most admired and valued. It was impossible to accept his protection any longer. As soon as Tante was well out of the room, Rachel slipped out of bed and began to put her few belongings in a shawl, resolutely ignoring the pretty new dresses.

It took less than half an hour to leave the room looking as if she'd never been there except for the dresses in the armoire and the notes she'd written for Harry and Tante, thanking them for being so good to her, telling them not to worry, that she was going to relations. That was a lie, of course, which they probably wouldn't credit since she'd told them she had no close kindred, but they might believe she had some remote great-aunt in reserve.

Old Bess and the cow had been brought in for safekeeping at Gloryoak, the mare retired to pasture, and Rachel, with her small bundle, hesitated. Should she take Bess or travel on foot? She didn't know where to go. Harry, even Tom, might look for her at Tristesse, and Harry was sure to inquire about her from Tante Aurore with whom Rachel was disinclined to seek refuge.

Where then? With great effort, she concentrated on that. No time now to seek a teaching position, and Harry would find her if she looked for work around Jefferson.

She must go in the other direction, where, she remembered vaguely from remarks of Bradford's, there were a few small settlements. Perhaps she could work at an inn in exchange for her lodging, or pledge Bess for later payment after she had found a place.

That hope, but even more a clinging to Bess as the

one familiar living tie to her home and father, prompted Rachel to go quietly out of the house, taking the long way around to the pastures to avoid Tante's sharp eye. She wished she could tell the children good-bye, but if they tagged her they'd be able to tell Harry which way she'd gone, cut down on the lead she needed. Bess was grazing under an apple tree at the edge of the field, switching flies and enjoying the blessings of retirement, so sleek and plump that her ridged backbone seemed less prominent.

Going into the stables, Rachel was beginning to think her old saddle had been thrown out when she found it hanging in a corner, most respectfully oiled, but also in retirement, the worn bridle looped over the horn, the ancient blanket folded neatly across a beam. Harry must have given strict orders about her gear or the stablehands' pride would never have tolerated such dilapidation.

Collecting her things, Rachel dropped the saddle and blanket just outside the stable along with her bundle, entered the pasture with the bridle and was greeted with affection if not delight by Bess, who came to meet her and looked a bit reproachful when Rachel followed her usual petting and praise by slipping on the bridle.

"Sorry, old girl. Just get me away from here and I'll do my best to see you don't have to work hard."

Bess snorted but came peaceably, and within a few minutes Rachel was mounted and making for the nearest fringe of woodland. She'd get out of sight as quickly as possible and pick up the road afterward.

Now that she was on her way she had time to wonder if Harry would catch his brother, scarcely knew what she hoped. Certainly she wanted Tom punished, would do it herself if she got a chance, but it would agonize Harry to hand Tom over to the law. Tom doubtless would get off by pleading self-defense unless she testified about the circumstances and that he'd raped her. In which case Harry would see her, and the hurts she'd already caused him would be multiplied.

Rachel sighed wearily. If they didn't reach shelter by nightfall, she'd have to sleep in the woods. That wouldn't have bothered her once. Now she dreaded the possibility and thought mournfully how glad she'd be if Etienne were alive again and asked her to go *anywhere* with him. But she only felt that *because* he was dead, because she could never again be the wild spirit whose best delight had been "to walken in the wodes wilde."

A man appeared in front of her. For a moment she thought it was Etienne, called back by her wish, but then her startled glance saw hazel eyes, light brown hair, a bruised forehead.

"Rachel!" said Harry. "Rachel, my love."

IV

Never in all her life had she been so glad to see anyone, but the rush of joy was followed by the sinking realization that she wasn't what he thought; she couldn't give him sexual love, and at the same time she wasn't a virgin.

Holding Bess's bridle, he closed his free hand over both of Rachel's. "As soon as Tante makes your wedding gown, we're going to be married."

Rachel shook her head. "Harry, please. I'm not the kind of wife you should have."

"You're the only one I want." His mouth curved whimsically. "And you can't say I'm not old enough to know my mind."

She had to smile at that but then repeated. "No, Harry."

His eyebrows shot up. "Come down where we can discuss this properly," he said.

Before she knew what he was about, he had her

out of the saddle, looped Bess's reins about a stump, and drew Rachel against him. Rigid at first, ready to battle, she gradually calmed in the comforting circle of his arms, the slow deep beat of his heart making her aware of the strength and life in him.

"Let's see if I can guess why you refuse. You don't love me in a romantic way? I can handle that, my sweet. It's natural you should grieve for your first love but as our life together deepens, you'll live in the present—live with me."

She didn't answer, and he sighed. "Rachel, this is more now than a matter of love, it's family honor. Tante told me that Tom offered you shameful affront. If some of your reluctance to marry is because you feel dishonored, know this makes me want to wed you more than ever."

Feeling exposed, she tried to sound indignant. "Harry, I believe you'd marry me out of obligation even if you didn't like me!"

"No, my love. I'd give another girl money or whatever recourse was possible. You're different."

"Yes, I am." She pulled away and looked straight into his eyes though it was hard to do. "I wasn't a virgin, Harry, before Tom. Etienne was my lover."

Except for a widening of the pupils of his eyes, Harry showed no reaction, though he didn't speak for a moment. Then he said, "That could easily happen when you were constant companions and cut off from regular society. The lad was not much your elder though it's a shame he took advantage—"

"He didn't! He begged me to marry him."

"Oh!" Harry looked relieved. "You simply hadn't gotten to a minister."

"We were never getting to a minister," she said with defiance, "I didn't wish to marry."

"Rachel!"

She hunched her shoulders. "I knew you wouldn't like *why*," she said grimly, "even if you could overlook *what*."

His mouth twitched. Clasping her hands, he said gravely, "May I inquire why you are so prejudiced against the state most young ladies see as their life's goal?"

She told him at considerable length, judging that he'd asked for it. "Mmm," he mused, when she finished. "You really are a rather noble savage, Rachel, thanks to Bradford's dosing you with Rousseau. But you'll grant your life and its circumstances have changed drastically since you declined Etienne's suit."

She didn't answer. That was all too painfully true.

"You'll have all the freedom consistent with safety," he promised. "We can renovate Tristesse and spend some time there. But you can't return to your childhood, Rachel. You have to start over. Start with me."

What he said was undeniable. And she did care for him more than for anyone else in the world. If he still wanted her, knowing all that he did— Yet there was one thing more.

"I—I'm afraid I can't be a wife to you, Harry. Since —Tom, I can't help it, I really lose my head, just panic. I don't know if I'll ever get over that."

He tilted up her chin. "Soldiers recover from battle, women from childbirth, and you'll someday want me to make love to you." He laughed teasingly. "Better not wait too long, though. I may forget how."

He was so good, so sane, so strong and easy-tempered he utterly confounded her sad, proud heart. With a sobbing laugh, she carried his big brown hand to her lips. She owed him everything. In every way she could, she would make him happy.

Harry had searched for Tom all that day till it was apparent he'd gone to earth and wouldn't be quickly discovered. When the sheriff's party took up the hunt, Harry left Gloryoak men combing the area and hurried back to Rachel. A stableboy, drowsing in the shade, had seen her ride off into the woods on Bess. Harry had guessed her strategy and ridden straight down the road, pulling into the trees and waiting until he heard Bess.

No trace of Tom was found. He had won a considerable sum at cards in Jefferson the night before he came home, so he presumably had money. Reward posters were sent out for him, but though the sheriff investigated a number of leads, they led nowhere. Rachel hoped he would never be heard of again. Now that Harry knew his brother had forced her, he was likely to kill Tom himself, especially since he wouldn't want Rachel's violation to figure in a trial.

The wedding was held in the ballroom early in August, presided over by the Presbyterian minister who had buried Etienne. Rachel had demurred at white but Harry had insisted, so the gown was richly glowing satin with imported lace inserts and thousands of tiny seed pearls. Tante and four grandmothers had needed the better part of two weeks to make it. It was so exquisite Rachel felt transfigured when she slipped into it.

All the gentry and substantial folk for miles around had been invited, Dr. Martin and Ferris Pettigrew, Harry's lawyer. No one was scandalized enough by whispers about Rachel's strange upbringing and her riding into town with a murdered man across her saddle to miss the event. Rachel's pupils and their grannies who had made her gown were there. After the brief, poignant ceremony, several attractive young matrons laughingly told Rachel that she had the husband they had hoped for until they'd met "the really right men," their present spouses. The McLeod sisters of Belleforest, the nearest plantation, hadn't found husbands and were obviously chagrined.

There was a bountiful feast, several kinds of punch and a great silver bowl of syllabub. The best musicians from three counties played for the dancing and Gloryoak rejoiced, Tante Estelle said, more than in all the years she could remember there.

"Now, when you and Mr. Harry have some young ones, won't that just frost the cake!" she said.

Rachel's smile faded. She was beginning to understand the world well enough to know that if she showed no signs of having a child within a year, women would start gossiping, wondering what was wrong, condoling with Harry.

She held her shoulders and chin erect, brushing the softly gleaming pearls on her bodice. She certainly couldn't live as she intended and be much worried about what other people said. What most mattered was to please Harry.

He seemed suited, spending with her as much of every day as he could, often laughing in amusement or delight. And she was suited, too, much better than she would have believed possible in a life so different from the one she had planned. In some ways Harry filled the void left there by her father, for he discussed everything with her, from crops and his fear of the rising secessionist fever to Livingstone's explorations in Africa and Edward FitzGerald's beautiful translation of the *Rubáiyát*, which Harry liked so well and always seemed to be quoting.

Bess grazed contentedly in the pasture while Rachel fared out on Lady, now hers as a wedding gift. Since she had never ridden much, she quickly got used to a sidesaddle and found the nuisance a small price for the exhilaration of skimming through fields or loping down a lane. Riding the high-mettled but affectionate mare was challenging exercise and compensated considerably for roaming the bayous and lake.

Free now to indulge Rachel, Harry seemed to find continual pleasure in giving her everything he thought she might enjoy or need. After making the wedding dress, Tante Estelle was relieved of sewing, and the best seamstress in Jefferson came to stay at Gloryoak with her sewing machine, while she designed, fitted and made two riding habits, one a severely tailored bottle-green broadcloth, the other of ivory-beige pongee, exceedingly fetching with its nipped-in waist and flowing lines. When Rachel protested that she had too many dresses, Harry pointed out that fall and winter were approaching so she'd best prepare.

The result was half a dozen poplin and woolen gowns and evening dresses of pearl-colored silk piped with pearl satin, rich plum silk ornamented with medallions of black lace, and a triple-flounced purple cashmere. Mrs. Mapes labeled some of the plainer dresses "walking" or "carriage" gowns, but Rachel didn't worry about such distinctions. She was delighted with them all and enchanted with the nightgowns of linen cambric and Valenciennes lace, the linen drawers and embroidered chemises of cambric muslin and flannel.

Mrs. Mapes wanted to make corset covers instead of the last but since Harry refused to have Rachel lace even if she wished to, Rachel preferred the simple, pretty chemises. Then there was a merino cloak of dark gray lined with cherry silk, one of fawn-colored cashmere trimmed in velvet and a dark-green velvet lined with gold satin.

Mrs. Mapes' sister was a milliner who created a

variety of bonnets from white chip and blond straw for the rest of the summer to silk, velvet and wool for winter. Harry's bootmaker laid aside his other orders to make her everything from dancing shoes to riding boots. With all this activity, few days passed without some new present which led Rachel to vow guiltily that she would never buy another article of clothing.

They made a trip to Tristesse to collect Bradford's books and the few mementoes of Rachel's mother. Selah, before the wedding, had been sent to take the cow to Tante Aurore and help her fetch any of the furnishings of kitchen things she could use. The house was nearly stripped of the small much-used articles that had made it home.

Rachel's pirogue was gone, too, so it was a rather melancholy trip. The men cleared vines and spreading bushes away from the small graveyard on the knoll, and Harry knelt with her there, by her parents' graves and that of Désirée, his father's mistress.

"We could put a wrought-iron fence around the plots," Harry suggested. "Would you favor headstones?"

"Headstones seem so hard and cold."

"Well, then," he said after a few minutes' thought, "why not a large stone container where you could plant flowers and sweet herbs but where the names could still be engraved?"

"That would be perfect! Harry, how is it that you always know exactly how to do things?"

He smiled, held her hand to his face. "I'm afraid I don't, my sweet. But at least I've gained the wisdom to wait."

As he was waiting for her? They had not yet spent a night together. He came to her bed each evening for an hour or so while they talked and he held her in his arms but he rode his passion with a tight rein, getting up and having a cigar when he began to tremble and his kisses grew ardent.

Rachel knew this torment couldn't go on. She felt a cruel cheat, all the more because he was so unfailingly kind. He had given her everything, married her when he knew Tom had raped her, and Etienne been freely given the body which, in spite of all her willpower and disgusted self-scolding, grew stiff and shrinking when Harry's protective affection turned to ardor.

The night they got home from Tristesse, she returned Harry's kisses, stroked his shoulders, tried to stay soft and relaxed, telling herself this was Harry, her husband, the man she loved, her friend whom she wanted to make happy. It worked till his tremulous hands touched her breast. She went rigid though she kept her arms about him.

Immediately he broke away. "No, Rachel! Not that way!"

"But, Harry, please! If you just go ahead, maybe I could get over it. I want to, I hate this! Please, Harry."

"I can't," he said simply, with a strained little laugh. "When you stiffen like that, darling, I remember Tom —God, my own brother! And even if I wanted to take you then, almost with force, I can't." When she would have argued further he laid his fingers on her lips. "No use, love. Your fear unmans me."

He reached for his dressing gown, turned back to touch Rachel's head as she sobbed against the pillows. "Sweetheart, don't take on like that. We've years and years ahead of us, years I won't chance tainting because I desire you so. I'm sure in time, when your body learns along with your mind that I won't hurt you, all will be well with us."

"If—if I drank some wine—"

"Rachel, Rachel!" he chided. "Don't try so hard.

When you're finally mine, I want to be proud of the way it happened." With that he kissed her half-buried cheek and left her.

Rachel continued with her school, and an empty cabin was being equipped with desks and chairs, a large plasterboard coated with black paint, a globe, and several large colored maps. The class had increased. On the occasion of the wedding, Harry had given their liberty to a score of men and women who were, so he let it be circulated for the benefit of critics, close to paying out their freedom anyhow.

Two of the men departed to find work in cities, but though the others stayed at Gloryoak, most of them wanted to learn a little reading and writing and ciphering. Tante Estelle and Selah instructed this group two nights a week. Rachel sometimes gave a geography lesson and Harry spoke several times on such applied economics as interest, credit and savings, but he told Rachel firmly that they must not be too involved with the freedmen's school.

"People can see the advantages of educating young slaves so they can perform more varied tasks, keep accounts and so on," he explained. "And one might educate a freedman or two for the same reason. But we'd be thought seditionists for sure if we personally taught the school."

"But Harry, who cares what such bigots think?"

"I do, love. Because if war breaks out, as I fear it may, and shortly, reason will fly out the window. I shall have to fight, of course, and I don't want to leave you among hostile neighbors."

The calm way he spoke about the likeliness of fratricidal civil war sent cold chills through Rachel. "If there is a war, what will your brother Matthew do?"

she asked faintly. "Since he's in the army, won't his allegiance be to the United States?"

"That's what he'll have to decide," shrugged Harry. "I can't guess, myself Matt's a strange one. I used to worry over his hotheadedness, but he seems to have toned down considerably."

Matthew had been Bradford's favorite and was, Rachel suspected, Tante Estelle's. Since leaving for West Point ten years ago, he'd been home only for short visits, but everyone who knew him recalled him as vividly as if they had seen him only yesterday.

"Have you written to him about our marriage?" Rachel asked.

"Yes, but even though the Butterfield Overland Mail Route has vastly improved service, once letters from here reach a Butterfield station in west Texas, it still takes weeks for an exchange, even if Matthew isn't in the field after Apaches."

She hoped he wouldn't think she had married Harry for his money, and she wondered if Harry had told him about Tom. That news, any of it, would be terribly hard to send a third brother. Rachel suspected Harry would give the barest facts and leave details to their next meeting.

"Is Matthew like you?" she asked her husband.

He raised a quizzical eyebrow. "Would that commend him to you, my dear, or be a handicap?"

"He can't be as good," she said, refusing to be baited.

Harry gave her a long searching look. "I hope that doesn't mean dull. Though I suppose I feel dull when I compare myself with Matt! He was always out there ahead of everyone else. Riding, shooting, cutting a shine for the ladies. But he had a tender heart, and I never knew him to do a mean or underhanded thing. He's literally given the coat off his back to someone having hard luck, and he almost drowned keeping Selah afloat when they got caught out in a storm on Caddo years ago."

Presented with such a contradictory picture, Rachel laughed and said, "You have me thoroughly intimidated!"

"No need. He'll be utterly your servant."

His other brother had certainly not been. To cover this thought, which Harry, from his stricken look, must be having, too, Rachel shook her head in mock despair. "Perhaps my best gambit will be to look as if I'm drowning or as if I need his coat."

Harry chuckled. "Don't you dare, minx! It's my privilege to see that you're undrowned and well-coated. I asked Matt to do all he can short of mutiny to get Christmas leave. We'll make a merry season of it, love." She knew he was thinking this might be the last peaceful Christmas for years, that if Lincoln was elected that fall the country might plunge swiftly into war.

"Oh, a very merry season," she teased, trying to lift his spirits. "We'll invite all the belles, but you remember they're for Matt and not for you!"

"I have my belle," he said, and brought her into his lap. She snuggled against him and for a few close moments they were warm and happy till that strained trembling began in his arms and she knew he ached for her.

Matt rode home to Gloryoak in October, after the black gum had turned dark red, just as the sweet gum was blazing yellow. The dogwood bore red berries and red leaves, the sumac was flaming, and the great oak was the brilliant orange that would later sere to brown. Rachel was cutting late roses from the garden by the sundial. She glanced up at the music of hoofs, shielding her eyes to gaze at the big gray horse cantering swiftly up the long walnut-bordered lane. His rider matched him in size and grace, moving easily with his mount's deceptively smooth gait.

Rachel could not look away. There was something vaguely hauntingly familiar about this man, though she was sure she'd never seen him before. He had eyes the strange shade of skies when a blue norther was blowing in, cheeks so lean they seemed gashed beneath long slanting cheekbones, and a hard mouth that shaped to a smile of pleased surprise as he swept off a broad-brimmed felt hat to reveal thick curly hair that looked black till she saw the red in it.

She'd never seen him before. No woman could have forgotten him. Even in her innocence, Rachel sensed that. But there was something—

"Ma'am?" He swung down from the saddle and bowed, his manner belying his rough clothes. "May I hope that Gloryoak has acquired such a beauty?"

"I'm Mrs. Harry Bourne," she said, wondering why she pronounced the name with a qualm.

His eyes glinted. "Why then," he said, laughter welling from his bronzed throat, "I claim brotherly privilege!"

He trailed the stallion's reins. Before she realized his intent, he swept her to him.

His mouth stifled her scream just as his broad shoulders and chest frustrated her hands. Pressed to him like that, the sharp bite of rose thorns against her arm and breast filled her with panic. She was being crushed like the flowers. His mouth, caressing at first, had gone cruel at her struggles, forcing her lips apart so she felt exposed, vulnerable. Terror flooded her mind. She gave a convulsive shudder, felt the ground sliding away, her arms going limp. . .

"Here, now, for God's sake, ma'am!"

She opened her eyes and found herself propped on a garden bench, supported by one of the arms that had lately been her prison. "I cry pardon if I kissed the bride a trifle roughly, but I can't believe any woman faints at a kiss these days!"

Drawing away from the odious assistance of her assailant, Rachel glared. "Indeed, sir, that was more mauling than kiss! I think my ribs are broken, and you've ruined my roses as well as scored them into my flesh!"

She held out her arm and shook back the flounce to show bloody scratches, but what he stared at were the bright droplets where the soft swell of her breasts showed above the piqué ruching of her gown. He bent his head. She felt his warm breath, his mouth, and when those sunlit gray eyes looked into hers, the blood was gone.

"If you must be wounded, let it be by roses," he murmured. "But never again by me." He drew her to her feet, collected the scattered roses. "I've made a mess of them! Shall I cut you more before I find my brother?"

She snatched the roses from him before he could toss them away. "I—I'll save them for potpourri. Your brother?" Then his earlier remark came back and her hand went involuntarily to her lips, still bruised and softened by his. "You're Matthew!"

He bowed again. "Your servant, sister."

"Indeed," she flashed. "If you were my servant, I'd have you whipped!"

"If you're of a mind for that," he mocked, "doubtless Harry will oblige. Show him your wounds and swear I offered violence."

"You did, sir!"

"Only when you fought like a catamount."

Was there no squelching him? "I've no wish to set

brothers wrangling, and I suppose that soldiers have heartier manners than common," she said, tossing her head. "But be warned, brother-in-law! If you ever constrain me again, I'll take it out of your hide."

"So Harry's found a lass with bottom to her!" cheered the newcomer unrepentantly. "Damned if I thought he had it in him, but slow fires burn deep. Where'd he find you, Mrs. Bourne? Not, I'll be bound, sitting primly by your mama at a dance?"

With my lover dead across my knees and a sheriff hauling me from the saddle.

Shallow-buried pain rose up. She stared at him, unable to speak. His smile faded. His eyes seemed to delve into her mind. The air was charged and for those few still moments, there was no one else in the world. She had never been so possessed by another's spirit, not even by Etienne's when they melted in primordial ecstasy where self was lost.

"Matthew!"

Harry was coming forward, Selah and Tante Estelle behind him, though Tante rushed past. throwing herself into the tall man's arms. He kissed her. swung her in a circle, laughing. before he embraced his brother, clasped Selah's hand.

Rachel watched as if she were a ghost.

Matt was not in uniform because he'd resigned his commission. "And the first thing I did as a free man was beat the hell out of a fellow officer," Matt said. Catching himself, he begged Rachel's pardon. but Harry was too concerned to much note his brother's profanity.

"That finishes your career, then." he said, and sighed resignedly. "Over a woman. no doubt?"

Staring at his scarred, worn boots. which had now been polished to gleaming by devoted hands, Matt gave his brother a crooked grin. "No. It was over an Apache."

Harry knit his brow, slapped the side of his leg. "The chief who saved your skin from a band of roving hostiles? That event impressed you enough, apparently, to occasion a letter home."

"Cochise did get me out of an ambuscade," Matt said. "But to understand how it is with Apaches, you've got to remember they live in small bands and range widely for food. To start with, the Western Apache and Chiricahua Apache are pretty different. The Chiricahua separate into three major groups while the Western Apache belong to five principal groups that divide again into a score of bands that splinter again into local units. These smallest groups raid and war, sometimes joining with their nearest neighbors, but it's very rare for a whole band to unite. Groups are separated by numerous mountain ranges and the fact that each needs a large area from which to hunt and gather food."

"They don't grow squash or corn?" asked Rachel.

"Western Apaches have been farming for a long time," Matt said. "They grow six different kinds of corn, which is the main crop, and beans and squash. The Chiricahuas grow almost nothing. All Apache depend heavily on wild foods. Mesquite beans, acorns, piñon nuts, mescal hearts, berries, wild onions and potatoes, the fruits of most cactus, seeds and roots. Collecting these foods takes a lot of time."

"But from what we read, there's still time for raiding," said Harry.

"Apache have been driving off Mexican horses and livestock for two hundred years," shrugged Matt. "But Spaniards and Mexicans have enslaved a lot of them to work in the mines or as servants. I doubt you know how in 1836 the governor of Sonora got a trap-

per named Johnson to hold a feast for the Chiricahuas
who had been friendly to the Americans. When the
Apache were all crowding around some stacks of gift
cornmeal, a heavy gun blasted away, loaded with bul-
lets, nails, stones and chains. Trappers finished off the
survivors except for a few who escaped and spread the
story. The wonder is that an Apache ever trusted
Americans again, yet the great chief Mangas Colora-
das did—and got a hundred lashes from gold-hungry
miners. That brought on the slaughter of innocent settlers, which I'm sure you read of, brother—but did you
know the Apache side?"

"You seem to have taken it much to heart, Matthew."

Matt turned his glass wearily in his hand. "Our
Indian policy is disgraceful, Harry. I know our people must be protected, but I've no stomach to battle
Indians for the score of years it will take to subjugate
them. Since the only other prospect of war is between
the North and South, I felt there was no future for me
in the army."

"But you haven't finished with Cochise," Rachel
reminded him.

Matt sighed, downing the rest of his drink. "Cochise,
as I may have written you, Harry, had been supplying
wood to the stage station at Apache Pass and protecting the route from other bands. Anyhow, a bunch of
Western Apaches raided a ranch, drove off cattle and
kidnapped a half-Apache boy. I was away from Fort
Buchanan at the time, and a young shavetail, just out
of West Point, was sent out with a detachment. He
didn't know one band from another and didn't care,
but he met Cochise at the stage station and demanded
the boy's return. When Cochise claimed innocence, the
lieutenant arrested him and six of his friends. Cochise
got away and took hostages for his men. The damned

West Pointer hanged six Apaches, including two of Cochise's nephews and his brother. Cochise killed his hostages. I got back to Buchanan and as soon as my resignation was accepted, I asked the lieutenant to a meeting." Matt rubbed his knuckles reminiscently. "It was worth it."

Rachel listened, intent on the sound of his voice rather than what he said.

"Too late I came to love thee . . ." The cry of Augustine echoed in her heart during the next days while her heart flamed like the autumn around them. *"Yea, too late came I to love thee. And behold, thou wert within me, and I out of myself, where I made search for thee."*

She told herself she couldn't love him, that he was a brigand where women were concerned, and if she cared again for any man, it *must* be Harry. Sick with shame, she wondered what her husband would think if he knew his brother's presence filled her with a restless fever. If his hand brushed hers, sparks flashed between them. If he came near, her blood slowed, weighting her till she felt powerless to move. Tortured when he was present, irritable when he was not, she took to spending much time in her room alone with her father's books.

She was stricken with the kind of madness, the physical disorder, seen as disaster by Euripides. "Oh let not love with murderous intent come to my door." It was a malady, a sickness that would wear itself out, but she must give it no chance to flourish. There was, however, no way to avoid Matthew at meals.

"Have you taken a dislike to Matt?" Harry questioned her a week after his brother's arrival.

Rachel jumped. "Why, no," she stammered. "What makes you think that?"

"You scarcely speak when he's with us, and I don't recollect your ever engaging him in conversation."

I cannot look at him, meet his eyes. When our glances touch, fire runs through me. I dream of him; dream that he held me as Etienne did, that he's stroking and kissing me and sending me mad. His voice wakes hidden secret nerves. I can't speak more than a few words to him or everyone would know.

"You've had a lot to talk about," she evaded. "I enjoy just listening."

"Do you, sweet?" Harry kissed the tip of her nose, chuckling. "I'm proud of your knowledge, Rachel. Perhaps I'm vain, but I'd like my cynical young brother to know my wife is learned as well as beautiful. He told me yesterday he wondered what you teach in the school since he'd tried to discover your opinions on a number of subjects and could only conclude that you had none."

"He said that?"

"He did, love, and with justification from what I've observed. He's asked your thoughts on everything from the Atlantic cable and the Suez Canal to cherry bounce, and I declare your answers would lead one to think you'd never heard of the first two and thought the last was some kind of game."

It was the first time Harry had ever criticized her and it smarted.

"Very well," she said ominously. "If you gentlemen desire my conversation, you shall have it!"

It happened that Dr. Martin was in the neighborhood that day and joined them for dinner. When the doctor and Matt began discussing the shortcomings of military medicine, she kept Harry from reminding them the subject was less than agreeable for mealtime by launching into Florence Nightingale's struggles with prejudiced doctors and officers when she introduced basic hygiene into hospital wards in the Crimea and reduced the mortality rate from cholera, dysentery and typhus from fifty percent to two percent.

"Um—yes," said Dr. Martin. "I understand she intends to found a training home for nurses."

"A pity we can't train doctors, too," Rachel remarked, "for she seems to know a good deal more than they do about saving lives."

She next asked what he thought about Lister's studies of the coagulation of blood and Pasteur's observation of tiny organisms called bacteria.

"Most interesting, ma'am." The doctor's frizzy sideburns made his round cheeks seem even plumper. "But one must watch these new theories with caution." He escaped with relief to Matt. "Since the Republicans have won state elections in Maine, Vermont, Indiana and Pennsylvania, it seems almost sure Lincoln will be elected this week. Tell me, sir, do you think he will attempt to hold seceding states?"

Before Matt could answer, Rachel said, "Isn't it strange how things alter? Back in 1812 some New England states were threatening to secede and the South detested them for not supporting the war against Great Britain."

Matthew gave her a strange look. "When you have one region dependent on agriculture and the other preoccupied with industry and shipping, there's a natural clash of interests. To your question, Dr. Martin, I hope that any states wishing to leave the Union can do so in peace, but I don't expect it. Mr. Lincoln said over two years ago he didn't believe the government could endure permanently half-slave and half-free. I think he'll see it as his duty to unite the divided house even if it takes flesh and blood to make the mortar."

Harry nodded moodily. "I fear you're right, brother."

"Well, if the Yankees push us, we'll trim their wicks!" cried the doctor. "If we can't outfight a pack of vinegar-blooded shopkeepers and puritans, it'll be a sorry pass!"

"We'll be fighting strong young men, doctor. There are twenty-two million of them, more than double the South's population, from which one must subtract about thirty percent slaves. They'll be worlds better provisioned and supplied, and they have a balanced economy, good railroads and naval supremacy."

The doctor put down his brandy, eyes rounding. "Dammit, Matthew! You're not suggesting they could beat us?"

"No suggestion about it, sir. Fact."

Dr. Martin swallowed so his Adam's apple wobbled in the soft folds of his neck. Quivering, he heaved to his feet. "I never thought to hear such talk at Glory-oak," he breathed. "Why, Matt, it's high treason!"

Matt raised a dark eyebrow. "That's what some say about secession, doctor."

"If it comes to war, may I ask on which side you'll fight?"

"Is there a mandate I must fight for either?"

"And you a soldier!" gasped the doctor.

"No longer, sir." Matt shrugged bemusedly. "But if I wanted to win, I'd have stayed in the uniform I lately quitted."

"I—I scarcely know how to answer you, Matthew."

Rising, Harry dropped a hand on the arm of each man. "Doctor, I dare say you've forgotten Matt's freakish tempers. If Texas goes to war, he'll be in the first and finish at the last. Let's talk of something else."

Matthew cast a droll glance at Rachel. "I'm sure my sister-in-law can supply a topic," he murmured. "Shall we argue whether the Neanderthal skull is really a hundred thousand years old or marvel at this new writing machine someone has invented that strikes letters onto paper?"

"I have another call," said Dr. Martin. He bowed to Rachel. "Thank you for your most gracious hospitality, ma'am." He shook hands with both brothers though there was a stiffness in his clasp with Matt. Harry and Rachel saw him to the door. She then made as if to go to her room but Harry drew her back with him to where Matt was pouring more brandy at the sideboard.

"I'd trounce the both of you were you a dozen years younger!" he said with feeling. "A pretty pair you are! Rachel going on about army hospitals and coagulating blood, and you, Matt, ruffling poor Martin's feelings every which way!"

"Shocking," agreed Matt, twinkling back at his half-earnest brother. "The doctor will spread it around you've a bluestocking for a wife!"

"And a seditionist for a brother," thrust Rachel, but she couldn't help bursting out laughing.

Harry swung her in a whirling circle, his usually calm eyes lit with eagerness. When they collapsed, breathless, on the sofa, he held her proudly close and grinned at his brother.

"At least you can no longer think my wife has no opinions."

His lean dark face a mask, Matt said carelessly, "Well scored, Harry. I look forward to learning my formidable sister-in-law's attitudes on a great many things." Finishing his drink, he saluted them both. "I'm sure you'll gladly excuse me," he nodded. "I promised to stop at Belleforest this evening for some taffy pulling."

Belleforest had two most marriageable and attractive daughters. Harry grimaced.

"You may get caught in more than taffy if you ride there often, my lad."

Matt chuckled. "Come, Harry, the McLeod damsels may have set their caps for you true enough, but you're the heir of Gloryoak. A poor ex-captain like me may think himself lucky with a mouthful of candy."

His eyes touched Rachel's lips. A pang coursed through her, a stab of wild jealousy at the thought of his spending a gay flirtatious evening with the young McLeod women. She started to slip from Harry's arms, but he held her closer.

"You're so lovely." His voice was unsteady and he swept her in his arms as the door closed on Matthew. "I want my taste of sweetness, too. Oh, my love—"

V

She awoke the next morning feeling as if she'd had a nightmare till the aching stiffness of her body brought her sharply awake and remembering.

Harry. After three months, she was physically his wife. She felt she'd shriek if he touched her. Thank God he wasn't in her room—please, God, let her not see him till she had herself reasoned back to a normal state.

It wasn't his fault. True, he had placed her on her bed last night, kissed and fondled her, but it was she herself who had led his hands to her breasts, she who had lured and invited till he drew back, sweat beading his forehead.

"You—you want me?" he choked. "Oh, Rachel, you want me?"

She had been tormented enough in her body, angry enough at Matt and despairingly sorry enough for Harry to gamble against the rising terror she felt.

"Yes," she moaned, fighting panic with her last bit of will. "Yes!"

Then his hands were no longer Harry's, the urgent questing body bore no relation to the husband-friend she admired and loved every way but this. She was being devoured, smothered, impaled. She clamped her jaws hard together to keep from screaming.

It's Harry, she repeated, the familiar name her only anchor in a tide of rising horror that swept her back to Tristesse, Etienne's crumpled form, jostling masked men, those pawing, bruising hands, greedy mouth. . .

Harry! Harry, Harry.

His long-controlled passion crested in a few minutes but what was to Rachel an endless battle against striking out, fighting him. Tautly rigid, silently calling his name, she came slowly back to the reality of his lying beside her, cradling her in his arms.

"Oh, my love," he said. "Oh, my darling! You've made me so happy, you're wonderful beyond all telling!"

She couldn't answer. He lifted himself anxiously on one elbow. "You're all right? I didn't hurt you?"

"I'm all right."

He kissed her eyes and throat and hands, for the first time enjoying his bride, permitting himself to behave like a lover, though for the present his desire was quieted.

"Next time it'll be happier for you," he promised. "I'm afraid I was carried away tonight."

He pushed her hair back from her face, watched her till, to keep from crying out that she'd hated it, that she'd been afraid and always would be, Rachel let her eyelids droop, said sleepily, "Harry, dear, I'm so tired. Could we have the candle out?"

"Of course, love."

He snuffed the candle, told her good night and soon

slumbered heavily, his arm weighing her down as it sprawled possessively across her.

Sleep was long in coming to Rachel. *Next time.* She hadn't thought beyond getting through the first time. Now, sinkingly, she realized that Harry thought her fear was broken.

Would she ever grow used to lovemaking again? Would it ever be as it had been with Etienne? How could her body, so joyously attuned with his, be cold and locked to her husband?

She lay unhappily in her husband's arms, drifting into a restless, dream-filled sleep when she seemed to be looking up at a man whose face was hidden. She was not afraid, perhaps she was, but the excitement of his touch, the tingling shocks going warmly through her, overpowered her fear, turning it into a higher peak of longing.

"Harry?" she cried. "Etienne?"

The shadowed face lifted. Matt gazed down at her. Gripped with terrible sadness, she awakened and found herself alone.

Harry had business in town and left directly after breakfast. Matt had not come to the table by the time Rachel left for school. She thought vindictively that he must have found the taffy pull at Belleforest decidedly fatiguing. At noon, after seeing the last of her pupils off, Rachel returned listlessly to the house, picked at her solitary lunch and decided she simply couldn't mope about Gloryoak the rest of the day. Harry would be late and she certainly didn't, after that disgraceful dream, wish to encounter Matt.

She hadn't been back to Tristesse since the headstones with their plants had been set up. She told Tante Estelle where she was going, said no, indeed, she didn't need someone with her, and asked to have

Lady saddled while she changed into her dark-green habit.

She was homesick, she told herself, eyes stinging as a great wave of longing for her father and Etienne swept over her. She had been so happy with their simple life. But Father and Etienne were dead; the peaceful fabric of that life had been ripped forever that morning the intruders burst in.

For her there was no going back, but today she'd ride to Tristesse, at least. If anything survived of the dead, she might sense Bradford's gentle presence or feel something of the mother she could not remember.

The boy who brought Lady to the house was the same one who'd watched her run off on Bess, and he eyed Rachel nervously. "I could just follow you on old Tam, Miz Rachel," he offered.

"Thank you, Jason, but I'm not running away," she assured him, smiling in spite of her megrims. "Tante Estelle knows I'm going, so no one shall blame you."

Reluctantly, he gave her a hand up and handed her the reins. "You take mighty good care now, Miz Rachel," he warned. "Master Harry kill me too dead to skin if you was to get lost or have any trouble."

"I expect I'll be back before he is," she assured him. "Don't fret, Jason. I'm just going to my old home for a little while."

Waving to Tante Estelle, who stood disapprovingly at the door, Rachel rode down the lane and soon picked up the rutted road to Tristesse. It was overgrown with grass and vines, almost invisible in places. Feeling desolate and alone, Rachel conquered the impulse to whirl Lady about, take the clear, broad road, perhaps start for Jefferson and meet Harry on his way home. But instead she nudged the high-stepping mare down the path that Bradford's infrequent journeys had kept open.

The road grew even more obscure as the woods grew thicker and the ground boggier. Great bald cypresses reared above water and willow, oak and tupelo and sweetbay grew in the damper places. Leaves were beginning to carpet the ground, and squirrels were busy against the winter. There was a hint of frost in the sunshine, though haze softened the crimson of black gum across the lake. Up ahead were the twin cypresses that marked the Tristesse pier, and Rachel's heart twisted painfully as the pillared beauty of her old home showed through the magnolias. Reining Lady, Rachel waited silently. Easy to fancy that Father was inside at his books, that stew simmered in the black iron pot and Etienne might stride up at any moment with a gift of honey or game.

But nothing happened. Tristesse seemed transfixed in enchanted sleep. She felt like a trespasser, as if she no longer belonged here, yet this sense of alienation drove her to stay. Hitching Lady to a post, she first walked up the knoll to the little graveyard. Gracefully carved stone planters were softened by rambling roses, thyme, rosemary and lavender. Bradford's and her mother Louella's names were linked together on one long stone. Harry had ordered Désirée's name on the single planter, a little distance from the Delyses. How like him to be kind, Rachel thought, even when there was no one left to see. Tante Aurore had never visited her sister's grave.

Rachel knelt and prayed, but got no feeling of response or peace. Slowly, she touched the headstones, then descended the little hill, going up the stairs and into the house.

Her footsteps echoed past the sitting room and guest chamber, and she turned into the dining room, which had been her father's office and where she had sat reading or sewing while he talked or studied.

Could that smell of tobacco linger so long? She
touched the pipe still lying on his desk, the pile of
books. Mill's *On Liberty,* Tennyson's *Idylls of the
King,* Trollope's *Barchester Towers,* de Tocqueville's
L'Ancien Régime. She had left these when moving
most of his library to Gloryoak. It seemed that the
pipe, chair, desk and books should be there to leave
some palpable trace of the man who had used them.

The kitchen was cold. Tante Aurore had taken
away nearly everything movable. Rachel glanced in
her old room. The four-poster where she'd slept for so
many years was stripped of bedding and the draperies
were pulled.

There was still the blood stain from Etienne's
wound, close by the spot where she had fought and
writhed in Tom's brutal hands. Here she'd dragged
her lover's body across the floor. There was nothing
for her now but that. Blindly, she ran down the hall,
colliding against a hard figure. She screamed, struck
out in mindless terror so that she kicked and struggled
until she was swept up in steely arms, one hand
trapped against her captor's chest, the other pinioned.

"What's wrong?" a harsh voice demanded. "Have
you gone mad, flying down the hall like that and jumping on me like a—wildcat?" The voice gentled, took
on a teasing note. "A small wildcat to be sure, and
very, very pretty!"

"Matt!" She opened her eyes, so relieved that she
went soft and trusting against him. "Matt, I was frightened! I'm so glad it's you!"

His eyes were gray fire. With a groan, he lowered
his head, taking her mouth with his as he pushed
through the door of the guest chamber. When he lowered her to the bed, Rachel tried to sit up, tried to
say no, but his hands on her breasts woke sweet wildness within her, a burning urgency. She helped him

thrust her clothes aside, knew one moment of old dread when he entered her, a dread engulfed by the rising tide of savage need that swelled and surged, built to unbearable heights, then crested and broke in great waves of delight. She sobbed and laughed and clung to him, the frozen armor of her body shattered.

She didn't know what would happen now, couldn't think of Harry, her marriage, anything. She only knew she had been dead and was alive again.

But Matthew was looking at her with a haggard face. "Oh, my love!" he said. "Oh, my darling. And to think I followed you to see you came to no harm!"

"Matthew, it—wasn't harm." With a tremulous laughing sob, she touched the hollow of his cheek. "I thought I'd always be afraid. I still was, even last night with Harry."

"Last night?" Matt's eyebrows knitted. "My God, girl, you can't mean that's the first time you—" He broke off. "So that's why you went crazy when I kissed you that first day! But even when you fought me there was something about the way you felt in my arms—I'd have sworn you knew how to please and pleasure."

"Etienne was my lover."

"That Cajun boy who's buried in the family plot?"

"Your father's grandson and your nephew," she elaborated.

"Did Harry know?"

"Yes. I told him because he felt responsible for— for what Tom did."

Matt sucked in his breath, his arm tightening around her. "Tom raped you!"

"Yes."

"And after that you were afraid. My God, poor Rachel! Poor Harry! Married to you for months and only last night getting you to bed!" Matthew stared at her in the dim light, brushed her lips with his and sprang up. "Well, Rachel, you've had your dealings with my family! If you're able to receive my brother now, we'll forgive ourselves this afternoon. But it cannot happen again."

The words stabbed her, though she knew he was right. Impossible to betray Harry, impossible for either, brother or wife. But how, after this, to never yield to that sweet hunger, never feel Matt's lips or hands again?

"I love you," she said forlornly.

"Don't think that!" He drew her to her feet, straightened the basque of her habit as if she were a child. "Harry adores you. He's a far better man than I am in every way."

"But—"

His eyes were filled with such pain that she winced, began arranging her clothes and hair, a taste of ashes in her mouth. "Rachel, I've wanted you ever since we met, but I'm not a green boy. I thought I could keep my hands off my own brother's wife. None of this was your fault. You think you love me because I broke through your prison. But it's Harry you must love. Come. Let's go home."

She paused as she went past him, but he would not look at her.

That night at dinner, he said he was leaving. "There's a wonderful place west of the Pecos and south toward the Rio Grande," he said. "I scouted there when I was stationed at Fort Lancaster. Good grass and all the land a man could want since there's no rush to settle."

"Isn't that where the Comanches go every fall on their raids to Mexico?" asked Harry while Rachel gripped her napkin tight, feeling as if her heart had stopped.

Matt shrugged. "The Comanches do pass through the Big Bend," he admitted. "But I'd look for a place well-removed from their usual route. Milton Faver's the only white man ranching in the whole region, now that Ben Leaton's dead. He depends on spring water. But I'd locate between mountain meadows and the Rio so if the springs went dry I'd still be able to get my cattle to water."

"You seem to have thought about it in some detail," Harry observed. "Why don't you stay at Glory-oak, Matthew? There's plenty to be done."

"Guess I've been too long in the West. I feel crowded, Harry. Even the air's heavy and moist. Besides, I'd never make a planter."

Harry studied his wine, then lifted his shoulders and laughed. "Then all we can do is wish you well with your cattle. I had no business making plans just because you'd left the army. When are you going?"

"In a couple of days."

"A couple of days?" Harry reacted as if to a slap. "There can't be that rush, brother! Won't you stay for Christmas and let us celebrate the New Year together?"

For the briefest second, Matt's gaze touched Rachel, piercing her desolation to send her blood pulsing. "I wish I could stay, Harry. But I need to get settled in and buy cows that'll give calves in the spring."

"When people move west, they often never see their families again." Harry reached for Rachel's hand. "Won't you add your persuasions, darling? I wish we might have this holiday before Matt seeks his fortune and warclouds burst."

All that afternoon his name echoed within her.

Matthew. Matthew. The marvel of feeling alive again
in her most secret parts vied with guilt, her resolution
to be faithful to Harry.

She knew the only way she and Matt could keep
away from each other for long was to put physical distance between them. He was right to go, and quickly.
Yet the thought was like a knife tearing through her.
Matthew, Matthew. Without you I shall be only half.

"Please stay," she said at her husband's urging.
How could he not guess, what with the way her hands
trembled and her voice frayed? "Just till New Year."

Matt's eyes widened, then narrowed, and his jaw
set. He looked as if he hated her. "Alas, sister, I must
beg your pardon and be on my journey. I'm sad, believe me, not to share your holidays, but I hope to return in a few years and bring gifts for the children
who'll fill Gloryoak by then." He grinned at Harry.
"You've not been wed so long, brother, that two's still
not the best company! I thank you both for your graciousness, God knows, but I miss the open skies."

"Then we must hope you'll visit us soon," said
Harry, taking Rachel's hand. "Who knows, you may
bring back a wife and children of your own!"

"I doubt it," said Matt.

"Why, boy, you'll need someone to inherit those
cattle and vast acres!"

"Your children can have them," Matt said. "The
only lady I ever fancied in the marrying way already
had a husband."

Rachel held her breath but Harry nodded. "I
thought it was something like that more than Cochise
that made you want out of the army," he said. "The
officers' world's a small one. Paths always cross again."
They talked then of cattle prices and far-flung army
posts guarding the fringes of the Big Bend of the Chi-

huahua Trail from Mexico to San Antonio, and danger of Comanches, but Rachel heard little of it.

Don't go away. I can't bear it. Nor can I bear it if you stay. To see you like this, to want and need you though it must not be. Too late came I to love thee— yes, too late came I to love thee.

Three mornings later, on Sunday, Matt said his good-byes, kissing Tante Estelle, trying to make her smile through her tears, before he shook his brother's hand. They embraced with the quick rough embarrassment of men trained not to show their feelings. Matt dropped a kiss on Rachel's cheek, swung into the saddle.

"Be happy," he said, looking down from his big gray horse. "Harry and Rachel, I wish you very, very happy." He rode down the lane, stopping at the far end, and waved before he put Storm into a canter.

It was too cruel, for him to go away like this. Walking to the house with Harry and a sobbing Tante Estelle, Rachel tried to tell herself it was over. Matt had done the only wise and honorable thing. But she had to see him, alone, one more time! Kiss him again, feel the strength of his arms, his long hard body. Just once, just for an hour. Then, forever, she'd be a good, proper and virtuous wife.

"I have some letters to do," Harry said as they moved down the hall. "Will you excuse me for a few hours, my love?"

"I was just thinking I'd enjoy a ride," she said. "If I go now, I'll be back for lunch."

"Perhaps I should come with you."

"Oh, no, do your letters," Rachel urged. "If it stays warm, we might picnic at the lake this evening."

"We'll do that then," Harry agreed, stopping by the library door to kiss her. "Take care, my dear. I don't like to plague you by sending a boy along when I can't escort you, but do be cautious."

Would he never stop talking? Rachel said impatiently, "I'm sure I'm safer alone than with someone who might startle Lady. Don't fret about me, Harry." She gave him a fleeting kiss and hurried to change.

She took the shortcut Harry must have used that day he intercepted her on the road leading west. Consequently, though Matt had nearly an hour's start, she'd been little over an hour on the way when she heard a horse whicker. Lady responded, speeding up, and within minutes, Rachel gripped her reins tight against the saddle horn, gazing into eyes that froze and burned her. Storm champed the bit, and Matt brought him sternly under control.

"Well, madam? Have you a message from my brother?"

She stiffened at his icy tone but desperation made her reckless. After what was between them, what did words matter?

"Tell me good-bye, Matthew. Hold me and kiss me and tell me good-bye. Give me that, at least, to remember."

He watched her for a long moment. She held out her hand imploringly. His face changed, grew more relaxed. Swinging down from the stallion, he looped the reins over a stump, did the same for Lady and lifted Rachel down.

"One time," he breathed. "One time for all our lives. Oh, Rachel! It took all my strength to tell you good-bye at Gloryoak. I'm not strong now."

But he was strong to love her. He was her man, her only man, and though she might never see him again, *this*—this ecstasy melting him into her would always be the real truth of her as a woman.

They were coming back to the road when Harry stepped in front of them. He had a pistol and his face was death.

"I was ashamed for letting my downcast wife go riding alone," he explained in a clipped brittle tone. His eyes rested on Rachel, so full of agony she would gladly have died to erase it. "Did he open your body for me? Is that why you finally took me?"

She couldn't answer.

Matt said, "Harry, when I knew how it was I decided to go away. Can't you forget this?"

"No."

"I won't fight you," Matt said. "Kill me, and it's your right, but don't hurt Rachel. It's not her fault."

"Yes, it is!" she cried. "I came after you today."

"And you love him." Harry's smile was more horrible than the dead expression. "Will you give me a kiss, Rachel?"

"Harry—"

"Kiss me."

Half expecting him to shoot her as she did so, she moved forward and kissed his cold mouth. He touched her cheek. "My dear, remember this. You are the most beautiful thing that ever happened to me. Go get on your horse."

She thought she understood, caught his hand. "Harry, kill me, too!"

"I'm not going to kill my brother, love," he said as if surprised. "But I want to speak to him privately. Now, please, leave us."

Uneasy but forced to obey, she walked toward the road. She was scarcely mounted when a shot exploded. Scrambling down from the saddle, she ran to where Matthew was swathing his shirt about Harry's neck and jaw. There was blood on both of them. Harry's eyes were sightless, unblinking in the sun.

Rachel fell beside him, calling his name. But he would never answer. Never again.

"I tried to stop him," Matt said. "I wrestled his arm down but he still shot himself beneath the jaw."

"Shot—himself—?"

"My God, yes!" Matt brushed a bloody hand across his face. "He told me to—to take care of you. I was to stop at the nearest inn and wait for news of his suicide. You were to 'find' him and bring Selah." Slipping his arms beneath his brother, Matt carried him toward the road and the waiting horses.

"Matt," protested Rachel, "if you take him home, it'll look as if you'd killed him."

He gave her a look that made her shrink. "Didn't I?" he said, and laid Harry's body across the saddle.

Sheriff Carey's black eyes bored into Rachel, who stood with Tante Estelle near Harry's bed where he lay covered with a sheet. Turning back to Matt with a shake of his head, Carey mused, "So, Mr. Bourne, your brother followed you, commended his wife to your care and shot himself in spite of your trying to wrest the pistol from his hand. I'll credit you with imagination, sir! I've never heard such a story in all my life."

"It's true," said Rachel.

Carey preened his moustache and gave her an unpleasant smile. "You're an unfortunate lady, Mrs. Bourne. Mighty unfortunate. Or maybe it's the men who get killed when you're around."

"You'll respect my brother's wife." Matt's voice was quiet but Carey's sneer faded.

"She'll get the respect she deserves. I'll let you attend the funeral, Mr. Bourne, since if you'd meant to run, you could have. You sure can't expect anyone to believe a rich healthy man with a new wife shoots himself so his brother can step into his boots. I want your promise to turn yourself in."

Matthew nodded. "The funeral's in the morning. I'll be in Jefferson tomorrow afternoon."

The sheriff gave a mocking half-bow and turned to go but Tante Estelle hurried forward, blocking his way. "Sheriff, you know I raised both these young men. I love them both. And I swear before Jesus on his cross that if Mr. Matt says it happen so, it happen so!"

"Well, mammy!" It was probably the first time she had ever been called that in her life, and Carey knew it. "Since you know your boys so well, maybe you can say why the elder one would kill himself?"

"I don't know," she said stubbornly. "But what Mr. Matt say, I believe."

"I'm afraid you're prejudiced, mammy."

Selah loomed in the corridor where he had been standing. "I serve Mr. Harry all my life, sheriff. But Mr. Matt don't lie."

"Loyal," shrugged Carey. "And doubtless wise to play up to the new master."

Rachel barred the sheriff's way, moving as if in her sleep. "My husband killed himself, sheriff, because I had been unfaithful to him."

Tante Estelle gave a moaning gasp. Selah's great shoulders flexed, and the look in his eyes was terrible to meet. "I didn't kill my husband," Rachel ended. "But I was the cause of his death."

"That I'll believe," Carey said. "But I want the man who pulled the trigger. So, Mr. Bourne, in spite of all these testimonials in your favor, I'll expect you tomorrow."

He swaggered out. Selah went to his dead master, kneeling by the bed. Matt confronted Rachel. "Why

did you do that? It won't help me. And it's the last
thing Harry would have wanted!"

"I can't let you take the blame."

Tante Estelle caught each of them by the arm. Her
tawny eyes were blazing. "You neither of you have a
lick of sense! I saw you flowin' together like filings to
a magnet, and I blessed you, Mr. Matt, for going away
'cause there was bound to be trouble otherwise. I fig-
ured when Miss Rachel had babies—" Hunching her
thin shoulders Tante put away all of what might have
been and spoke with the practicality of one who'd seen
many deaths and learned that life goes on afterwards.
"You stop thinkin' on yourselves and remember why
Mr. Harry did this. He was sick to his soul—*that*
you'll have to live with all your years long—but he
loved you still. He wanted you to have each other and
be happy. How you can do it, God knows, but you
owe it to him to try."

When Matt brought Tante's hands to his lips, there
were tears in his eyes. Then he went quickly out.

Rachel stared at the older woman. "Oh, Tante, I
want to die!"

"No," said Tante with sudden hardness. "You're
one who'll live. And you'll laugh and love, though you
don't think so now. Come along. I'll give you a bit of
laudanum. Sleep's the best thing for you now."

Glancing at Harry's covered form, Rachel wished
she could sleep forever.

VI

If only. If only—

That afternoon, night and next morning, all through the funeral, Rachel's agony of regret was muffled but not soothed by laudanum. She had a sense of not inhabiting her body, an illusion heightened by wearing a too-large black dress of the former Mrs. Bourne which Tante had aired and pressed. In spite of these efforts, the odor of camphor and age clung to the stiffly rustling taffeta, the black veil that let Rachel, fortunately, be present without baring her face.

Matt had no such protection. His face must be his mask. Because of the circumstances, only a few people were there besides the inhabitants of Gloryoak. The McLeods were there, the daughters casting sympathetic glances toward Matt, and so were Dr. Martin and Ferris Pettigrew, the lawyer.

Harry's grave was next to his mother's, not far from

Etienne. When the minister said the last prayer and the grave was filled in, Matt looked at Rachel.

She put back her veil. It was like gazing into eternity. She loved this man. Standing near his brother's and her husband's grave, she loved him. But his eyes were bleak as winter. He kissed Tante Estelle and strode to where Selah held his stallion.

After everyone was gone, Rachel knelt by Harry's grave. He had deserved so much better—a wife who could make him happy, give him children, a quietly blessed life. But like a bewitched traveler in the bayous, he'd followed an elusive dancing light, his dream of her, which in the end left him in darkness. She had loved him like an older brother, worshipped him as a guardian. Now that they were alone, she wept for him, her face against the earth of his freshly dug grave.

If time could just turn back to yesterday! How gladly she would have let Matt go if Harry could be alive. By killing himself to leave her and Matt free for each other, he had made it almost certain they never could be together.

A piercing wind blew and rain misted down. Rachel was surprised she could still feel such things as damp and cold, but she didn't move. Tante Estelle came scolding, brought her inside, got her out of her muddy wet clothes, gave her a brisk scrubbing and clean nightgown and got her to bed with a cup of warm milk and more laudanum.

"Now, don't you go wrecking yourself!" Tante scolded. "You'll have to give evidence at Mr. Matt's trial, and if you act like a sick pullet, it won't help anyone. Best way you can show Mr. Harry thanks is to prove he didn't love a flutterbrained coward."

"But Tante, I *am* afraid!"

"For sure. It's what you do when you are scared

that counts. So get your rest, child. Sun'll come up in the morning and you got to meet it."

Rachel didn't wake to sunlight, though, or even daylight. Drowsy with laudanum, she was dimly conscious of the glare of light, scuffling movements, before strong hands seized her, tearing away the bedding, pushing aside her gown. A cruel hot mouth muffled her scream, forcing her lips apart as a hard knee spread her legs. He entered her savagely with sharp punishing lunges as if using a weapon to hurt and subjugate her.

Tom.

She would know that body anywhere, those rough, grasping hands. It hadn't occurred to her, or probably anyone, that he might hear of Harry's death and come back to Gloryoak.

This was the nightmare, only worse. Writhing beneath him, trying to twist herself this way and that to dislodge him, Rachel wrenched her head down, bit his arm. He swore and struck her on the side of the jaw so her own blood mixed with his in her mouth and she lay dazed until he shuddered and collapsed on her, pinioning her with his weight.

Could she reach the lamp, stun him with it? There was a poker by the fireplace, the cast-iron door jamb, a bronze statuette on the mantel. If she held on to her nerve, surely she could stun him long enough to make her escape.

Keeping one arm over her, Tom raised himself on one elbow, lazily tracing the curves of her thighs and breasts, his clear blue eyes as callously cheerful as a boy's who's pulling wings off butterflies.

"So here we are, my pretty whorish sister-in-law. Poor old Harry beneath the sod and me as master!" He paused, grinning, to let that sink in. "If you study to please me, your situation won't change much except that I can appreciate and develop your talents. To outsiders, you'll be my respected if somewhat foolish, widowed sister-in-law."

"And if I don't please you?"

He raised a careless shoulder. "You'll be my demented female relation who must be restrained to her room. A great pity, but so fortunate that I'm dutiful in seeing to my late brother's widow."

It was horrible but it could work.

"You seem to forget you're wanted for murder," she said, seizing at a sudden hope.

He chuckled. "Self-defense. And nobody cares about that Cajun now my upright brother's dead. Don't raise your hopes on that score. I talked with Sheriff Carey. He's an old friend of mine. Without Harry to push those charges, they might as well have never been made."

She could well believe that, but snatched at a new thought. "Can't you get Carey to let Matthew go?"

"My dear, why should I?"

Dumbfounded, it was a moment before she could speak. "Why, he—he's your brother."

"And I was Harry's, but did that keep him from putting a price on me?" Tom's eyes gleamed. "I hid out in New Orleans for a while, but I always planned to come back and settle with that pious muttonhead. I was on my way when I heard Matt had saved me the trouble."

"But Matt didn't!" When she'd told the story, Tom chuckled again.

"Harry's just stupid saint enough to have done it. But I've made sure Matt will hang. We were never friends. He was always ruining my fun. Don't need any contenders for Gloryoak or you. I scattered plenty of whiskey around the town, and set talk going. Matt's riled our red-hot secessionists by saying they can't whip the North, and he hasn't hid his views on slavery. Carey won't stop a band of righteous citizens who crave to avenge the esteemed Harry Bourne."

That meant that now—right now—Matt was in danger. Twenty miles away. She couldn't wait for a foolproof moment. When Tom, yawning, started to sit up, she snatched the lamp, smashed the heavy glass globe against his head with all her strength behind it.

He pitched forward, sprawling. Oil from the broken lamp was catching fire near his head. Rachel didn't want to burn him or the house. She ran for the ewer by the wash basin, tossed water on the flames, finished smothering them with an edge of the wet rug as Tante Estelle rushed in.

"What in the world—"

At sight of Tom, Tante Estelle choked. She looked from him and the broken lamp to Rachel. "Did he—"

"Yes, but I'm all right. Tante, he's stirred up some drunks in town, has them thinking about taking Matt out of jail and hanging him! I've got to do something!"

Tante Estelle was tearing sheets into strips. "Help me tie Mr. Tom good and get him in that little room. I'll lock it tight and he won't be getting out for a while. Hurry, child!"

Tom's head was bleeding, and he breathed heavily. "It may be a few days till he wakes up," Tante said as they hauled him into the small windowless chamber. She tossed the bedding over him and locked the door.

"Get into your riding habit," she told Rachel. "And stick a few things in one of those quilts. I'll send Selah for your horse, and he'll ride with you to town."

Rachel scrambled into her warmest habit, stuffed underthings, a wool dress and her hair brush in the quilt, slipped into her hooded cloak and boots.

No sound came from the adjoining room. Evidently Tante meant to pretend surprise when she would be finally compelled to "find" Tom. Whether he lived or died, Matt wouldn't be safe. If Rachel could get him free, they'd have to run, at least till tempers cooled.

Tante came back, helped her drag her bundle down the hall and thrust two small leather bags in her hands. "Tuck these in your habit, Miss Rachel. There's enough to get you and Mr. Matt well on your way. It's money old Mr. Matthew left me, but I'm never going to need it."

"Tante, I can't take your savings!"

"Sure you can! That boy in jail's worth more to me than anything." The little woman's golden eyes blazed. "You break him out and don't let any grass grow under you till you're long gone!"

"Oh, Tante!"

"Come on. Selah's ready. He's got a pistol 'case it's needed."

It was after midnight when Rachel and Selah tied their horses a little distance from the jail. The hope that Tom's cronies had drunk themselves into a heap faded at the sound of howling laughter and ribald song coming from a public house on the outskirts of town.

Rachel shivered. When they had worked themselves up to it, when they had stopped being men and became a mob, then they'd come. They must be drinking up Tom's largesse before they got down to business.

"Sheriff's not in the jail," Selah reported, back from reconnoitering. "Door's locked but the key's left on the outside, all easy for that trash yonder."

"Then I'll go get Mr. Matt. Where's his horse?"

"Back of the jail. I'll put my saddle and bridle on him, Miss Rachel, and you make all the hustle you can. I hear those pigs across the way hollerin' for a rope. Any minute now they're comin'!"

Rachel glided in shadows, forced the awkward key, prayed the creaking door wouldn't be heard.

"Matt?"

A sharp intake of breath. "What are you doing here?"

"Can't you hear them across the road?"

"Just drunk."

"Tom's back. He paid for the whisky and the talk." How she wished she could see Matt's face. "You're not going to get a trial, Matt. The sheriff left the key in the lock. Hurry! Selah's getting your horse."

"Have you got a pistol?"

"Selah does."

"Then I think I'll borrow it and wait for those gentlemen."

"They'll kill you!"

"Maybe. But not with a rope."

"What are you trying to do?" she asked painfully, wishing she dared touch him. "Offer yourself to God's judgment in trial by combat—with that rabble?" When he didn't answer, she pushed on. "Matt, Tom raped me again tonight! He means to keep me shut up at Gloryoak. If you won't come away with me, you'd better kill me. It would be kinder than what'll happen otherwise."

Silence again, but this time she felt his presence. He was at least considering another road than his hell-bent one. She forced herself to keep still, let the darkness and the jeering voices across the street argue for her.

At last he sighed. "All right. We'll go. But it'll be one hell of a long long way. Far enough to forget."

She didn't think there was that distance in the world, but at least for now he was turned from death.

She found the key to his cell on the sheriff's desk and, after what seemed an eternity of fumbling, got the lock turned.

They rode southwest after parting from Selah, who said he'd go with them except for his wife and children at Gloryoak. "That trash'll forage around in the bushes but won't much happen till daylight," he said. "And not much then, I reckon, with Mr. Tom eggin' them on. That sheriff won't fancy trailing an army man. By the time Mr. Tom's able to kick up a fuss, you can be out of reach."

Rachel could tell Matt was frowning. "You're sure Tom won't know you and Tante helped us?"

"He won't know a thing we don't want him to," chuckled Selah. "Tante's goin' to be so thunderstruck when she finds him, goin' to take care of him so good, that he'd never reckon she helped plunk him in that little room." The men shook hands. "Some day maybe you come back?" Selah asked wistfully.

"I'm glad you can want me," Matt said in a strangled voice. "But I won't be back. Give Tante my love."

The shadow that was Selah vanished into the darker shadows of the night and Rachel and Matt rode south and west. And silent.

Rachel came to hate that quiet. It made her think of Harry, and she kept seeing his stricken face that last day. She remembered the heavy weight of Etienne's body against her knees, the way Harry had comforted her. Strangely enough, though she shuddered from the physical memory of Tom's last assault, it had exorcised the vicious horror of that first attack. He was a man she had managed to knock senseless and from whom she had escaped. He would never haunt her dreams again.

But Harry would. He'd haunt her waking hours,

too, till she made some peace with herself. How could that be, especially with Matt so remote and forbidding?

Shunning plantations, settlements, even lone cabins at first, they had ridden through pine forests so dense sun scarcely filtered through at noon, their horses' hoofs muted on needles fallen from pines thrusting two hundred feet into the air, or mulch of leaves from giant sycamore, cypress, walnut or pecan. There were cotton and corn fields, too, when they reached the rich bottom land of the Brazos. Sleek cattle and horses grazed in lush pastures, and Rachel glimpsed more than one distant great white house like that they had forsaken.

The silence between them was terrible, but speaking was worse. Rachel's mind could barely distinguish reality from illusion. Of course they'd talked a little. She'd told all she knew about Tom's return and had given Tante's hoard into Matt's keeping.

"Poor Tante!" he said, "She loved all three of us boys. The best one's dead, one's a fugitive and the rogue's the one she's got left! But Tom was fond of her in his way. If they have trouble, it'll be because of how he treats other people."

That seemed likely, but Matt answered Rachel's questioning look with a shrug. "Tante's free. And there'll be a nice sum left her in Harry's will. She can leave if Tom worries her too much."

For several days they slept in the woods. Selah had packed their saddlebags with provisions and some of Matt's belongings. After that Matt judged it safe to stop at inns or houses.

At the first inn they learned that Lincoln, as expected, had won the election. After they were settled in the inn's one private room that night, a small loft reached by climbing up a ladder, Matt took Rachel's hand. It was the first time he had touched her except by way of necessity. Her blood began racing, sending her nerves tingling.

"Rachel, you're young, healthy and of a nature to be happy when woes don't blight you. You'll forget all this much quicker if you start a new life without me. Tante Estelle's money would keep you till you found a position or I could leave you with army friends at one of the Western forts."

She tried to free her hands but he held them tight, so she searched his face in the dim light while she fought the lump in her throat. "Do you want to be rid of me?"

"That's not it."

"Then what is?" she demanded. "Do—do you hate me, Matt?'

He pulled her against him. She thought he would kiss her but instead he buried his face in her hair, rocking back and forth despairingly. "I love you, Rachel, but I don't know what can come of it. After what's happened, can we ever be happy together?"

"Happy or not, I'm staying with you unless you ask me to leave."

He still would not kiss her, but that night she woke to find his arms around her. Tempted to arouse him in his sleep, she started to stroke him, then turned away. She would not play that kind of trick, though instinct told her that loving could cleanse a lot of wounds. When he made love to her—if he ever did—he must choose to.

When the two riders crossed the Colorado, they came into grazing lands of mesquite grass watered by occasional springs and creeks. Wild turkey gobbled in live oak thickets and deer fed in the glades, but Rachel begged Matthew not to shoot the graceful deer unless they had no other food. They found honey in a hollow hickory tree by the Guadalupe River, and this gave them a wonderful taste of sweetness, though they left honey enough behind for the bees.

Not long after, they gazed down on the valley of San Antonio, where the old city of sun-dried adobe wound along the river watering many canals which nourished garden patches, flowers and trees. The town was laid out in streets that intersected at right angles toward the town center of two plazas surrounded by flat-roofed stone houses, with the church and public buildings in the middle.

Twenty-four years ago the Alamo had fallen, and hundreds of Santa Anna's dead soldiers had been dumped into the river. The Texan corpses had been burned. Now the city was peaceful and Rachel gazed longingly at glimpses of green leaves behind high walls and barred gates.

"Matthew—Is—is this far enough?"

"No!" His lips had been tighter than his fingers on the reins. "But we'll be married here. Whatever else, we'll do that!"

They'd been wed by a rheumy white-haired Presbyterian minister who didn't ask where they came from, only where they were going. When he heard their way lay west into new country, his tired eyes lit up and he hurried out to his kitchen, returning with some kernels of corn, which he put into Rachel's hand as if they were gold.

"This is San Jacinto corn!" he told them proudly. "When you get to your settling place, plant it!"

He laughed to tell them how Santa Anna had vowed to Sam Houston that he would lead a great army back to victory, wiping out his defeat at San Jacinto. Houston had showed him an ear of corn, said it had been his ration for four days, and did Santa Anna think an army could whip men who would die following a general who had only corn to gnaw on?

"Then we called to Sam to give us the corn so we could plant it and name it after him," the minister went on, eyes misting as they shone. "But Sam, he said to call it San Jacinto corn and plant it everywhere in honor of that battle where we won our freedom."

"We'll plant it," Rachel promised.

They had thanked him and gone to buy necessities; grain for the horses, tamales stuffed with chicken, a meal of *cabrito,* or young kid, a hatchet, salt and corn-meal.

Though they were haunted by each other's company, it was a shared and naked dread, a feeling they did not have to conceal. But when they spoke with people, they themselves seemed unreal. This was so painful they did not linger in town but paid their money to pleasant, joking people and rode away, past the river echoing with the sounds of women and children bathing.

Matt had chosen the stage road that ran four hundred and fifty miles from San Antonio to El Paso, the last half of the way through desert and bare mountains. He explained that a few garrisons had been built along this route in the '50's to protect travelers and discourage Indian forays but that Comanches still ranged over western Texas and made an annual raid into Mexico during the autumn Comanche Moon. In spite of deserts and Indians, the Butterfield Overland Mail had carried passengers and mail for several years now from Saint Louis and Memphis as far west as San Francisco, stopping off at the isolated Texas forts.

Rachel and Matt followed the Nueces through cedar- and oak-covered hills where clear water sparkled over limestone outcroppings and frothed over shallows. When they and their horses grew tired, they camped to let the big gray stallion and dainty chestnut mare graze in the deep grass along the river while they rested and feasted on wild turkey or trout with bread Rachel made in the frying pan.

During the last part of their three-hundred-mile journey, Rachel had been openly asking Matt if they had come far enough. On the second morning of their Nueces camp, she breathed in air sweet as that of East Texas but with a wilder tang of cedar, plum, buckthorn, mallow and mustang grapes.

"We might," she ventured, "build a cabin here."

Matt seemed not to hear, and Rachel dared not speak again. But that afternoon when he saw a herd of whitetail deer in the glade, he would have shot one had not Rachel gasped and caught his arm.

Their eyes stabbed into each other's. Rachel moved back from him as if burned. Matt went pale. As the frightened deer bounded off with their white tails signaling danger, Matthew stared at Rachel. "No," he said. "We can't stay here!"

He caught up Lady and Storm, and they moved on that very afternoon.

The country ascended, thick with deer and rabbits, still ridged with limestone, but with fewer cedar, oak and elm. Rough-leafed hackberry trees with warty trunks and twisted shapes grew in ledges of stone, sending feeder roots into tiny crevices, until the roots, though constricted and gnawed by the rock, gradually split it. Less hardy trees would die before winning their battle with the limestone, but their seeds would start other trees growing in the fissures, letting moisture seep in, till the giant slabs finally crumbled into soil where gentler trees and plants could feed.

"See how that tree's pushed up the rock!" Rachel called to Matt.

At first she had been no more able to talk than he,

but as their journey lengthened, the midnight of her despair was seared with flashes of fear for this man she loved, this man she had not met till she was already married to his brother. On this plateau four hundred miles from home her heart cried out to him, though she spoke only of hackberry and limestone. Somehow they must start speaking naturally again, look at each other without the crippling dread that gripped her now. Somehow they had to live. Somewhere they had to stop running! Matt looked at the stunted, fiercely rooted tree which had pried up the huge rock slab. A hint of a smile softened his long mouth.

"That's a boulder-breaking tree, a pioneer. Too busy sucking water and food from around the rocks to worry about whether its roots get scarred or if its limbs are pretty."

Six days out of San Antonio, they reached Fort Lancaster, located on a ledge of limestone above a pretty little creek which flowed through stands of pecan and oak. The quarters were built of limestone, and Rachel saw two officers' ladies chatting while their children played nearby. She halted her mare and gazed at the women who seemed so at home and gay in this wilderness. Even the bare parade ground seemed to create a sense of purpose.

This was wild new country, dangerous, yet beginning to be settled. Surely she and Matt could start fresh here and have human company though they were far from home.

Rachel looked at him, reading his feelings in the down-bending of his mouth, and though she was disappointed, she urged Lady after him.

"Would you like to stay?" he demanded, turning in the saddle. "I'm sure some of the officers I knew are still here."

"Could you stay?"

"No."

"Then neither can I."

Out of sight of the fort, they camped on the creek, and Matthew caught and broiled a delicious bass, but Rachel had no appetite. Were those ladies at the Fort the last white women she might ever see?

They crossed the Pecos into a different world. The frequent springs and waterfalls ceased. They were in prime Comanche country now and lit no fire at night or where the smoke could curl up and be seen from a distance. It was lonesome plains and desert hills with rabbits and antelope below hunted by high-wheeling hawks and eagles dropping from a dazzling sky.

Two men rode up one noon, a ginger-haired white man whose red lips showed through his curling beard and whose yellow eyes strayed often to Rachel. He wore bandoliers, as did the Mexican with him.

"That real coffee?" he asked with a tight smile.

"Have a cup," offered Matthew. He could do little else. When a traveler stopped at your camp, he immediately became your guest and was entitled to hospitality.

"Much obliged," grinned the gingery one.

He climbed down, followed by his companion. Rachel poured coffee into her cup and Matthew's and gave them to the strangers, who drank with gusto and showed no signs of leaving.

"I hope you'll pardon us," said Matthew, beginning to tighten the horses' cinches. "We need to be moving on."

"Oh, do ye?" asked the yellow-eyed man, and his gaze went over Rachel in a way that made her turn her back and busy herself with clearing up the food. "And where be ye headed in such a hurry?"

Matthew jerked his head west. "What's in that direction?"

"Nothing or a lot, dependin' on what you want," drawled the stranger. "If you go due west, you'll soon hit the Comanche trail. Runs from the Staked Plains down across the Rio Grande into Mexico. Leads through the Big Bend, and there in the Chisos the Comanches split up and half raid Chihuahua while the others steal everything they can carry or drive off from Durango. But if the Big Bend don't tempt you, you can go on west by Fort Davis to the Guadalupes. El Capitan leans over the big salt lakes, then there's El Paso, and then you can cross into New Mexico. Hell, stranger! You could keep goin' if you wanted to till you got to Californy!"

"I reckon the Big Bend will do us," Matt said.

The ruddy man squinted curiously. "Eagles nest there, and coyotes have their dens. Indians, rustlers, bandits, they all pass through, but none of 'em settle. There's plenty of pronghorn and rattlesnakes, but it's no place for people."

"That's fine. More room for cattle."

"You'd be lucky to sell before they were stolen," the stranger shrugged. "But supposing you did raise a herd, you could sell to the army posts, Fort Stockton or Fort Davis."

He nudged his friend in the ribs. "You and me like elbow room, don't we, Manuel, but there's too much down there even for us!"

Manuel laughed and nodded. "No people. No one to rob."

He brought his hand free from under his vest, holding a pistol. Red lips shining in the mat of his beard, the white man pulled a Walker Colt out of his belt.

"Stranger, you can travel lots faster alone. Get going." He smiled toward Rachel. "We'll take right good care of your lady. Rather not have to kill you and get her all upset."

It all happened in a moment.

Matt launched himself at the gingery man. "Ride!" he shouted to Rachel.

She swung the frying pan into Manuel's face but he knocked her aside and brought his gun crashing down on Matt's head. Staggering to her feet, Rachel tried to fight them off Matt's prostrate body, but the white brigand dragged her up by her hair, laughing as he roughly fondled her breasts.

"Spunky. We may keep you a while. But it'll be more fun to break you in with your man watching. Manuel, stake him out."

"Let him go!" Rachel cried. "I—I'll do whatever you want, but please don't hurt him!"

The man held her close to his foul-smelling body, playing greedily with her breasts. "Why, honey, you'll do what we want anyway if you want to have a chance. Kick up a row and I'll geld him." He gave her a shove. "We're hungry. Get our dinner."

Matt was tied now, feet together, hands lashed to greasewood bushes. Sick with fear and knowing that their only hope was in her keeping calm and finding some chance to overcome their captors, Rachel began mixing corn bread. The coffee was boiling at the edge of the coals. Matt's knife lay where he'd used it to cut up the rabbit they'd fried that noon. If one of the men would just leave camp! Surely they wouldn't relieve themselves this near their food. But she couldn't do much unless Matt was conscious. To her vast relief, he stirred but went still again when Manuel glanced toward him.

Had he immediately comprehended their situation or was he still senseless? The wolf-eyed man stretched lazily and sauntered off. Manuel squatted between Rachel and Matt and began to pick his teeth.

Setting the fry pan bread on rocks by the coals, Rachel used her skirts to shield her from Manuel. Lifting the coffee pot, swinging about in the same instant, she sent the scalding liquid over her guard. Screeching, he clawed at his face. She grabbed Matt's knife, calling his name as she slashed the thongs binding his hands, hacked at those on his feet.

He was conscious, thank God. Manuel was lurching toward them and the other brigand was running back, firing his pistol. Matt kicked Manuel off his feet, reached for his heavy Colt, and aimed from a kneeling position that braced his arm. He did this as the advancing bandit's first shot struck Manuel and the second hissed close to Rachel.

Matt didn't miss.

The man's rusty hair vanished in blood along with the top of his face. He reeled, his hands flailing the air, then pitched forward. He kicked feebly and was still.

Matt went to stare down at Manuel. "You're gut-shot. Shall I finish you?"

Sweat beaded the dark face. "Gracias, señor."

"Ride ahead," Matt told Rachel. "I'll bring our gear."

She tightened Lady's cinch and mounted, avoiding the sprawled body, beginning to shake now the danger was past. In a few minutes she heard a shot and winced.

Awful men. Better dead so they couldn't prey on others. But—terrible, unbelievable, that life could end so quickly. When Matt caught up to her she was crying.

"Rachel!" He rode alongside and grasped her bridle. "Are you hurt?"

She shook her head, sobbing harder. Weeping for Harry and Etienne, for all who had met sudden violent death.

Matt swung off Storm. He looped the horses' reins to a mesquite, spread his cloak and lifted Rachel down.

It was the first time he had taken her since that day she overtook him on the road, the day Harry died. She wanted him to be slow and loving, smile at her in the daylight, and let the grief and guilt and sadness heal. But he took her in haste and though she cried out, opening to him, he would not stay in her after his wild fierce crescendo.

For some minutes, he lay drained, but when she hesitantly touched his face, he got to his feet, straightened his clothes and helped her up and into the saddle.

VII

The swelling rounded hills picked up colors of sun and sky, stretching on in a nothingness of grass bleached gold.

For the first time, fear of the wild land gripped Rachel, so that she halted Lady, stroking her mane, and peered into the glittering distances, as alien to her, after cypress swamps, moss-grown giant trees, and rich black planting soil, as any foreign desert could have been.

"Matthew! Where—where are we going?"

He stared west for a few minutes, the sun glare causing the corners of his eyes to wrinkle. An eagle spiraled toward the sun, climbing till he was a tiny speck. Matt turned in his saddle.

"The Big Bend! We'll swing south before long."

Where only eagles nest and coyotes den?

But at least there was a river. Trees would grow there, a garden, fruit . . .

Rachel spoke to her mare, rode up beside Matthew but he did not look at her, and all that day they said nothing they did not have to, while the weight on her heart crushed heavier.

Had killing the robbers brought back memories of Harry's death? Would they never be free of it? To grieve a while, to suffer, that was bound to be, but were their lives to be haunted forever, their love poisoned at its roots? Rachel stared at the broad shoulders of the man in front of her, almost hating him because he could not master his guilt but instead set it between them.

How could she forget? How could she even live, if he refused to hold her in his arms and cherish her? How long could she go on like this, riding drymouthed under the hostile sun in a wilderness she could not have imagined, with the back of the man she had loved always turned against her?

At twilight, Matt raised his arm and pointed where a white track stretched beyond the limit of vision, dimmed into hills and shadows.

"That's the Comanche Trail."

He rode forward and she let her mare keep pace so they took the road at the same time. It was a strange, savage trail, worn by horses and cattle and mules, littered by their bones. Probably, Rachel thought, bones of captives bleached with those of animals, for this was country where Indians drank the blood of their horses when all else failed, or desperate white men drank their own urine, which drove them even madder with thirst.

Matt and Rachel kept to the trail as it wound into palisades of fiery rock, mountains topped by bleak stone citadels, stretches of spiny knife-edged plants, and dozens of wind-twisted, water-seeking plants that clung to life in defiance of the arid, rocky terrain.

They saw lizards and jackrabbits, glimpsed a coyote, watched as a crested bird with a long tail pursued some hapless insect through the cactus. As the land climbed, the sparse desert growth yielded to dwarf walnut and desert willow while pine and juniper, live oak and thick coarse grass grew along the mountain slopes. There were whitetail deer, squirrels and chipmunk, and Rachel cried out in delight at a graceful straight-horned kind of antelope with black markings on its face.

They had been rationing their water for days, but it was now almost gone. They were always thirsty.

"The animals must drink somewhere," Rachel said.

"Yes, but only they know where," said Matt. "It can't be far to the river now."

The Rio Grande, a name she had only heard, a foreign name. She shivered in spite of her dry throat, gazing around at the vast silent country. It was hard to believe that human beings, even Indians, had ever been there, and passed through that tortuous landscape.

On the eighth day from the Pecos, Matt woke Rachel early. They shared a cup of coffee he had already made, chewed a little bread.

"We have to keep going tonight," he said. "The horses can't last much longer without water."

The sun gleamed purple, rose and gold off a carved range of flat-topped mountains to their left as they moved into low flats that seemed to stretch south to infinity and west to hills capped by natural fortresses like those they had ridden among.

A snake raced in front of them with startling speed, disappearing among the tumbled rocks. Lady shied. Rachel quieted her but could not still the revulsion that scaly diamond-patterned creature, slithering on its belly, had aroused in her.

Cursed be the earth for thy sake . . .

She stared at the parched, tortured land, overgrown with thorns, and in her mind she saw the black rich earth of Gloryoak. *Thy brother's blood cried to me from the ground.*

Brother's and husband's blood. Rachel groaned inwardly, recalling that plea of the first murderer. *My punishment is greater than I can bear.*

But she must bear it or die. There was no going back to the moment when she could have stayed at Gloryoak. Now there was only this desert, shimmering, shifting distances, far-off purples colored by light that turned, as one neared them, into barren earth and stone.

But just ahead! A hint of green? Senses alerted, Rachel scanned the horizon. Beyond the monotonous grays and blue-greens of scattered desert moisture-suckers rose fresh bright forest green.

She turned her head and her cracked lips moved. "A tree!"

Matthew nodded.

They rode toward the tree, the horses moving faster, scenting water, and half an hour later, beneath the gaze of an astonished beaver, Storm and the little mare stood in the Rio Grande, drinking its waters, while upstream, Matt and Rachel sank their faces and drank.

They splashed themselves, laughing, drinking again and again, then fetched the horses to keep them from foundering. The grass on the bank grew thick and green, and the horses settled into it while Matt and Rachel, wet with the Rio's waters, looked about them.

The great-trunked, luxuriantly fronded, giant mesquite that had signaled across the flats knotted its thirsty roots in a small stone cliff above the river,

which curved back, rising in height, to bluffs following
the water, bordered by rushes, grass and trees.

On the Mexican side, a sheer granite wall formed
one side of a canyon through which the river ran, but
this wall ended abruptly a short distance to the east,
so at that point, the river looked easy to ford.

Round holes, perhaps made by wind and rain,
pitted the great stone barrier. It seemed impossible
that people could have lived in them, yet indentations
led to some of the caves, scored with a regularity that
made them seem like footholds.

Rachel's wondering gaze followed Matt's to a huge,
angular collection of sticks and limbs jutting from one
of the upper caverns.

From even higher above came a raucous scream.
Out of the burning, cloudless blue hurtled an eagle,
dropping on something out of sight along the towering
cliff. In a moment the great bird reappeared, a rabbit
in its claws, heading for the haphazard nest on the
cave's edge.

"It's not the time of year for young eaglets," Matt-
thew said. His eyes reflected the wild sky, lingered on
the gold gleaming bird, passed to the ford crossing into Mexico.

Shrinking against the tree, Rachel gripped the
rough bark to hold back a pleading cry. They mustn't
enter another country, wander in other deserts, or go
without food and water until their skin dried on their
bones! Yet if Matt went, she would have to follow.
Even if she could have hoped to stay on alone, and
live, she would have to go with him. This man commanded her life. Or death, if it came to that.

Could they love each other again? Could they live,
here on this river, so far from home? She was asking
all these things when she called to him across the little

space, "Is this far enough, Matthew? Is it far enough?".

He slowly turned to her. "We'll stay here," he said. But he could not answer her deeper question.

They stayed a week by the river, taking shelter under a half-cave in the bluff, their blankets spread on limbs covered with rushes. Exploring their side of the river, Rachel found a warm spring filling a rock hollow not far from their camp. Here she bathed, washed her hair and scrubbed hers and Matt's travel-stained garments.

They barely spoke, they didn't lie in each other's arms and Matthew wouldn't really look at her. That day he had taken her after killing the bandits must have been the flow of life asserting itself after a brush with death.

The horses' gaunt frames filled out with lush graze and rest. Matt shot a wild pig. Its flesh was strong and flavorful.

"Where shall we have our house?" she asked Matt one morning as they ate quail and bread from the last of their flour.

"This is too close to the river," he said. "Indians and outlaws from both sides must come this way."

"We haven't seen anyone since—since those men."

"One meeting with that kind's enough," he answered dryly. "Remember, we followed the Comanche Trail. They go down it only once a year, but it's best not to be on that route."

She remembered the hidden folds of the Chisos through which they had passed, and shuddered. Somehow, being near a river, even this boundary between two wild regions, gave her a feeling of being closer to people, for in dry country people came to water just as she and Matt had done.

And Comanches? Outlaws?

"If you find water," she asked, "then what?"

He frowned. "This is no place to raise cotton. Once we have some kind of roof over our heads, I'll get some cattle. Fattened up, they should sell at Fort Davis."

"How will you buy cattle? We can't have much of Tante's money left."

"I can hire out for a while to some Mexican rancher, take my pay in cattle."

All through their conversation he looked past her, across the river, his tone as remote as his gaze. Rachel got to her feet. "And what shall I do while you're earning cattle? Stay at this water hole you hope to find back in those awful mountains?"

"It would be the best thing." He still wouldn't meet her eyes. "I'd shoot plenty of meat for you before I left and cure it so it would keep."

"What if you don't come back?"

"Rachel, life out here is one big chance, whatever we do!"

"Matthew, look at me."

He did not. But the line of his jaw hardened and a pulse throbbed at his temple.

"That's what I mean," she said in a dying voice. "Oh, Matt, if you can't even look at me, how can we live? Here, Mexico, anywhere? Why didn't you let the bandits have me?"

His eyes came to her then, so tortured that she flinched, wished her words back. "We'll live," he vowed. "I'll cover your life with mine, as I'd put my cloak over your body. But what else will happen is past my knowing." And she dared not try to force herself into his arms.

VIII

The old coyote still had all the cunning that had kept him alive in these mountains for so long. His gray-yellow coat blended with catclaw and earth as he waited near the water for the creatures he knew would come to drink there.

He'd made the little well himself, digging several feet into the sandy earth to free water seeping down from a cleft in the towering rocks above. Here he could drink, and also eat, as the small bones scattered about testified.

Two field mice scurried forward with the speed of creatures whose lives depended on eluding the swoop of birds or pounce of beasts. The old coyote had one in a spring and a flash of teeth. The other shot into a clump of prickly pear where it had its nest, protected from the coyote and others of his soft-nosed kind.

One mouse was not enough. The coyote lolled back to wait. Suddenly, his ears pricked. Something was coming. Something with a strange strong odor he did not recognize. He moved deeper into the catclaw and waited to see whether he could eat this strange thing or whether he must flee it.

Guadalupe's breasts had dried up, so though her child tugged at her nipples till she could have screamed from the pain, he got no milk. He'd wailed with hunger and thirst, poor little thing, till she'd almost left him in order not to have to hear him or watch him die. Only the stubborn hope she might find water had kept her moving.

Today, she crawled more than walked, the two-year-old slung behind her in her shawl. His tiny bones must be as hollow as a bird's. He was in a stupor that was surely next to death, and if he died, she'd lie down with him cradled at her breast, and Mary Mother would be merciful to them, though people had not been.

She was from the village of San Ysidro, on the Rio Grande, one of several river villages that had immunity from Comanche raids in return for hospitality and trading guns and ammunition for stolen mules and livestock.

Such places were hated by ranches and settlements which suffered the annual Comanche scourge, and they considered the people of San Ysidro traitors. Ten days ago, San Ysidro awoke to knives, fire and slaughter. A force of men from southern ranches and towns, most of them mounted on horses marked with Don Celestino Cantú's Tres Coronas brand, had destroyed the little river village and every living thing in it, even the dogs and chickens.

Only Guadalupe and her small son, through the irony of being outcasts, had survived. Juanito was a beautiful little baby, though he had been sired by a Comanche autumn before last, a warrior who'd found Guadalupe bathing in the river and took her in a manner savage as he was.

Guadalupe's parents were dead, and when her body began to swell and she told the old aunt with whom she lived how it had happened, she hadn't been believed. Women would not speak to her. Men made signs and accosted her till she wouldn't go out except to visit the church and pray, early in the morning, before the village was awake. For San Ysidro had a church with a fine bell from Chihuahua, though a priest seldom traveled to the isolated village.

At first Lupe had prayed for the people she'd known all her life to be kind to her again; then she'd prayed for the baby to be stillborn, and after he came, so lovely and perfect that her sad heart smiled to see him, she began to ask the Virgin's help to leave the village and journey to some new place where she could bring up little Juan in peace.

That had been her prayer on the morning the raiders came. She'd hidden in the confessional, at first thinking the horsemen bandits or Apaches, but then she heard shouts in Spanish, taunts of the men from the south and the useless pleas and screams of the people of San Ysidro.

Because of the early hour, no one even looked in the church. When the attackers were gone, driving cattle and horses laden with everything of value, Guadalupe crept out of the church.

A horrid stench came from a pile of blackening corpses burning in the center of the village. Most had been stripped so that old and young, male and female, lay twisted together as if blown there by a terrible wind. Dogs, cats and chickens sprawled among the broken bodies. Guadalupe's old aunt lay across the threshold of her one-room adobe house, naked, one arm lopped off. Guadalupe choked back nausea. Her aunt had treated her like a drudge, but to die like this . . . Closing her aunt's staring eyes, Lupe dragged the body inside the hut, covering it with their old straw sleeping mats.

Crossing herself, Guadalupe moved on, peering in each house. No one lived. When the Comanches stopped here in the autumn they would find ruin worse than they were used to spreading. It would not go well, next Comanche moon, with those brave men of the ranches and towns who had plundered San Ysidro.

Guadalupe went back to the church and gave Juan her breast while she tried to think. She couldn't stay here. She couldn't try to shelter with those who'd killed her people or hope to make her way to a large place like Chihuahua or Durango. If thirst, hunger or Indians didn't kill her, bandits surely would.

But she *could* go over the Rio Grande to search in the mountains for a sheltered place where she could raise little Juan. Some Texans had once stopped to eat and drink in San Ysidro and they had paid silver money and done no harm. They were said to have horns, but she'd glimpsed none, and even if there were Texans in the mountains, they couldn't kill her deader than the men of the south had killed those of San Ysidro.

She hunted till she found a little corn the raiders had missed or scorned, dragged a smoldering but reasonably good serape from a body that had rolled a little way from the pyre and hunted through the houses again till she found a goatskin water bag. There was nothing else left of any use. The raiders had taken blankets and clothing, smashed furniture and pottery, destroyed what they could not carry.

"I can't take you to a worse place," she told Juan, balancing him in a sling made of her shawl.

At the Rio, she filled the water bag, and though the taste of goat grew stronger as she traveled north, and she held her teeth together to strain out the hair as she drank, the water kept her alive and she blessed it.

She was hungry but in no danger of starving. She ate the smallest, most tender pads of prickly pear, and twice she made a hole in the earth, lined it with stones and made a fire in the Apache way her people knew, whirling the point of *chaparro prieto* in the dried bloom stalk of a sotol till it burst into flames. When the earth oven was hot, she trimmed the heart of a sotol from its stalk with a sharp stone, then covered it with more hot stones, and let it bake overnight.

Once, she spotted large black honey ants and followed them to their nest where the workers deposited sweet juice secreted by gall wasps in the crops of storage ants who hung from the top of their chambers, too swollen with honey to move. She dug out many of these tiny storehouses and ate them, squeezing some of their juice into little Juan's mouth.

But water was giving out, and when she could not drink, she could make no milk for the baby. She was a week from the Rio, apparently far from any help, and now she couldn't find her way back to the river where at least there was water.

One gorge looked like another, and it seemed she had been down all of them, but she found no *charco* or *tinaja,* no creek or river, though she followed two dry streambeds for miles to find their sources dried up, as were the dirt or rock-bottomed holes which rains would turn into ponds.

But she must find water while she could still move or they would die. She threw away the useless water bag because of its weight, half-crawled along a ravine, found that it opened into a high, broad valley rimmed with peaked red sentinel cliffs.

She hadn't been here. She would have remembered such good grass stretching for miles between the jagged walls. Water was more likely to be near the rocks.

Painfully, she made her way along the cliff, but the dull red granite was dry as dead fire. No damp showed anywhere.

Then she heard the sharp, quick-stifled cry of some creature, saw a yellow-gray flurry of motion subside into the brush, the glint of sun on water.

That gave her strength. A few minutes later, she fell by the coyote's pool, sprinkling her baby's parched face and mouth with the cool miraculous water, sipping it herself, not minding the sand she got with it.

"Juanito! Juanito!" she croaked as he stirred and sucked toward the water she dribbled from her fingers into his mouth. "We will live! With water, we shall live!"

The coyote trotted away. No thirsty prey would visit the pool while that strange creature splashed about. He must fill his belly someplace else.

All Lupe did that day was rest and rejoice in the water, though she was careful to sip slowly, not too much at one time. A tree had fallen near the pool, and under its bark she found slugs and ants, which gave her food without effort. Her milk began to come back, responding to little Juan's tugging, which grew stronger as he drew in nourishment.

She was very lucky! The Virgin must have listened and guided her to this tiny, precious pool, which replenished itself from some underground seepage; there was no fear of it going dry since it held water even during this season of no rain.

If this was the only water hereabouts, there must be other thirsty creatures. Lupe found a half-cave under the bluff, where powdered dust was warmed by the sun, and she drowsed there with her baby in her arms, in between trips to the pool.

Sometimes she heard a sound and opened her eyes

to see dainty pronghorn water. Squirrels came, chipmunks, rabbits, foxes both red and gray, and once she saw the sharpnosed black mask of a racoon. Tomorrow she might set snares to add meat to her food, but on this day she was content to sleep on the age-old dust and now and then glimpse the animals who shared this wild place with her and lived from the pool's refreshing waters.

As the sun dropped behind red pinnacles, turning the opposite cliffs a glowing gold, Guadalupe gathered bunches of long grass and made a nest for herself and Juan where the rocks of the cave would hold their sun heat longest, for mountain desert nights were cold. After a last drink, she cuddled Juan close, settled in the grass bed, and pulled serape and shawl about them as best she could, covering them over with more grass.

She could live in this valley as long as she wished. It was off the river, unlikely to be traveled by marauders. And if wild creatures were to be her only company apart from Juanito, at least they didn't care who his father was!

No longer driven by the need to find water, she crooned a bit to little Juan, and slept in more comfort than she had known since her village died and more peace than she had felt in months.

She woke with the sun in her eyes, a crunching sound in her ears. As she sat up, clutching her startled baby, a tall shape loomed between her and the sun, casting shadow over the two of them.

A man! With gray Norteño eyes and black hair with a gleam of red. She had never seen anyone so tall. He held a pistol, and a carbine was in the scabbard of the saddle on the big *grulla* drinking at the pool.

The man's face did not seem threatening, nor did

his voice, when he spoke softly in a language she couldn't understand. But when he pointed across the mountains, then at her and his horse, raising his eyebrows, she shrank away, shaking her head. He must be saying he could take her home, across the mountains she had traversed so painfully.

"No," she said. "No!" And he understood. It was one word that meant the same in both tongues.

He shrugged, went to his horse and from the saddlebag got some smoked meat, which he put down on a boulder near Lupe.

Then, speaking slowly, he gestured that he would be back, and turned his horse. Her heart was beating fast as she watched him ride out of the passage to the valley.

Leave the water? Hide? She could not! But suppose he were evil? Suppose he brought back other men and they did with her as the Comanche had? Or as the men of the southern ranches had done in San Ysidro?

She thought of his gray-blue eyes, his long straight mouth. The memory reassured her, though he was too stern to be handsome.

Did he ever smile? Surely, had he meant her harm, he would not have given her meat, or spoken gently, or moved with quiet care, as one approaches a wild bird or animal.

She went to the spring to drink, then sat on the boulder and chewed hungrily at the cured strong-flavored javelina meat, as Juanito suckled eagerly. It was time he was weaned, and she gave him a bit of the meat.

Sun warmed the crisp air as Lupe stretched and yawned.

It wouldn't do to be lazy. The big stranger might not come back, or if he did, it might be some days. She must collect food and make some kind of shelter. But first she washed herself and her hair.

IX

When Matthew and Rachel rode through the jagged defile into the valley, Rachel watched for the girl of whom he had told her, with expectancy and foreboding.

What would this first human be to them? What was a girl doing alone in this wild place, with a small child?

There was good grass here, brownish yellow, and trees in the towering red cliffs that enclosed the meadow, while higher mountains rose beyond but lapsed from sight as they rode further into the green basin. Matthew stopped and moved his head to the left.

Rachel followed his gaze. There in a cavelike hollow of the bluff was some thatched kind of shelter, a slanting roof of limbs, stalks and grass supported on one side by the cliff and on the other a heaped wall of rocks about eight feet long.

"She's been busy," Matthew said. "Yesterday all she had was a big grass nest. Look, there she is at the pool."

Rachel peered at the young woman who had come to her feet in a swift, flowing motion, a toddler in the curve of her arm. A dark madonna, Rachel thought, glancing at Matthew with a stab of jealousy.

Any man must be struck by this girl's soft lovely grace, her warm flesh, cloud of black hair, and dark, sad-looking eyes. Only the copper child nestled against her hinted that she was not as shy and tender as she looked—the child and that competent shelter in the cliff above.

The girl looked from Matthew to Rachel, evidently startled to see a woman. *Disappointed, too?* thought Rachel. But something in the way the young mother held her child stirred sympathy in Rachel, and she got down from her mare, smiled at the girl, and held out her arms for the baby. The girl smiled, too, shyly, bowing her head, then beckoned and turned to lead them to her camp.

But she didn't give her child over to Rachel's holding. She raked hot earth and rocks off a pit to reveal a smoking cabbagelike pulp, as any great lady might invite guests to a feast.

During the next week, Lupe taught Rachel many food secrets of the river people, using Matthew's knife as a key to the thorn-armored treasures of the desert. In grease from the game Matthew shot, they fried pads of the prickly pear after the spines had been carefully scraped away.

Lupe showed Rachel how to cut the cabbagelike heart of the sotol and bake it in a rock pit till it was mealy and tasted rather like a sweet potato. Lupe also enjoyed chewing the stalk of the yucca cut from where the bottom leaves sprouted. Rachel tried it and found it rather like sugar cane.

As they spent time together, they learned words of each other's language by acting out or pointing to things. To Rachel's chagrin, Lupe seemed to remember best, or perhaps it was because Matt talked to her, too, and something in his deep voice imprinted the sounds he made.

Matt, having studied Latin like Rachel, knew many root words, and within a few weeks they could speak and be understood. Usually their conversations were part Spanish, part English, punctuated by gestures and laughter.

Reeling as if drunk, Lupe pointed to the sotol base and said, "Makes fire *agua*—water." She touched a tall dull-green stalk. "Mescal makes crazy water, too."

Matthew laughed across to Rachel. "I don't think it'll ever replace wine and brandy," he said. "But spirits are useful to have around."

This basin, Matt decided, was the best place to settle. For temporary living, he and Rachel made a shelter like Lupe's at the other end of the semicave. Without any spoken agreement, it was accepted that the Mexican girl, for now at least, would be part of their household. There was no doubt that her knowledge of food plants and the country was as valuable as the meat Matt brought in, and Rachel won both Matt's and Lupe's startled respect by improvising a slingshot and bagging rabbits.

Besides the coyote's pool, Matt found a stream, fed by several springs, running from a fissure between two sentinel cliffs at the western end of the broad valley. Digging as the coyote had, at damp places under the bluffs, he'd made two other pools, which promised to serve as water holes.

"There's water here for cattle," he told Rachel. "It's

far enough off the river not to be traveled much by bandits or Indians, and the grass is good. If the herd gets big, the overflow could graze on the higher slopes or spread toward the river."

"Where will you get cattle?" Rachel asked.

"Cattle?" echoed Lupe, cradling little Juan.

Matt made horns and made a mooing sound. Lupe giggled.

"Vacas!" she said delightedly. "You—need *vacas?"*

Matt nodded. "I have no money—no pesos."

She pointed south. "Many *vacas*—many!"

"No money for cows," Matt said again.

Lupe's teeth flashed. "Comanches no pesos." She made a shooting motion of her long warm-skinned arms. "Comanches get *vacas!"*

"I'm no Comanche," said Matt. He looked reprovingly at the girl, gesturing south. "Your people, Lupe! You want me to steal from them?"

"They kill—fire my town!" she spat.

Before, to explain why she and her baby were wandering alone, she had said her town was "dead." Now, in broken English scattered with Spanish and gestures, she told her whole story, and though Rachel and Matt missed details, they understood the main burden, and that the men who had burned San Ysidro must live in extra fear now of the September Comanche raids, for the Indians would be angry to find their trading outlet and resting place destroyed.

Lupe glanced challengingly at Matthew's pistol and rifle resting on a sheltered ledge of the camp.

"Take those," she said. "Go to Don Celestino Cantú. He pays pesos or cattle for you to kill Comanches—bandits. Don Celestino always need *bravos— pistoleros!"*

Matt's eyes widened. "A paid killer," he said. Then his gaze caught on Rachel's who looked back at him.

We've run to the end of the country, and what will you do now?

Matt turned to Lupe. "Where is this Don Celestino?"

"Cross Rio Grande. Go south. Keep Sierra del Carmen on your left but in sight, and you find Don Celestino at Tres Coronas." She smiled. "And his *vacas*. *Vacas* Comanches steal in Mexican Moon."

"Don Celestino burned your town?"

"Many horses wore his mark."

"If he's got men, why doesn't he fight off the Comanches?"

Lupe shrugged, lifting Juanito so that he peered over her shoulder with bright black eyes. The sturdy boy was plump again, recovered from his ordeal of thirst and hunger.

"Don Celestino's land big." She made a wide circle with her arm. "Vaqueros one place, Comanches raid other place. Many Comanches. Too many to fight."

"So every year they steal and kill and carry back slaves?" demanded Matt. "The Mexican government —soldiers, army—why don't they stop Comanches?"

"Mexico City far from Rio Grande," said Lupe. She looked up at Matt. "Your *soldados*—they stop Comanches?"

Matt had to laugh. "They try. So far with little luck."

Rachel felt cold inside, not only because Matt and this girl laughed together as Rachel and he no longer could but because she felt as if they were stranded on a hostile planet where the inhabitants were barbarous, alien and deadly.

"If you get cattle, Matt," she said slowly, "you'll have to defend them from bandits from both sides of the Rio. And from the Comanches as well."

"Apaches, too," said Lupe. "Some live in the Chisos."

Rachel made a despairing sound. Comanches once a year were bad enough, along with occasional bandits. But Apaches living almost as neighbors—

"Well, shall we live in Mexico, then?" Matt stared coldly at Rachel. "Or go back to East Texas?"

Rachel bowed her head. There was no safe place for them. Their love and Harry's death decreed that. It was just, that they begin with nothing—only their lives —and go in fear, atoning for the dead man at Glory-oak.

As if he guessed her thoughts, Matt's voice softened. "This is where we are, Rachel. Sometime, somewhere, we have to make a new start. This land is open. It can be our home."

Or it will make us its own, our flesh its soil, she thought, but she raised her eyes to this man with whom she had fled across eight hundred miles and managed to smile.

"All right, Matthew. How shall we begin?"

"We'll plant those few kernels of San Jacinto corn," he said.

So that corn, descended from the ear Sam Houston had given his men at the defeat of Santa Anna, was the first food planted by man in that valley.

Matt killed a deer and javelina before he left and jerked the meat so it would last the women along with what Rachel could get with her slingshot and Lupe with her snares. Matt removed the deer hide with great care, cutting so the leg and neck openings could be sewed up tight and the skin shaped and sewn into a large bag, rather like the goatskin water bag Lupe had been forced to discard.

"I'll leave either the pistol or the rifle," he said.

"Leave us your big knife," countered Lupe. "We can open sotol and mescal with it and skin rabbits."

"How can I leave you without a weapon?"

"You'll need yours," Rachel said. "Most likely no one will find this valley, but if bad men do, they'd kill us anyway. One gun in our hands wouldn't help."

"I'd damage some of them with the knife," vowed Lupe.

"And I might stun a few with my sling," said Rachel laughing. "You shouldn't worry about us, Matthew!"

Lupe's exultant chuckle swelled her firm breasts under the coarse white blouse. "We here when you bring *vacas*—first *vacas* of many! You make great rancho here, Don Matthew! Greater than Don Celestino's!"

When Matt was ready to leave, he stopped before Lupe. "You'll help my wife?"

The girl nodded with fierce intensity. "Yes, Don Matthew. We are *compañeras*."

"And I'll help her and her baby," Rachel said, with emphasis. Matt faced her in surprise, then laughed from his belly for the first time in months.

"By God, you mean that," he said. "Kiss me, Rachel. Wish us luck!"

In their kiss, the old sweet desire flamed again. Her body went soft, molding to his. After a moment, Matthew stepped back, steadying Rachel, and said huskily, "I'll be back! Nothing will keep me from coming back to you!"

He mounted his big gray horse and rode off. At the mouth of the valley, he turned to wave. The women watched until he was out of sight and then walked back in silence to the camp.

During the next few days, they made bricks for their growing house—mixing mud and dry grass, pressing it into wooden forms, letting the bricks dry in the sun, then stacking them into walls. Each day they worked from morning until early afternoon at this task, ate and rested and then did quiet work or gathered food.

It would be just one room to begin with, but others could be added. Even to Rachel, with her stifled memories of Gloryoak and Tristesse, the adobe walls seemed beautiful, the promise of a real home. In the adobe they could have a fireplace, windows of some kind, furniture. If Matthew brought back cattle and got an army contract, there would be cash, in time, to buy things they couldn't make.

If Matthew brought back cattle.

If Matthew came back.

She forced the whisper away and sat down to sing to little Juan, letting him clasp her fingers. He was a handsome, well-formed child, his dark hair already covering his head, and he smiled back at Rachel, showing white fine teeth.

When would she have a baby? Was something wrong with her, or was it simply that she hadn't been with a man at the right time? Matt hadn't made love to her since the day they'd encountered the bandits. But now that they were settling down and making a home, surely he'd really become her husband. And when they had a baby, he'd have more to think about than the past no one could change.

Rachel and Lupe got along well. They sang and talked, learning more of the other's language and ways. Every day the walls grew higher, and they added to their homemaking supplies. They tanned hides of the animals Matt had shot by covering them with a mixture of brains and horse dung. When this mixture leached off the hair, the hides were scraped with flints and hung to dry.

From clay they found at one end of the valley, they

made bowls and plates and storage jars, firing them in hot coals. Rachel's were awkward at first, but she quickly acquired a deft touch and soon was not ashamed to put her work beside Lupe's.

Lupe showed Rachel the various plants that could be used for remedies—lechuguilla brewed as a tea for rheumatic pains, charcoal from mesquite wood for diarrhea, sunflower seeds to poultice sprains, prickly pear pulp on the forehead to ease headaches. Rachel had a few needles and some thread, but they used bone awls and sinews to lace the hides into blankets, for the nights were chill in spite of the warm days.

When Lupe visited her snares, Rachel stayed with the baby, working near the camp. One day she was sewing rabbit skins together when Lupe came hurrying up, tossed down a rabbit and cried, *"Miel! Miel!"*

Rachel shook her head, not comprehending.

Lupe touched her lips and smacked them. "Sweet. Very sweet." She thought a moment and made a buzzing sound.

"Honey!" Rachel cried. "Lupe, how wonderful!"

They stored the rabbit in the adobe larder they'd built in a niche of the bluff where food could be safe from animals and got out the deerskin bag Matthew had fashioned. Lupe collected several dry cedar limbs, then held a green slow-burning one in their banked fire to use for lighting the other torches when they were near their prize.

Rachel took the bag, the fire limb and the dry ones while Lupe hoisted Juanito into his sling and led off down the valley.

Where the palisades closed, bees were coming in and out of a crevice in the rock, about ten feet above the ground.

Lupe put Juanito on a protected ledge some distance from the bees, warning him to stay there, and began piling rocks into crude steps until, on tiptoe, she could reach the crevice.

"The torches!" she called to Rachel. "And hand the bag where I can reach it. Have care for the bzzz's!"

Rachel put the bag over a rock close to Lupe, lit two of the dry limbs from the green one, handed the first to the girl, and clambered up beside her.

"I put torch in cave, you keep smoke around us to keep bees off," Lupe instructed. She held to the rock with one hand and stretched upward, thrusting her torch inside.

Through the smoke of her own torch, Rachel saw bees pour out in an angry whirring, but she moved the torch, acrid with resinous smoke, and the bees veered away. Lupe gave her torch to Rachel, got the deerskin bag, and clambered up, till only her small brown feet protruded from the cave.

Rachel flourished the torches to ward off the bees, lighting another when one began to burn down. The last torch was halfway gone when Lupe, wriggling and panting, gradually emerged. Clinging to the rocks with one hand, she eased the deerskin bag out of the cave and lowered it to Rachel.

Mussed and smeared with honey, Lupe slid to the ground and took the torch. "I'll carry the bag and keep the smoke around it and me," she said, *"Por favor,* take Juanito and go ahead! Plenty of *miel* is left for the bzzz's, but they're angry!"

Half an hour later, they were proudly back in camp with their treasure. They hung the bag from a tree and kept it covered with skins, with a wall of prickly pear stacked high enough to ward off any raiders.

"Don Matthew will have sweet now," said Lupe, giving Juanito a taste from her finger.

She sounded innocently pleased but Rachel turned away, fighting a swift stab of jealousy. Lupe was lissome and beautiful. She knew how to live in this country better than Rachel could ever hope to learn. Matthew's sweet might be more than honey—

Then Rachel remembered the way he had kissed her, the surging need between them, and from deep within this memory she smiled at the Mexican girl.

"Matthew likes honey. But no more than Juanito does! Look at him hunt for more!"

Lupe nodded, smiling as she fondled her child. But Rachel walked toward the pass, where Matt had waved good-bye, and stared out at the fierce mountains stretching in every direction.

What had happened to him across the Rio Grande? When would he be back? She could not let herself think that he might already be dead, that she might never know how or where he died. He must come. And he'd bring cattle, the start of their herd, just as she and Lupe had begun their home.

X

Matthew crossed the Rio, filled his water skin where he and Rachel had camped and paused to watch the eagle plummet from the heart of the sun to something below.

The mate of the eagle screamed, soaring, climbing into the blinding brightness, and the wild splendor of the flight, the upward beat of the pinions like the visible throbbing of God's savage golden heart, seemed to Matthew the song of the great bird, not its raucous shrieking.

Matt eased the reins and urged Storm onward. "I'll see you in a month, brother," he called to the eagle. "Or I won't see you again at all. But I suppose men are like big ants to you, fastened to the ground."

Once across the Rio, he turned south, the chiseled pink and purpled mesas of the Sierra del Carmen to his left. Resting middays, he rode in the early mornings and from midafternoon till twilight. On the third morning he saw cattle grazing, scattered widely because the grass was poor.

Then he saw the first men he'd met since the bandits, three men in peaked sombreros riding toward him at a gallop. Leather men, brown-skinned, in their high-cantled saddles, hide-covered stirrups for brush work and leather pants and vests. They may well have been among the raiders who destroyed Lupe's village.

Their ropes were leather, too, braided rawhide, and they began circling him, their reatas whistling. Matt halted Storm, controlled the excited horse by a tight grip of the knees, thighs and hands. One of those ropes snapping tight around a man's neck could break it or, more slowly, strangle him.

"Don Celestino Cantú!" Matthew called authoritatively, and blessing Guadalupe for the Spanish she'd taught him, commanded the men to take him to their patrón.

"He knows you, señor?" demanded the most ferocious looking of the horsemen.

"He wants to know me," Matt said carelessly. *"Andale,* hombres!" He spun Storm and rode between two of the leather men, confidently, not looking back, as if certain they must obey him.

It was a tribute to his audaciousness or their fear of possibly angering their master that no rope settled over his shoulders. He was allowed to ride free, a vaquero on either side and one behind, through scattered herds of longhorns, spotted and dun and gray and black, marked with the Cantú triple crown, but wild as the Big Bend pronghorns.

What held his eye more, though, were the horses. From the distance he saw a herd of several dozen grays, which was strange enough, but several miles further on, a score of chestnuts ranged together. As his guards steered him south, Matt saw bands of bay, black, gray and white horses, all grazing unfenced.

"*Caballos,*" he said at last, to an impressively mustached rider, and asked why they were grouped like that.

He missed some fine points of the answer, but he did learn that the best stallion of each color was kept with matching mares because Don Celestino wished to breed the best possible line of each color. This was difficult, though, because the Comanches ran off some of the stock each year.

"And it won't be long till they come again," said Matt pleasantly.

The vaquero shot him an angry glance and spurred forward, so that Matt had to urge Storm to a faster pace.

Storm responded eagerly. He was jaded from the long ride, but he never liked other horses to get ahead of him. Matt didn't like eating dust, either, and when a sprawl of buildings showed white against the far purples of the Sierra del Carmen, he touched Storm with his heels and sent him forward.

Knowing the vaqueros could rope or kill him, Matt was careful not to overplay his hand. He waited for them where he halted before the great abode, and he smiled as they scowled and muttered, except for the mustached one, who laughed.

"Don Celestino will indeed wish to see you! At least for a moment!"

There was the sound of a lifting bar and the massive door, carved with the Cantú emblem of three superimposed crowns, swung open.

Huge and heavy as the door was, it could not dwarf the man who stepped out, though except for a fine white shirt, he wore the leather of his vaqueros. There was grandee blood in him, the pride and toughness of conquerors, though he walked with a limp and his hair was gray.

"Felipé, Abram, Luz!" His voice cracked like a whip at the men, who swept off their sombreros and looked as abashed as children. "How is it that I see you with dust on your faces from riding at the tail of a gringo?"

"I told them you wanted to meet me," Matt began. He showed his teeth in a smile, though he felt cold in the pit of his belly. He wished his Spanish were better.

Don Celestino's thick gray brows lifted and he studied Matthew with hawklike intensity, his mouth grim in his lean, weathered face. He dismssed his men with a gesture.

"Get down," he ordered Matt. "No man stays higher than I."

Matt climbed down obediently. He was a bit taller than Cantú, and much younger, but he would have hesitated to fight this man, whose very presence exuded power.

"Why should I want to know you?" demanded Cantú.

"First, señor, my horse needs water."

Don Celestino whistled to his vaqueros. "Luz," he instructed the mustached horseman, "unsaddle this man's horse, give him water and grain and leave him in the corral."

"*Mil gracias,*" Matt said, moving stiffly toward the long veranda, supported by adobe pillars that ran the length of the house. Wood benches and a few rawhide chairs stood on the porch. Earthen jars planted with vines were by each pillar, and trees grew along the porch, providing shade for summer.

Stables and outbuildings spread to the right, clustered about by enough dwellings to form a small village. Around the small whitewashed church were graves marked by crosses and stones and decorated with bits of ribbon and colored pebbles.

Near a well where women filled their jugs, dogs, cats and scrawny chickens dodged plump toddlers. Little girls made and played with shuck dolls, or tugged babies about while boys as young as five and six lassoed everything in sight that couldn't elude them, from roosters to their younger sisters. Matt gazed past the bustle to corrals where the best bulls were kept, out toward the herds ranging beyond his vision.

Someday he might have a place like this. How Rachel would love the vines, the thick adobe walls that held warmth in winter and coolness in summer. She'd love the children playing, the chatter and laughter of the women . . .

"You approve of Tres Coronas?" jabbed Cantú's dry voice.

Matt turned. "It's good to see people—families—living here, and able to laugh. But I suppose they don't laugh much during the Mexican Moon. Nor must you, when Comanches run off your fattest cattle and best horses."

"You have a warm heart, to feel for our troubles," mocked the older man, his eyes narrowing. "But I would rather lose stock to Indios than Texans!"

Matt swung toward the older man, probing his eyes, and found in them a spirit he could talk to. "Don Celestino! If I can help you keep your herds this fall, wouldn't it be worth a tithe of what the Comanches would take?"

Don Celestino threw back his head. Laughter erupted from him, bright angry laughter tinged with wry admiration. He stopped as abruptly as he had begun and stared at Matthew, who returned his gaze until Cantú, with a brusque nod, limped to his door and swung it open.

"Enter, Texan! It is at least worth conversation, this offer of yours!"

The barred windows had panes of real glass, so although the corners and hallways were dim, light splashed brilliantly on polished wood and glazed tile, heavy silver candelabra and goblets, rugs woven in ochre, cream, black and gray. This main room had high beamed ceilings plastered white, as were the walls, and a great fireplace at either end. It was a room of mixed beauty and crudeness, family treasures from Spain or Mexico City next to goatskins and clay jars, crystal in a rough-hewn cupboard, an alabaster Virgin on a slab of unpolished onyx.

Don Celestino clapped his hands, sinking into a carved chair made comfortable with hand-embroidered cushions and he signaled Matt to take another. A barefooted young girl, prettier than Lupe but without her distinctive, almost haughty refinement of mouth and nose, hurried in, bowing her head to await Cantú's will:

"Will you have chocolate?" asked the Don. "Perhaps tequila or mescal suit Texans better."

"I would like water first," said Matt easily, smiling at the girl, who regarded him with intrigued wariness. "And then, Don Celestino, I will drink whatever you commend."

The Don gave an order. Bowing, the girl, whom he had called María, went out, her bare feet soundless on the tiles. Resting his chin on his hand, Cantú regarded Matthew.

"Your Spanish is poor. You do not seem of the Rio Grande."

"I have traveled a long way, but I shall live near the Rio from now on."

Cantú smiled. "Many who thought that died instead."

Matthew thought involuntarily of the first man who'd fled his homeland with a brother's blood on his hands. *God put a mark on Cain so that no one would kill him.*

"I expect to live," he said. "So I need cattle and horses."

"Plainly," agreed the Don.

The girl brought in a silver tray with mugs of frothy chocolate smelling of cinnamon, Matt's water in a cut-glass goblet, and a plate of small cakes decorated with currants, nuts and candied fruit. Don Celestino crunched several of these reflectively, his eyes half-shut, then grew stiff and serious again.

"Tell me, señor, how would you discourage the Comanches?"

Matt had his answer ready. "I'd dig out the sides of the ford so only a few at a time could climb up the Mexican bank, and I'd pile up earth and rocks to protect men who'd pick the warriors off as they rode forward."

"But there'll be hundreds of Comanches!"

"Not all at once. When our fire opens, several dozen may be in Mexico, more will be in the Rio, where they'll make easy picking, and if the others get across they can still only reach the bank a few at a time. How many men have you, men who can shoot?"

The Don laughed. "There must be a hundred men scattered over my lands, tending sheep and cattle and horses. But they are not *bravos,* señor. I doubt if twenty could be taught to fire a carbine."

"Well, choose twenty and let me train them," said Matthew.

"There aren't twenty carbines on Tres Coronas."

"No wonder the Comanches steal you blind!"

"I'm a rancher, not a soldier," said the Don stiffly. "It's the government's place to protect us, but though troops come out from Chihuahua now and then, it's never at the right time. They fear the Comanches anyway."

"Give me men and carbines and we'll give the Comanches something to fear," promised Matt.

"I'll ponder it," said the Don. "I'd have to obtain the guns but— Be my guest overnight. I'll give you an answer tomorrow." He clapped his hands. The girl came quickly. "Take the señor to a room," ordered the Don. "See he has everything for his comfort. He'll join Donã Anatacia and me at dinner."

So this *hidalgo* had a wife. "Do you mind if I look around?" asked Matt.

"I'll have Luz come to you in an hour with a fresh horse. He's in charge of my north ranges—and, señor, he is very good with a carbine, machete, reata and knife."

"I'm glad to hear it," said Matt following the girl.

The house was a hollow square, one room wide, around an inner court planted with vines, shrubs and two great cotton-woods. Matthew's room had a tremendous bed, a heavy carved chest, rush mats on the floor, and a rawhide chair. Above the bed hung a gruesome-looking crucifix with real teeth and thorns making the figure grotesque.

Bringing towels and a pitcher of water, María placed them on the wash stand by a large washbasin. Someone had already brought in his saddlebags. She was back in a few minutes with a silver plate of dried peaches. Giving Matt a shy smile, she waited to see if he wanted anything more. When he thanked her, she bowed her head and vanished on those silent brown feet.

Matt shaved, then stripped to the waist and scrubbed with one of the coarse homespun towels. Refreshed, he pulled the rawhide chair to where he could gaze out at the big cotton-woods in the inner court.

Would one like those grow where he planned to make his headquarters? Munching the tasty leathery peaches, he reflected that this kind of fruit would be a blessed change from pitahaya and cactus *tunas*. He stretched out on the bed, grinning at the rustle of the corn shuck mattress. What a mixture of luxury and Sparta this place was, like Don Celestino himself.

Would the Don gamble on Matthew's plan? And if he did, would it work?

Matt yawned and stretched. The Don might not like gringos, but he was smart and tired of losing stock. Having raided and destroyed San Ysidro, the Comanches' return station, he wouldn't increase his risk of loss much by attacking the Indians.

Of course, he might use Matt's plan, without Matt.

And if he, Matt, didn't return to the women in the valley, what would happen to them? At least there was water and they wouldn't starve. If he didn't come back by late autumn, they'd probably stay the winter, and when spring rains put some water in the desert stretches, they could make their way toward Fort Davis or Fort Stockton. Matthew pushed that speculation out of his mind.

He *was* going back. With cattle. If Don Celestino wouldn't hire him, some other Comanche-harassed rancher would!

Matt was dozing when the girl called from the door. "Señor! Luz waits outside!"

Stuffing his shirt into his pants, he picked up his hat and followed María along the corridor that led around the house, with doors to each room opening onto it. They passed through the big central chamber, and she held the crown-emblazoned door as he stepped out.

Mounted on his tough, scrubby little mustang, Luz held the reins of a handsome black who showed Arab blood.

"Señor," he greeted Matt, but he did not smile.

Wonder what's bothering him? Matthew puzzled. Hates gringos? Thinks I want a job here?

Taking the reins, Matt smoothed the neck of the fidgeting horse, speaking softly to him until the laid-back ears pricked up. Only then did he mount. The black moved with nervous pride, but he had a good mouth and didn't fight the bit.

"Soldán is Don Celestino's," Luz said. "The Don has pain in riding so the horse gets little use." He laughed, tilting his head with the peaked sombrero trimmed with snakeskin and tarnished silver. "A marvel Soldán let you mount. He has a hate for strangers."

"Perhaps his manners are better than yours," Matthew smiled.

Luz shot him a look of grudging respect and encouraged the dun with a touch of his large sunburst spurs.

Don Celestino's herds were mixed—Spanish "black," usually linebacks, with a stripe of white, brown or dun from tail to shoulder, some with brownish faces, many-colored "Mexican" cattle, which were fatter and heavier-horned, and some longhorns, bigger still, though they seemed mostly bone with horns that often measure as much as nine feet from prong to prong.

When Anglo settlers brought their own cattle in

from Arkansas, Missouri and Louisiana, these had mixed with the Spanish black cattle and Mexican stock, both descendants of seed brought by Spanish explorers. From this mingling came longhorns, as quick as deer, as wary as wild turkeys and capable of protecting their young from wolf, coyote and panther.

Sheltering in scrub timber when not grazing, scenting moisture under dry creeks and following it to water, a longhorn would sense a coming norther and wait in the thicketed breaks until the freezing blast was gone. Longhorns, like mustangs, came in all colors. They were just as wild and ranged all parts of Texas that had graze.

"The Spanish blacks are from the blood of fighting bulls," said Luz. "See how their horns set close together at the base, reaching out to battle? Have you ever seen a bullfight, señor?"

Matthew shook his head.

"A pity," commiserated Luz, gazing at the blacks with loving admiration. "We have bullfights at certain fiestas. Don Celestino brings up some promising young *torero* from Mexico City or Chihuahua, and he meets the bravest of our bulls in the round corral." Luz nodded approvingly at the blacks, deep of chest and narrow of flank. "The *toreros* say our bulls are as good as those they meet in the great bullrings—eager, fast, *muy valiente!*"

As they rode on, Luz explained that Don Celestino tried to keep his best stock farthest from the likely route of the Comanches. After branding, yearlings were put with a herd of their quality, and in recent years, in an effort to improve his cattle, the Don had begun castrating inferior males and selling or slaughtering them and scrub females for beef and hides—those the Comanches left.

Jacales, sometimes occupied by lounging vaqueros,

were scattered about. Luz called greetings to the men and told Matthew they took turns at minding these outlying herds, though their families always lived near the main ranch.

"The *pastores* stay with their sheep all the time," explained Luz, wrinkling his nose as they approached dirty cream-white blobs that gradually became recognizable. Four dogs ran out, barking, but their clamor didn't alarm the placid herd, which went on feeding wherever the cattle could find a blade of grass.

A bent man with white matted hair and beard and skin like weather bark ran forward, signaling his dogs, which were making strange noises.

"The dogs think they're sheep, except for their teeth," Luz continued. "They're taken at birth and suckled by a ewe, so they grow up with her milk in their bellies and her smell in their nostrils. They are both faithful and valiant, but if such a dog tastes sheep blood once he may become the worst and most cunning of their slayers." Lolling in his saddle, Luz called to the old man in superior but friendly fashion. "Hola, Inocencio! Your sheep look fat."

The shepherd grunted something and gestured toward his hut.

"*Gracias,*" declined Luz, "but I must show this señor Tres Coronas, so you will understand we must hurry." He tossed the shepherd some tobacco and a hard cone of brown sugar. The old man accepted these with delight and carried them off to his shelter.

As they rode on, Luz said, "Inocencio isn't half-witted, though he may sound so. When only a boy, he spoke rudely to Don Celestino's father, who had his tongue torn out on the spot. Since then, Inocencio has preferred the company of sheep."

"I don't blame him," Matt said, shuddering inwardly, though he knew a cruel master in the South might treat a slave child so.

Moments like this made him acutely aware slavery must end, yet how? If the North kept pushing, if those manufacturers and shippers kept squeezing the South with legislation designed to ruin her, the South would have to leave the Union.

And if such a war came, Matthew Bourne, what would you do?

It would be his duty to fight for the South, but what of Rachel, their home and the life they were struggling to build? Matt shrugged the threat away. Right now his concern was over fighting Comanches and convincing Don Celestino it could be done.

They had been moving in a wide half-circle, and were now facing the distant mesas of the Sierra del Carmen.

"This is the special herd," waved Luz, pulling up a distance from a long shallow basin that formed a kind of natural pasture, with the best grass Matthew had seen since leaving the valley.

"Señor, have you ever seen anything like that?" The vaquero gestured with pride and disgust at the animals grazing under the vigilance of half a dozen horsemen.

Matt turned and gaped. He'd seen cattle similar to these grazing in England's deep green grass, Durhams and Herefords, and he'd seen some attempts to improve range stock by importing blooded cattle. He remembered how Colonel Tom Shannon, given two fine shorthorns by Queen Victoria from her own herd, had picked them up at New Orleans and brought them to Texas in ox wagons.

"What do you want in this country with cows that can't walk?" Matt's father had asked his old friend Colonel Shannon.

"Good beef," answered Shannon, eyeing his royal

treasure with pride and some ruefulness, for he still had a long way to go.

The cows had thrived and produced calves, but neighbors didn't want the short-legged, pampered breed to "ruin" their own hard-foraging stock, and most of the shorthorn bulls that weren't killed or walked to death by the tough native bulls were shot out on the ranges. It was a shock to see them here in Mexico.

"Don Celestino had some of these brought all the way from England," said Luz. "He's mixed in the best from Tres Coronas stock, for shorthorns die of fever that doesn't bother our cows. Don Celestino wants an animal with shorthorn meat and the hardiness of Spanish cattle. So they graze over here, so far behind the sheep that Comanches have never seen them."

Staring at the chunky creatures who looked so out of place in this austere land, Luz brightened suddenly, raised a hand to the nearest vaquero, who waved back but didn't ride to meet them.

"That is Quil," said Luz, gazing speculatively at Matt. "Quil is a Seminole-Negro. He hates gringos, for he was the slave of one before he killed him and ran away. He's our best man with horses and can throw bulls to the ground by their horns. And he's better with his knife than any of us at Tres Coronas, though we are not slow, señor."

"Interesting," said Matt, starting to rein away, but Luz caught his arm.

"Not like that, señor! Not so easy!" His teeth showed, very white, but ground down by chewing cornmeal containing flecks of volcanic rock from mortar and pestle. "You wanted to see Tres Coronas! We want to see you! It takes more than talk to kill Comanches."

Matthew reined in, fighting his anger. "Did Don Celestino plan my—test?"

Luz shrugged and grinned. "The Don left it to me," he admitted cheerfully. "But it was clear that I should establish your valor, if any. Can you do more with a knife than skin rabbits?"

"I might try you," said Matt dryly, "but I think you're too rotten to skin!"

Luz's eyes sparkled. "Will you try Quil, señor?"

Matt was no knife man, but this was the test. If he refused it, he could not hope to rally Tres Coronas men against the Comanches. His mind shot back to the army and an unusual knife fight he'd once seen. It offered a chance—if he could hold steady.

"It's your fiesta."

Luz motioned to Quil, who rode over. He wore no spurs and seemed to exert no pressure on the bit to control his compact bay mustang.

"Quil," said Luz, eyes glowing, "Don Celestino wishes to test this gringo's courage. *Por favor,* entertain him with your bowie!"

A broad-faced handsome man with long straight hair, Quil had such massive shoulders that Matt was surprised, when Quil dismounted, to see he was only of average height.

As Matt swung down, Quil spoke slowly in a tone that was perfectly flat, a means of conveying and receiving information.

"You need a knife to match my bowie."

From a brass-tipped belt scabbard, Quil drew a twelve-inch blade almost two inches wide at the guard, running straight till it began to curve several inches from the tip, where it ended in a startling saberlike point. The original had been burned with its owner at the Alamo, but as a type, the bowie ranked first among fighting knives, far above the "Arkansas Toothpick," and could split skulls and decapitate.

"It's quite a blade," Matt said. "I've never used one."

Quil turned to Luz, who watched eagerly, his hands resting on his saddle horn. "It's no contest, my bowie against this man's, if he's no knife fighter."

"All the better," said Luz. "Today we test spirit, not training."

The Seminole-Negro responded in that expressionless voice, "What use to prove spirit if he dies?"

"One dead gringo," Luz shrugged happily.

"I appreciate your concern," Matt told Quil, whose face, black warmed with copper, was unreadable. "But I know the risks. I'll take them."

Quil gave a short, sharp nod. "Don't try for my head," he warned. "And remember, there's bone in the chest."

The main target, Matt knew, was hips to throat, ripping upward, or slashing sideways and down, keeping one's own knife low to parry strokes while waiting for a chance to drive the blade home. Experts could duel for hours without doing each other real harm, but the loss of a thumb or finger could open the way to swift, bloody death.

Luz held the horses and raised his hand toward the other vaqueros to halt them at a distance. Matthew took the bowie, shifted it in his hand until he got some sense of its shape and dimension, narrowed his eyes against the glittering length and breadth of the bowie which flashed in Quil's hand as he pointed it out and upward.

When Matt refused to be drawn to attack, Quil feinted high and thrust low, keeping head and body well back. Matt caught and turned the strokes, getting the measure of his man. In spite of quickening breath

and thudding heart, he felt detached from the fight,
detached even from his body.

Quil plainly meant to fight to some end, either
Matt's death or surrender or a signal from Luz. He
used neither surprise tactics nor especially savage on-
slaughts, but dueled away in a cool workmanlike fashion which suggested he was bored with his opponent
but bound to see his job through.

Matt took a long breath. *Now—*

Shielding himself with his left forearm, he took
Quil's blade in it, between the bones, twisted his arm
to hold the bowie trapped. That was when he could
have slashed Quil's throat or belly. Instead, he
dropped his own knife, relaxed his arm, stood almost
fainting with pain as Quil, trembling, worked the blade
free, ripped off his shirt and bound it on the savaged
arm.

"Lord God, why do that crazy trick?" he demanded
in English. "Crazy damn fool! Crazy—"

Matt made it to his horse, leaned against the saddle
a minute, drenched in cold sweat, his teeth chattering.

"Did I pass your test?" he flung at Luz.

Luz swept off his sombrero and bowed from the
waist. "Señor, you are beyond testing and beyond be-
lief! Can you ride?"

"Yes," said Matt. But he was glad of Quil's strong
hands that boosted him into the saddle.

XI

Matt rolled up a last thin round tortilla, dipping it into the succulent mingling of roast kid, beans, rice and thick chili sauce. He smiled unashamedly at the Don, who watched him with amused interest and clapped for María who brought them silver bowls of caramel custard. Doña Anatacia had sent her excuses, probably, Matt thought, because he was a gringo.

"You have a good table, Don Celestino," Matt complimented him. "Worth crossing the Rio for."

"It's pleasing to see a guest eat with appetite," returned the Don. He pushed back his carved chair and led the way to the veranda, where María brought them crystal goblets and a tall amber flagon. She stole a glance at Matthew and scurried away when he thanked her, though at the door she glanced back and smiled.

"If Luz saw that, you might get worse than a wounded arm," observed the Don, pouring brandy.

"And by the way, Don Mateo, what happened to your arm?"

"What do you suppose?" asked Matt, sitting stiffer and narrowing his gaze.

"Perhaps you caught a steer's horn?"

"A two-legged steer with a bowie knife?"

The Don nodded appreciatively, stroking his lean hard jaw. "So you found Quil. Did you bury him?"

"No. He bound up my arm. I'm surprised Luz didn't tell you how faithfully he carried out your orders."

Don Celestino laughed, sipping the richly colored thick brandy. "I only told him to make sure you were strong as your words, señor! When you came back alive, I knew you must be!" He sobered, and his dark eyes fastened on Matthew with a grip like an eagle's talons. "If you've found my hospitality a little strange, please know that I defended my country against invading United States troops in 1848 when you took much land from us, and my only son died in that same war. He was sixteen, a cadet, and when he and his classmates could defend Chapultepec no longer, some of them jumped from the parapets rather than surrender."

"I'm sorry," Matt said slowly, "but where does it all end? You're of the blood of conquerors who put Aztecs to the sword, and they had conquered the earlier Toltecs. My people have driven many peaceful Indians west, but that won't keep me from fighting Comanches who want my scalp. We are where we are and we do what we must—if we can." He finished his goblet. "This is fine brandy, Don Celestino."

"It is made from my peaches. When—if—you go back to your place, I will give you some young trees for planting." The Don filled up their glasses and settled back. "Now, having established our philosophy, how shall we act?"

Next day, escorted by several vaqueros, Don
Celestino drove off in a wagon to Chihuahua. He
would, he said, point out to the Governor of that Mexican state, who was his friend, that Tres Coronas was
assuming the responsibility of the army and was entitled to weapons; also, more to the point, if Tres
Coronas rebuffed the raiders, Chihuahua would escape
much harassment.

Matt, accompanied by all the men who could be
spared from work, rode toward the Rio. A wagon rattled behind, drawn by mules and driven by Luz's
mother, Carmen, whom they called Madrecita, a
fierce-tongued, leather-hided woman of indeterminate
years and great bulk who addressed all the vaqueros
as if they were feeble-minded children. She was to
cook for them, and the wagon was full of her gear,
supplies, shovels and axes.

"Andalé!" she shouted continuously at the mules.
"Fornicators with your own mothers, stumbling stubborn *estupidos!"* And when the mules stepped fast
enough to placate her, she turned her adjurations on
the men.

"Don't think to loaf on this job and make it a fiesta
while I toil to stuff your greedy bellies!" she told them
as they made camp by the Rio that day at dusk.
"Don't loiter till Comanches swoop down and scalp
us all, though, *Valgamé Dios!* the lice in your hair
would make even those Indios wish they had left you
in your corruption!"

"Poor Madrecita," said Luz tenderly. "Let me make
you a nice cigarette." The tough, leather-clad vaquero
carefully shaped a corn husk around strong black tobacco, lit it from the cook fire and handed it to her.

Her exasperation faded with the stingingly aromatic
gusts of smoke, and soon the men were dipping tortil-

las into a bubbling iron pot of reheated beans she had brought cooked from the ranch.

"No meat, Madrecita?" asked Luz's younger brother, a supple, handsome boy called Changa because of his monkeylike tricks and agility. Even when the saddle-hardened older men had grown weary, Changa had skylarked about, swooping from his saddle to pick up sticks, playing with his rawhide rope, trying to ride down and lasso anything that moved, from a horned toad to an Inca dove.

"Not tonight, *niño,*" the woman answered as tenderly as her gravelly voice would allow. She handed him a hunk of hard brown sugar, ignoring Luz's snort. "But the Don has given permission to kill a beef. Do it early tomorrow and we shall have meat, and *tatema* later, when the work is finished."

"What's *tatema?*" Matt asked.

"You don't know it?" demanded Changa, his dark brows rising. "Then you have a treat coming! *Tatema* is the head of a cow, covered in mud and baked in the ground till it is wonderfully delicious."

Matt decided the others could have his share, but thought it best not to say so. After supper, the men smoked a while. Changa sang, some of his verses racy and romantic, others about famous vaqueros and bandits. He had a pure, lilting voice, and his wrinkled mother watched him with adoration and pride as if she could not believe this handsome singer was the same child she had borne.

As Matt couldn't catch all of the words, he listened mostly for the melody, but suddenly the men began to glance at him and nudge each other.

Señores, voy a cantar con muchísimo decoro,
Estos versos son compuestos al gringo
valiente . . .

Sirs, I'm going to sing with much decorum.
These verses are composed about the valiant
  gringo . . .

The men listened, intent, while Matthew flushed
with embarrassment and wondered how Quil, his face
impassive in the firelight, was taking this praise of an
outsider.

Don Matthew held the bowie between his bones.
He did not flinch for any consideration.
He did not drive his knife into our comrade's
  heart
But dropped it in the dust
For this as much as his valor
We will remember the gringo.

"It is a good *corrido*," Quil said, breaking the quiet.
"Let's hope you'll soon be composing verses on how
Tres Coronas defeated the Comanches." He looked at
Matt, who smiled back. This Quil was a friend worth
having, if he would be a friend, not just a scrupulously
fair comrade.

Luz banked the fire, and the men spread their
serapes about the wagon, from which Madrecita's res-
onant snores issued almost immediately.

Matt was bone-weary, but his mind reached forward. He'd achieved the first part of his goal to get
Don Celestino's support of his plan. But would it
work? And if it did— He thought of Rachel, with a
warming in his loins which chilled as he remembered
Harry.

Rachel was Matt's wife, his love, though his own
brother had died because of that love. Still, they had
to go on. It was for Rachel he must get the cattle, for
her and their children that he must build another

home. But if they could be happy, if he could ever hold her without shame and guilt—that was another matter, a more painful one than defeating the Comanches.

The dozen men went to work the next morning, shoveling and hacking away at the Mexican side of the bank. The river churned away rocks and earth, so the men were soon standing up to their knees, then up to their thighs in water, and the work grew increasingly difficult as the current ran stronger and deeper.

Changa, who began late after slaughtering a beef, worked hard for a while but then began splashing his companions with water. Several splashed back, swore or shouted good-natured threats, but Changa kept on till Luz and Quil exchanged glances, whooped and grabbed the brash youngster.

Holding Changa by wrists and ankles, they swung him back and forth a few times and hurled him into the deepest part of the river. When he surfaced, spluttering and choking, he laughed louder than anyone, and he returned to his shoveling with complete attention.

After a meal of stewed beef and beans, the men began building breastworks on either side of the river where surviving Indians would struggle from the ford.

"Our shelter must seem part of the banks and rocks," Matthew cautioned as he moved along the lines of the ambuscade, which followed a slight defile. "Where you have to, pile up rocks, mix and jumble them until it looks natural. But leave holes to shoot through."

"When the Comanches come up from the Rio— those who do—they won't have time to examine our work," said Luz, brushing dust from his glossy mustache and straightening his back.

"True," said Quil, heaving a boulder in place with a smooth motion of his broad shoulders. "But we have to fool them from at least the other side of the Rio or they won't walk into our little surprise!"

Changa dug a hole for his mother and lined it with rock so she could make a fire. When the rocks and earth had absorbed enough heat, she put in the clay-covered steer's head, covered it with hot stones and earth, and built a small, slow fire on top. The *tatema* would be ready for tomorrow's noon meal. The men from the ranch all smacked their lips at the prospect, but Matt hoped to avoid his share of the treat.

That night, as they smoked and lounged, Changa began a song of how Tres Coronas tricked the Comanches, killed many and drove the others away.

Quil, whom the youngster followed like a shadow, snorted and kicked the fire into sparks. "Better save that song, *muchacho!* Sing it when it comes true."

Changa laughed, his white teeth flashing in the firelight. *"Ay,* friend, if one waits for a safe time to make a song, he may never sing it! Anyway," he added disarmingly, "if Don Mateo prevailed over you, Quil, in a knife fight, what chance do Comanches have?"

"I know the Comanches," Quil returned, sobering after a chuckle at the boy's question. "Scalps of many peoples hang on their lances; many are Mexican, some are from other Indians. But a great number are gringo." He looked around at the silenced men. "One's hair must cling very tight to the head before one laughs aloud at Comanches."

"I laugh at them!" cried Changa, but not for long, for a cuff from his huge mother sent him tumbling.

"Was not your father, may the Virgin intercede for his many sins, especially for his knocking my teeth out—was not he killed ten years ago by these Comanches? Work fast, hombres, and let us get back quickly to the ranch. I do not like this Rio!"

Two days later, the ambush prepared and Matt a bit queasy from his introduction to *tatema,* the party journeyed back to Tres Coronas.

"The Comanches leave the Staked Plains very happy," sang Changa, swaying happily as he rode his little bay mustang.

> They ride by the Pecos and Horsehead Crossing,
> They come through the Chisos and ride to the
>   Rio.
> How fat are the cattle they will steal, how
>   swift the horses
> How despised the Mexicans, easy to plunder!
> But this Mexican Moon holds blood for Coman-
>   ches,
> A surprise is waiting down there by the river . . .

"It's bad luck to saddle a horse before he's caught," cautioned Luz. But Changa larked on, and even the older, more solemn men were infected by his mood.

Matthew wished he were as confident as Changa. The ambush had a good chance of working, but if it didn't, the Comanches would spare no one in their southward pillaging. Usually on these raids they killed only those who resisted or made tempting targets.

Matt gathered his reins and sat straighter on Storm marveling with part of his mind that the pranking Changa didn't fall off his horse, and hoping with renewed intensity that Don Celestino would return with the guns.

Excitement, mingled with an edge of fear that intensified it, possessed the people of Tres Coronas as they prepared for once to take the offensive in their long struggle with the Comanches. Don Celestino had

into its fullness, the people of Tres Coronas scanned the north for a warning beacon.

Perhaps the lookouts had been caught or met with other disasters? Or, possibly—what they dared not even hope—possibly the Comanches would not ride this way. It was too much to hope that they wouldn't raid Mexico at all, but perhaps they would go toward the east, as some usually did, past Ojinaga.

"Even if they go that way," pointed out the older folk, sadly experienced in the methods of Comanches, "they may sweep around past us on their way north. Better they come while we're ready."

Matt thought of Rachel and Lupe. It was unlikely Comanches would stray there, where no pickings had ever been available, yet it might happen— He tried to close his mind to this nagging fear. Days he spent preparing the men or mentally singling out specific cattle he wanted for his pay. Evenings he dined with the Don and Doña Anatacia, then sat on the veranda, sipping peach brandy and savoring fine cigars. Except when he visited Chihuahua or very rarely Mexico City, the Don had no male to talk with on matters other than Tres Coronas, and he spoke nostalgically of his youth, when he had toured Europe and spent a year in Paris.

"The women!" he remembered, smiling, one evening after his sister had retired. "They understood men! But my father had arranged a marriage with a lady of good family from Mexico City. Not beautiful, but very devout and good. She died in childbed a year after we married. This country was too hard for her. To live here a woman must get tough as a cactus, and as dry!" Don Celestino winked. "And who wants to take a cactus to bed?"

Matthew thought of Anatacia, who was certainly no

cactus, though of this soil, and said, "I see many pretty women at Tres Coronas, sir."

"Oh, the little *chiquitas* may warm a bed, but they're not for marriage," shrugged the Don, in a way that implied he took such women as pleased him as casually as he would sip of his rich, homegrown brandy. He looked suddenly at Matt. "Your wife is beautiful?"

"Very." Matt's voice turned husky.

Don Celestino looked away. "You're lucky. Young, strong and lucky. You'd better not leave your wife often, Mateo, even to win cattle."

"I must make her a home," said Matt. But something in the Don's manner made him glad the older man would never see Rachel.

As they sat in the deepening twilight, Matthew stared, got to his feet. There, north toward the Rio, blazed the signal, a distant imperative warning.

"We've got to ride! I'll tell the men!"

"You may have a day or two to wait at the Rio, depending on how quickly the signals passed," reminded the Don. He caught Matt's hand. "Ay, Norteño! If only I could ride in the fashion required by this matter!"

"We'll do our best, sir."

Don Celestino's mouth quirked down. "I know you will, Mateo. For the cattle you need—and for your beautiful lady!"

Matthew put down his goblet and hurried to alert the men.

Thirty-two men with firearms and four boys to watch the horses rode out from Tres Coronas, along with another twenty men, armed with machetes and homemade lances, and the knives which everyone carried. In close quarters these men could be as deadly as those with carbines, and all could shoot, in case a marksman had to be replaced.

Some had been asleep when Matt called them, others had been drinking with friends or making love to their wives or playing with their children. But within an hour they rode under the huge moon that turned the country bluish silver, casting shadows of the horsemen.

Twice they stopped briefly to rest. At dawn they chewed tortillas and ate jerky by a water hole, fed their horses corn, and pushed on. It was sundown by the time they reached the Rio. Though both men and horses were exhausted, Matt decided to split the force and get it into position that night in case the Comanches were near enough for an early morning crossing. It seemed certain they would not attempt the treacherous ford at night.

"Luz," called Matt, "take half the carbine men and half the lancers across now. Eat and rest after you've concealed your horses a good way off and post a lookout. Just sit tight till the Indians come, and don't open fire until most of them are into the river."

"And watch where you fire!" warned Changa, grinning. "Don't try to pick off Indians who've climbed up the Mexican bank or you may hit me!"

"We'll all have to watch that," nodded Matt. "Men, there'll be many more Comanches than there are of us. We need the advantage of surprise. Don't fire until I do—but then shoot as fast as possible while taking aim. Lancers, you'll take over any dropped carbines, and fight where you have the best chance without too much exposure to arrows or firearms. You can take care of the stragglers and runaways."

"What if some of *us* run away?" clowned Changa, backing his mount as if about to flee.

"You might wind up a skinned monkey," retorted

Matt. "All right, men. Pick your side of the Rio, and let's get as much sleep as we can! Water the horses early tomorrow so they can be kept out of the way—and fight your damnedest!"

Matt awoke in dim light, surprised to find Quil lying next to him on the ground, until he remembered where they were, and why. He sat up, rubbing his eyes, his neck and shoulders aching from their uncomfortable rest on a saddle.

Quil stood up in one flowing motion. Tomás, the vaquero with startling red hair, was peering over the piled-up rocks and earth. He turned with a shrug of his shoulders.

"Nothing."

"So let's eat," suggested Matt. Gnawing some jerky rolled in one of the dozens of tortillas Madrecita had sent with them, he made his way to the arroyo where the boys had hidden the horses.

Yes, Don Mateo, they had watered the horses early, let them drink deep so they could wait till night to drink again. The Comanches! Was there any sign?

"Not yet," Matt told the lithe, sparkling-eyed boys, too young to fight but old enough to care for the horses. "Don't come out or move the horses until you get word—unless you hear lots of shooting, and it's over, and no one comes for you, even after a couple of hours."

The boys' eyes widened even more. For the first time they seemed to realize this was not a fiesta. Matthew grinned at them. "Just look out for the horses!" he said, and made his way back to the ambush.

All the men were up now, munching their dry food and inspecting their weapons. The sun barely rose above the gleaming edge of the mesas, but it was already hot. Tomás gazed over the barrier again.

"I hope they come soon. I'd rather fight than wait here quiet as mice all day, baking in the sun."

"Better the sun than hell," remarked a grizzled vaquero, one of the best shots. "Be sure that when the Comanches come, some of us won't live to complain about the weather."

"Old vulture!" began Tomás, then whirled back, his head tilted, listening. He raised a warning hand. In a moment Matt heard, too.

A sound like dim thunder reverberated from the north. The lift and fall of many hoofs. Half the men, led by Quil, went to the other side of the pass.

"Remember!" Matt called softly. "Watch where you shoot! And wait until I fire!"

Every man had found a hole, or made one, through which he could aim and shoot without exposing himself above the rocks. Twenty six men waited on either side of the pass, eight armed with carbines, five in reserve with lances and machetès.

Most of the men were breathing loudly, gripping their weapons. One hastily withdrew to relieve himself. The rumble in the earth came nearer.

XII

The Comanches came in sight, filling the approach to the river, light sparkling from silver ornaments and lance tips. Mounted on horses of every color, including a great number of spotted ones, the warriors were painted on their faces, chests, and arms, with vermilion, white, black, yellow, green and blue, in every combination of color and design.

A few had muskets, but all had bows and arrows in leather cases slung by a band over the right shoulder. Saucer-shaped shields flaunted turkey feathers; some were painted, some dangled horse and mule tails and others bore hair of different colors—scalps, some long and yellow.

Joking and talking, the first Comanches rode into the water. Matt tried to count as they poured past the low cliffs toward the ford.

Over a hundred. Another score. Another and still another. Taut as a wire, Matt prayed not many would be left outside the river area when he signaled for the assault. The dug-out ford would stall the Comanches for a while, but it couldn't stop them for long. The crucial thing was to choose the best moment, when most of the warriors were still milling around in the river, in order to pick off as many as possible during the initial shock.

Matt stopped counting when over two hundred warriors had jogged into sight. Some women straggled at the rear, probably brought to cook and serve their men. Along the destroyed ford on the Mexican side, the first Comanches floundered, riding up and down beneath the bank, hunting a way up, but on both sides the rock cliffs rose too steeply to be climbed.

Amidst loud shouts and exclamations from those hunting a way up, a brightly painted warrior kept urging his horse at the bank, until its hoofs, struggling for a hold, crumbled away clods of earth. Two other Comanches did the same with their mounts, and after thrashing that sent chunks of the bank churning down the river, the leader gave a shout, leaned forward in his saddle as if to lift his piebald, and clambered up the Mexican shore.

He was quickly joined by the other two, and they rode forward, so near that Mathew could see silver discs and bits of fur braided into long plaits that swung to their thighs, earrings of shell and bone and silver and legging fringes tipped with beads. The river was now swarming with painted raiders, and the women, waiting at the rear, seemed to be the last of his party.

In another minute, the leaders would be past the ambush.

Matthew thrust his carbine through the hole, squinted along the barrel at the gaily painted chief, and fired. The warrior flung up his arms and slumped forward. His horse burst into a gallop, its rawhide bridle dangling. The rider fell under the hoofs of the horses following behind as their owners pitched from their saddles.

Loading another linen-cased cartridge into the breech, Matt sighted at another Comanche, missed as the man fell under fire from the other side of the defile.

Load and shoot, load and shoot.

Horsemen swarmed up from the river, yelling, trying to find their enemy, unslinging their bows, brandishing lances, but unable in the uproar to locate their foe until many had fallen. Horses trampled dead men. Riderless mounts, neighing and rearing in their panic, bolted toward the plains, or lurched out on the other side.

The Comanches stopped surging up the bank and tried to turn back. They charged confusedly into their friends until the river was chaos, a tangle of horses and men upon whom Tres Coronas forces fired from four directions. The Comanche women, still on the Texas bank, whirled their horses and fled. The Tres Coronas men let them go, not from mercy but because there were armed warriors yet to fight.

Suddenly one warrior broke out of the milling welter, calling something in tones of scorn that drew others to him. He charged up the Mexican bank, lance atilt, and though everyone, including Matt, continued to fire, the warrior rode on, though blood poured from one shoulder and ran from his face.

Rounding the defile with a few survivors, the Comanche drove his lance into the nearest vaquero using an underarm thrust. Freeing it from the sagging body, the warrior poised it to rush at Matt, who, loading his carbine, was helpless in that instant.

Quil swung his rifle, knocking the Comanche to the ground. In a second, machetes hacked him to bits, but the rearing mounts of the other warriors had trampled down Tomás and two of the lancers. One Comanche got off a swift arrow that struck Matt's left arm, but Matt continued to fire with the arrow hanging from his flesh, and the warrior fell as Quil cut the throat of the Comanche grappling with him.

Other warriors had followed that daredevil charge. Enough broke through to keep the lance and machete men busy while carbines spat toward the banks and the river. A few warriors fought their way back past Luz's men and ran after the fleeing women, but when the last shot echoed along the cliffs by the eagles' nest, scores of painted bronze bodies lay scattered, tangled with their horses and with one another.

Not all were dead. Vaqueros, most of them marked by the battle, dispatched with machete or knife the wounded, who could neither ask for nor expect mercy, as well as horses too badly hurt to live. As knives flashed around scalplocks, Matthew started to protest, but Quil spoke in his ear. "It's not pure vengeance. The government pays a bounty on Indian scalps."

Matt tied part of his shirt around his freshly wounded arm and went to see how his men had fared. Tomás was dead, his red hair now a deeper scarlet; the grizzled old sharpshooter who had foretold that some must die lay with an arrow in his throat. One man groaned, his head caved in by a hoof. Matt cleansed and bandaged him with the rest of his shirt, then checked the other breastwork. One man was lanced through, but the others seemed to be out looting Comanches.

His carbine held above his head, Matt waded across the Rio, past islands of human and animal dead. Young Changa was having a prickly pear poultice bound over one buttock by Luz, who helped him tug up his bloodstained trousers before turning to Matthew with a laugh.

"Here's one monkey with a sore tail! He'll want to ride home on his belly!"

"How many dead?"

"Only one," called Luz over his shoulder, in a hurry to join the scalp takers. "You should have been a general of the armies, Don Mateo!"

Four men dead, one seriously hurt, many lesser injuries. Matt moved slowly down to the river, faint from loss of blood, revolted at the joking laughter of the vaqueros as they brandished Comanche hair. He could understand their joy at defeating a dread enemy who for years had killed or enslaved them at will, but . . . Matthew shrugged. The bounty paid for these scalps would be more money than most of these vaqueros had seen or would ever see again.

They returned to Tres Coronas carrying two hundred and twenty Comanche scalps.

Don Celestino insisted on making the ride to help Matt select his stock, but it caused his damaged leg much pain. His lips were pale and the grooved lines along his mouth seemed to grow deeper as he watched his men cut out the seed cattle he and Matt had picked. They also selected some of the heavier shorthorn strain, some Spanish "blacks," and several many-colored Mexican cattle.

"God wills that I must thank a gringo for protecting my herds and people," the Don said, as they rode back. "So I do thank you, heartily—and God, too, for I love this land of mine better than I've cared for any mortal except my son. If I could, I'd cover and protect it with my body. Some think there is silver in this earth and have offered me riches to let them rip it up. I would as soon tear open the belly of my bride."

"Other Comanches may come," Matthew warned.

"So will death and drought," shrugged the Don, his hawk eyes crinkling at the edges. "But you've shown my men they can outwit and vanquish these Comanches they have dreaded since they sucked from their mothers' breasts. And we have arms now. During the Comanche Moons, we'll post lookouts, and ambush again if we must." He looked speculatively at Matt. "Luz is my natural son. When Carmen was young, she had beauty as great as her present bulk, and there are other sons of my loins on this ranch who will have some share in it after I am dead. But if you'll be my foreman, I'll give you a house of your own, land for you and your descendants. You would grow prosperous much faster than you will in that mountainous bend across the Rio."

Startled, Matt gazed at the Don, saw the fierce old man was not joking and looked about the stretching pastures, rich with cattle, horses and sheep. He had to consider the offer, for it was a breathtaking one, but not for a moment did it speak to his heart, and so he shook his head.

"A thousand thanks, Don Celestino, but I must return to my own country and my own place."

"And your own woman?" smiled the Don.

Matt laughed. "My own wife," he corrected.

They rode in silence until they reached the sheep ranges and Inocencio ran out to kiss his master's hand —the hand of the son of the man who had torn out a child's tongue, so that Inocencio could only bleat his words.

The sheep seemed plump and content with their sparse grass. They had been sheared not long ago, and leggy young lambs frolicked about or pestered their mothers.

"This fall the rams will batter the ewes, and in spring you can see a sight that pleases me more than the entrechats and jetés of any ballet troupe—and I have seen the best of Paris, Havana and Berlin!" said the

Don. "Take a start of sheep, Mateo. Nothing gladdens the heart more than to see hundreds of lambs playing, full of good milk and gay spirits!"

"No," said Matt, giving Inocencio tobacco and brown sugar. "Thank you, but I prefer cows. I don't understand sheep."

"Follow your will," said the Don, "but one day sheep will earn more wealth than cattle."

His face was drawn now from the pain in his leg, and they pressed on toward the ranch, passing the *campo santo* by the church, where five new graves bore garlands and ribbons. The man with the kicked head had not survived the journey home. But the widows and families of those who had died were proud in their mourning. Their men could have died as sport for the Comanches or in defending their own hearths; as it was, they had fallen while protecting Tres Coronas and died as heroes. The Don had promised that none of their families would ever want.

Matt's cattle, two hundred head, and a dozen good horses, cloth, serapes, a big copper bottle and Chihuahua-purchased glass, hinges and tools, all the Don could spare, were readied for the journey home.

Don Celestino had ordered ten of his men to see the small caravan safely to Matt's valley. Matt was having a last meal with the Don before taking his leave, a meal served by María, who never seemed to take her dark wondering gaze from Matthew except when he looked up and she turned away in confusion.

"You didn't take her to your bed," mused Don Celestino. Doña Anatacia had not joined them so he could speak freely. "Your wife must be a fair woman indeed!"

Embarrassed for the girl, who was within earshot, Matt answered diplomatically, "María is too pretty a girl to court with one's mind on Comanches."

She looked at him with a glow of happiness, and when she brought them peach brandy in the heavy antique goblets, she knelt almost to his hand and murmured, "Go with God, Don Mateo. May our Lady protect you and all that is yours."

"Even your wife," smiled the Don, when María's skirts had whispered out. "It's well you go, Mateo! I'd lose all my people if you stayed long. You've gained not only livestock but men as well—if Changa can be called one!"

Matt blinked. "What do you mean?"

"Before they left with your livestock, Quil and Changa appeared before me. They asked my permission, if you consented, to stay with you and be your men."

So that was why Quil had asked Matt if he had any slaves!

"I knew nothing of this," Matthew said slowly, touched but not wishing the Don to think he had coaxed away the two.

The old *hidalgo* laughed. "Women need coaxing, men who are worth having do not. Nor does a man serve well if his wishes lie elsewhere. Quil is the best man I have ever had, at dull work as well as at tailing the bulls or throwing them by their horns. At trailing and taming wild horses he is without equal. Changa, for all his tricks, is more man than monkey."

"I'm glad to have them, of course," said Matt. "But I hope we won't have to fight any more Comanches!"

"Well, there are Apaches, and there will be bandits, both gringo and Mexican," shrugged the Don fatalistically. "But let us hope you will be established in power before the human wolves sniff your scent!"

"You've been very generous," Matt said. "If I can ever be of assistance, let me know."

"You mean that?"

"Of course," said Matt, surprised.

"Then come with me." Don Celestino rose and moved into the house, turning toward Doña Anatacia's rooms.

Matt stopped, blood pounding in his ears. Don Celestino spoke without turning. "Get me an heir, Mateo."

"But—the señora—"

"We have spoken. She would welcome your child. I shall adopt him, naturally."

Matt knew it was an honor. But to be picked for this like a prize bull, even by *hidalgos!* He didn't know whether to laugh or refuse.

As it happened, he did neither. The Don vanished through an arch. Before Matt could follow, a door opened. Anatacia's fragrance reached him along with her hesitant husky voice.

She stood in the doorway, her long black hair loosed over her shoulders. The filmy white robe barely concealed the proud thrust of her high petal-tipped breasts, the nipples erect. She was a magnificent woman, imperious in her need, irresistible.

"Mateo," she said again. Her eyes met his directly, though her lips trembled. "My brother wants an heir. But—that's not why I'm here for you like this. Love me, Mateo. This one time!"

She reached out her hands, wistful, imploring. Matt swept her into his arms and bent his mouth to hers.

The Don walked with Matt to the front of the house where Luz held Storm. And there was a wagon filled with the iron hinges, glass and tools that were part of Matthew's wage, and bundles with green leaves sticking out.

"A gift for your lady," explained the Don. "There are six small peach saplings there, and four young pomegranates, as well as seed from our best squash, melons and beans and sacks of cornmeal. Tell her I hope they thrive and bear much fruit, as I trust she will." The Don gripped Matthew's shoulders. Moisture made his russet eyes even brighter and more piercing.

"Vaya con Dios, gringo! If you tire of the other side, cross the Rio to Tres Coronas!" He turned as quickly as his leg permitted and went inside.

Matt shook hands with Luz. They wished each other luck, and Matt rode north.

He caught up with his herd at sundown, joked a minute with Changa, who'd devised a hollowed-out cushion to protect his wounded rump, and came alongside Quil.

"A nice start you have," Quil said, nodding at the mixed cattle. "Better to begin with fewer and work for a good beef animal that can stand this country."

Roans, grays, blacks, duns, linebacks and a sprinkling of red shorthorn mixes; horns from the curving, hooking sort to the straighter type of the fighting bulls to the smaller ones of the bred-up stock.

"Be fun to see what we get out of this bunch," Matt laughed. "We've sure got every kind!"

"At least no cow's a slave to others because of his color," Quil said, bitterness edging his voice.

"I come from a plantation with slaves," said Matt. "But I don't think it's right. I wouldn't have brought slaves to the Big Bend, even if I hadn't left in a hurry." He hesitated. "Quil, I'm glad you want to work for me."

"Don Celestino told you?"

Matt nodded. They rode on, their agreement more solid than any written, sealed contract. Ahead of the cattle, sometimes out of sight, sometimes grazing, the horses moved north. When they showed signs of scattering, Quil gathered them with a shrill whistle and rode among them for a while. Most of the horses had been broken by him. He knew their qualities and called them by name.

On the third morning they crossed the Rio. The scattered debris of skulls and bones, some still joined, others dragged apart, marked the spot where the Comanches had met defiance instead of dread. With whooping and gusto, the vaqueros hustled the stock across the river and up the Texas side, through passes and canyons, bleak desert and climbing rocks until, just as the last sun turned the palisades to flame, they drove the herd into the hidden valley.

Matt's heart thudded painfully. He strained to see a sign of Rachel and barely made out some kind of structure near the coyote's spring. Muttering something to Quil, he rode around the herd, past the cantering horses. His urgency passed to Storm. In spite of his long journey, the big gray horse neighed and surged into a gallop.

Wind stung Matt's eyes, but as he neared the old camp place, he saw the small adobe house. Rachel came out, her arms rising toward him as she called his name. She was thinner and browner, but beautiful still. Oh God! So beautiful!

Matt swung down from Storm to embrace Rachel, find her lips, feel the sweet softness of her body against his.

"Oh, Matt! I was afraid! So afraid you wouldn't get back!"

"Vacas!" exulted Lupe, pointing at the herd. *"Por Díos*, Don Matthew, I knew you would get them! And men! And horses! You are a grandee!"

"Not by a long sight," Matthew chuckled. "The men, except for two very good ones, will go back to Tres Coronas tomorrow."

"You'll find men as you need them!" Lupe assured him.

Matt, arm still about Rachel, gazed at the house. "You two built this?" he marveled.

"It wasn't hard," said Lupe. "Only time and work."

"There's only one room, but we've started the second," Rachel added.

Matt laughed. "You women must share the room till we've finished others," he decided. "The men can sleep in the cliff lean-to."

The cattle were fanning out now, as Matt had instructed, all along the meadow, and the horses had frisked to the far end, past the line of vision. The vaqueros were riding forward, sweeping off their sombreros as they saw the women.

"Can you feed ten men?" Matthew asked.

The women quickly stewed jerked meat with Don Celestino's gift of cornmeal. There were piles of strawberrylike pitahayas, and wafers made from baked and powdered sotol heart, of which the women had prepared a store. But what made a feast was the honey, into which the vaqueros dipped wafers and sometimes fingers, smacking their lips.

"Don Mateo," chuckled one man as the late moon rose on the circle lounging about the fire, "your women have prepared for your homecoming!"

"They've done well," said Matt proudly, letting Juanito crawl on his lap.

Watching Rachel's quick, graceful movements as she brought food, the hot craving in his loins grew more imperative by the second, and his mouth was dry in spite of eating and drinking. As soon as the meal was cleared away, he handed Juanito to Quil and caught Rachel by the wrist.

He didn't want to go into the house, close to the

men and their loud speculations. He led her along the valley to the coyote spring.

He spread his shirt and she her dress on the fine silt. She was naked and trembling, sweeter than the honey she had given him that night, and he stroked and caressed and kissed her until he could restrain himself no longer. As he entered her, as slowly as he could for she was almost virginally tight, she cried out in pain and pleasure, meeting his need, and he possessed her like the storm compelling him.

He was home. She was his wife. Their new life had begun.

XIII

The vaqueros left early next morning for Tres Coronas, though one of them, a sinewy, yellow-eyed rider with hair of raw gold, offered to work for his food until Matt could pay him. This Rico had a wildness about him, and Rachel was glad when Matt told him many thanks, but they didn't need another man. Rico left with the others but he looked back, and for a moment Rachel went cold in the pit of her stomach.

She moved hastily toward the peach and pomegranate trees. Changa, who had fallen worshipfully in love with both her and Lupe, came to help plant the trees, digging deep, wide holes to accommodate the roots, while Quil and Matt rode up the valley to get an idea of where and how to pasture the herd.

When the men came home that evening, they had decided the valley and bottom land would graze the cattle till midwinter and two slightly higher meadows outside the valley would carry them till spring, when some could be driven to Fort Davis. They spent the next few days digging two earthen tanks near pasture springs. After that came shelter for the people, for though the sun still warmed the days, it was cold at night.

Both Quil and Changa had worked with adobe. With three men and two women working at it, a new large room was quickly added onto the existing one. Its walls were three feet thick, double layers of bricks a foot and a half long, almost a foot wide, half a foot high and weighing about sixty pounds each.

Usually the women mixed clay and dried grass into the molds and left the lifting to the men, but when the men had to bring rocks to build the great fireplace or fell timber for the beams and doors, Rachel and Lupe stacked bricks.

When the walls rose eight feet high, peeled tree poles were laid across them, with peeled sapling sticks in between. On top of this ceiling went loads of earth which Lupe, Rachel, and Changa trod down with their feet, moistened with water, trampled again and left to be hardened by the sun.

As the men shaped and fitted door and window frames from rived cottonwood, fashioning a massive door and setting it on the iron hinges brought from Chihuahua, Lupe and Rachel plastered the big room inside and out with mud plaster, smoothing it with their hands. Lupe knew where there was a gypsum deposit near the river, and Changa rode with her to bring some back. Ground to powder and mixed with water, it provided a glowing whitewash, which the women rubbed on the inner walls with pads of soft hide. Uneven places in the earthen floor were filled and leveled, the whole was soaked with water and packed so that it dried almost as hard as tile.

The women were glad to move inside to cook, and this room, twenty by thirty feet, now served as their sleeping quarters while the men slept in the small original chamber and work began on the next room, joined to the main one by an inner door.

This smaller room was given to Lupe and Juanito and Rachel and Matt had the original room. Changa and Quil, sleeping in the main room now, decided bachelors were better off in separate quarters, and a long single-roomed building was started for them about fifty feet behind the main structure. They would eventually build other rooms that would join to shape a patio. The women worked on this while the men went hunting, for food had to be stored up as a reserve for the winter.

Squirrel and jackrabbit were eaten at once. Larger game, whitetail deer from the medium ranges, mule deer from the lowlands, and graceful pronghorn antelope from the high mountains, was dressed, cut in strips, and dried in the sun.

Bands of javelina rooted through prickly pear in desert flats along the river. The men made several expeditions after the piglike animal. Lupe showed Rachel how to treat the flesh as pork, frying the fat down to cracklings to be used like bacon or for seasoning and cutting the meat into slices and soaking it in salty water spiced with chilis.

These supplies of meat were kept in the coolest part of the main room. Almost every day something was added.

Rachel and Lupe hunted wild grapes, washed and drained them and hung them from a ceiling beam in a basket to dry into raisins. Wild onions dried in bunches. Wild plums were dried on the roof, then stored, and a respectable melon and squash harvest from the women's garden was cut up and dried on stakes. There was some corn, and what was not saved for seed filled several clay jars.

The honey tree yielded more honey and beeswax to make into candles. Sunflower seeds were gathered and dried. As the first snows showed on the highest peaks, Changa wandered in the mountains and brought home pouches of thin-shelled tasty piñon nuts from the little pines that grew along the slopes.

Water and grass for the cattle, food and shelter for the winter. The necessities were taken care of. Now the men made the first piece of furniture, a heavy plank table hewn of cottonwood. Next came two benches, and the night they first ate sitting down, Rachel lit two of the precious candles instead of the fat-burning clay lamp, and Lupe placed between them a clay bowl filled with bronze, rust and yellow leaves and pods set off with evergreens.

"A celebration!" cried Changa, smiling from one woman to the other and giving Juanito, who was teething, a crackling to chew.

"Yes, it's a real house now," sighed Rachel pleasurably.

It was as if they had all been rushing, working feverishly to be ready for the cold, long winter. Usually she and Matt were too exhausted to make love until they had slept a while, and their fierce nocturnal matings, begun while drowsy and quickly consummated, didn't really satisfy all her longing. Often during the day she thought hungrily of Matt or their eyes would meet with naked urgency, but she didn't want to go to their room in the day, when there was work to be done and the others would know what they were doing.

Now, though, there would be more time. And they wouldn't always be driven to their physical limit by hard labor. There'd be some strength for love. To-night—

Suddenly, Matt rose from the table. His eyes, the turbulent gray of a building storm, pierced her, held her transfixed as he came around the table, taking her hands.

"Excuse us, folks," he said.

"Matt!" Rachel whispered as he drew her into their room, undoing the front of her gown. "We—we shouldn't! What'll they think?"

"They'll think we're celebrating," he laughed softly. His mouth took away her last resistance. She touched him as fervently as he caressed her, and when they joined, it was a deep primordial melting that left Rachel unable to tell where she began and Matt left off. They were one flesh, one joy, and they had their home.

Next came beds, wooden frames set on legs, with leather strips crisscrossed tautly to hold serapes and the skins that were constantly being tanned and sewn into usable sizes.

Quil made Juanito a bed, too, carved it with coyotes and badgers and curious birds which the little boy traced with his fingers as he learned to say the names.

Rachel meted out enough of the precious Chihuahua cotton to make each person a small pillow. These were stuffed with moss, scraps of fur and grass, until they could accumulate enough down and feathers from quail and dove to replace them.

Almost everything had a use. Fat was used for cooking, of course, and for lamps, plain clay bowls with a sotol fiber wick. It was also saved for soap, as were ashes. These went into a wooden bin in the lean-to put up behind the house to hold things too bulky or dirty to go into the house.

Hoarfrost glittered on the palisades, and though snow seldom covered the mountain meadow for more than a few days at a time, and never fell on the flats by the river, the higher mountains held snow for weeks on end.

Squirrels, chipmunks, rats and rabbits fed on insects, grass and other browse and were prolific enough to maintain their kind while providing food for carnivores like the golden eagle. To a degree this protected the slower-breeding deer, antelope, Bighorn sheep, and javelina.

But if these creatures hadn't been checked by mountain lions, coyotes, foxes, badgers and skunks, grazers would have increased until there wasn't enough forage and water to sustain them. The men kept a close eye on the cattle, though unless the winter grew hard it wasn't likely predators would bother the herd until calving time. But in the higher ranges where they went hunting, Matt occasionally saw things that made him worry.

A deer on the slopes above them sank up to its belly in snow while a coyote ran lightly on the crust, attacked from the front, and cut the jugular vein with a quick motion of fangs, paying no attention to the men who'd left him his prey while they went after their own.

Another day Matt saw one coyote chase a large rabbit straight into the path of a hiding coyote who sprang out from behind a rock and made fast work of the unfortunate animal. After gobbling half the rabbit, the killing coyote left the other part for his accomplice.

The men hunted often, jerking and curing as much meat as possible. They brought in firewood from the mountains, seldom needing to fell a tree but hunting out lightning- or age-stricken giants—firs eighty feet tall and three feet wide, cypress, ponderosa pine, quaking aspen, maple. They smoothed the best wood with an adze and made it into shelves, chests, a big cupboard for the kitchen, more chairs and benches. And there were rawhide ropes to braid, riding gear to mend, shoes and boots to be patched.

The horses given by Don Celestino were wild, and Changa especially spent much time taming them, living up to his name of Monkey as he cleaved to animals who pitched, ran or rolled with only one desire, to be rid of the weight on their backs.

No one was sure exactly when it was Christmas, but Lupe made candy-cakes of honey boiled with nuts and dried fruits, and Rachel gave Juanito a ball stitched of leather filled with sawdust.

Lupe stared at the gift, then whirled to embrace the other woman. "Thousand thanks!" she cried laughing, though her eyes sparkled with tears. "In my village no one gave Juanito anything—my aunt even grudged him his life!"

Rachel thought back past the Christmas she and Matt had spent on the way here to her last Christmas in East Texas. Papa had been alive and Etienne. They'd sung carols in French and English, feasted on wild turkey and nut-filled fruitcake steeped in Papa's best brandy. Now her father and Etienne were gone and so was Harry, who had not been granted his wish of that one last joyous holiday together at Gloryoak.

Now, in this adobe house at the edge of the country, Matt's eyes met hers. He remembered, too. The sweet strong current between them flowed dark and cold for an instant. Rachel stroked Juanito's head and said to Lupe, "It doesn't serve to think of the past."

Still, they all did, those winter nights. Matt spoke of western army posts; Rachel sang Juanito songs and play rhymes she'd learned from her father, but it hurt too much to share the ones she'd learned from Etienne or the children at Gloryoak. If they remembered her at all, it must be as a wicked woman who'd caused Mr. Harry's death.

Lupe knew tales of witches who could take the shape of lions, miraculous healing by saints or the Virgin, the many tricks of Don Coyote and sad loves like that of *La Llorona,* who murdered her babies by a nobleman when he discarded her. She became a spirit of the night, luring young men to follow her beauty, then faced them with a skull countenance that brought death.

Quil told how the Seminoles had fought for their Florida lands till most were forced, with other eastern tribes—Choctaws, Creeks, Chickasaws and Cherokees —to the Indian lands north of Texas. Some Seminoles had managed to hide out in the Everglades, however, and were still there. And Quil told of mustangs he'd stalked for weeks till they let him move among them freely. He spoke only once of the master he'd killed before running away.

"He was full-blood Seminole himself," Quil said, his brow furrowing. "He'd been driven off his old lands, and you'd think he'd have had sympathy, but he beat his slaves until they died."

When the silence persisted too long, Changa sang ballads of the border and of Tres Coronas, including the new ones about Quil's and Matt's duel and the Comanche defeat. He sang love songs, too, careful to direct his languishing glances at the space between the two women.

One night a trilling hiss made the circle around the fireplace jump and begin to search nervously. "Rattlers should all be asleep," said Quil. "But that sounded like one!"

They found nothing, settled down again. Presently

the hiss came again. This time the men carefully went through the woodpile and poked into the dim corners.

Lupe shivered. "That was a *víbora!*" she insisted. "*A víbora cascabel!* We must find it or it won't be safe to go to bed tonight!"

"Snakes do like to curl up by something warm like a human," mused Quil. "I woke up one morning to find one snuggled under my serape. But there's no place else to look!"

They sat up a while longer, but no further hissing came, and they went to bed. Next morning, though, Changa didn't appear for breakfast.

"That sleepyhead!" said Lupe. "I'll call him!"

"He's not there," Quil warned, as Changa burst in from outside, waving a tattered saddle blanket.

"Look!" he lamented. "A cow, she got hold of my blanket and almost ate it before she woke me!"

"A cow?" Matt frowned. "Have you been sleeping with the cows?"

"That rattler hissed once too often after we went to bed last night," said Quil as Changa looked sheepish. "So I sent it out for some fresh air."

"And the cow ate my blanket!" Changa repeated in outrage, waving the scraps. "She liked the salt from my horse's sweat!"

Matthew roared with laughter. "Rattlers don't need blankets, little monkey!" he said.

After a minute, Changa laughed as much as anyone, and gave a long trilling hiss of his tongue.

The grass freshened with the approach of spring and grew high enough for easy cropping. The cows, most of them heavy with calf, were moved back to the mountain meadow after grazing the other pastures and dropped their calves in the home valley. The Spanish and Mexican cows could usually protect their young, but the shorthorn strain seemed feckless, more intent on browsing than watching out for their young.

The men kept careful watch, but a few sickly calves were run off by coyotes, and two golden eagles swooped on a stray, slashing its loins, tearing it into pieces they could carry to their young. For the pair of white eggs marked with purple and red-brown in the nest above the river had hatched into voracious youngsters covered with white down who were always hungry and kept their parents on a constant search for food.

Coyotes, too, had hungry young to feed. One morning the men saw half a dozen pronghorns chase a coyote against a cliff and kick it to bits with their sharp hoofs.

"He probably went after one too many of their kids," said Quil. An eagle scarcely waited for the men to pass before dropping onto the battered carcass.

Half the mares dropped colts, and new life flourished along with the grass. Only the human household showed no increase. Rachel began to wonder why she didn't conceive. She wasn't truly eager for a child as yet but she'd begun to imagine a boy with eyes like Matt's or a girl who might resemble her own mother. Quil watched Lupe with a kind of stoic longing, but whether he'd spoken to her of marriage was something Rachel couldn't guess and hesitated to ask. Lupe was so vital and warm and lovely it seemed a waste for her to be single, but a certain proud reserve in her kept Rachel from matchmaking.

Gradually the calves grew too big for assault except by the most desperate predators. Quil helped Matt select the hundred cows least valuable for breeding, and in June the men set out for Fort Davis with the sale herd.

XIV

Rachel hurried outside. When she came back, weak and clammy with sweat, Lupe wiped her face with a moistened cloth and said, "This will be great news for Don Mateo!"

"I think he'll be pleased," Rachel said.

"You're lucky." Bitterness tightened Lupe's face for a second. "I never had a lover or a husband, yet the village called me a whore!"

"But we all love Juanito! And he's such a strong handsome smart little boy!"

Lupe's eyes softened and she went to the door to watch her child playing with smooth pebbles Changa had fetched from the Rio. "Yes, I love him. A child lasts longer than passion."

Matt got home that evening with a thousand dollars worth of Mexican silver and the staggering news that the country was at war, had been for over a year, since Confederate troops fired on Fort Sumter last

April. Texas had seceded from the Union in February of 1861 as had ten other Southern states, including South Carolina, which had begun the withdrawals the previous December. Fort Davis was now garrisoned by the 2nd Confederate Cavalry, which had been organized at San Antonio, but it was doubtful they could be spared much longer at the remote outpost. Mail service had been stopped, and white people were fleeing the unprotected frontier as Indians grew bolder.

And Quil had gone north to fight for the Union.

Lupe cried out at that. Matt touched her hand. "He'll come back after it's over. I tried to give him a share of the silver, but he told me to save it for him —and give it to you, Lupe, if—well, if something happens."

Her dark eyes filling with tears, Lupe nodded mutely. Outside they could hear Changa talking to the horses as he rubbed them down. Rachel felt more nauseated than she had that morning. Something about Matt frightened her, the grim set of his mouth, the way he refused to meet her gaze.

"You'll be greater than Don Celestino!" prophesied Lupe, throwing back her shoulders and struggling to be cheerful. "It is sad that Quil is gone, but you can hire other vaqueros!"

"I'm afraid Quil's not the only one who has to fight," said Matt slowly. He looked at Rachel then with regret and pleading.

She felt as if she were floating above her body.

He took her hands. "Rachel, Tom's said he'd go abroad if war came. Harry's dead. That leaves only me."

"But you can't go!" Lupe burst out. "Rachel is—"

Rachel silenced her with a squeeze of the arm. "Do you mean to leave this summer?" she asked Matt in a calm, dead voice. Of course their happiness couldn't last. Of course as soon as she was with child, caught in that trap she had so dreaded and resolved to avoid, of course then her man, her only man would leave her. And how could she complain? After what had happened to Harry, how could she complain of anything?

"I can't leave you here," said Matt. "Maybe San Antonio—"

"No," said Rachel.

He stared at her, eyes narrowing. "You can't want to go back to Caddo!"

"I'm not going anywhere! This is my home, my place! I'm going to protect it and this house we've built and trees we've planted by staying, Matthew, just as you mean to defend the South." She turned to Lupe. "You don't have to stay. Matt can take you and Juanito to some settlement on his way to join the army."

Lupe took Rachel's hand and gave a soft laugh. "I was in this valley first, *pero no?* I welcomed you to my lean-to in the side of the cliff, gave you water from the coyote's spring, and food. This is the first place I've been happy. I shall certainly not go!"

Matt scowled helplessly from one to the other.

"But I can't leave you here! Two women in this wilderness? With Apaches and Comanches on the rampage and a war on?"

"Why worry?" offered Changa grandly. "I shall stay with them." Preening in his elders' astonishment, he said, "I have no concern in this war. Nothing calls me to Mexico. My only wish is to serve these ladies." He bowed to them in a way that made Juanito shriek with laughter. "If you will have a monkey, this one is yours."

"We'll keep you if you work." Lupe gave one of his outsize ears a flick of her shawl. "But don't think you'll be pampered because you're the only one left in trousers besides Juanito!"

Tears squeezed from Rachel's eyes but she laughed, too, fighting off the sick dread, the dizzying waves of illness. She wouldn't beg. She wouldn't cry. And she wouldn't tell Matt about the baby. Let him go about his miserable war and she'd see to her own matters.

"You must promise no more hissing like a rattler!" she warned Changa.

He put his hand over his heart. "Ladies, when you need to smile I'll be your monkey; when you need work or protection, I swear to be your man."

"If you look after the ranch and women, I'll see you're well rewarded," promised Matt.

Changa shrugged, glancing from Rachel to Lupe. Then he looked at Matt as if he marveled that any man could leave two such women.

"Don Mateo," he said, "I shall be rewarded if they smile at me."

Later that night, Rachel felt herself tensing when Matt took her in his arms, began to kiss her with the rough urgency of a man some weeks without his woman. Rachel could not respond. For the first time, his hands couldn't rouse her, send blood tingling hotly through her.

The lean hard body pressed to hers would soon be gone, for months, years, maybe forever. The hands on her breasts would grip a carbine. He wouldn't see the birth of their baby made in the winter's loving.

Matt! Matt! she cried silently. *How can you go? How can you leave me?*

His voice was impatient, as if he'd repeated a question. "Rachel, are you angry?"

Angry? One word to describe all that she was feeling, the grief and sense of being deserted, her fear of having a baby with its father gone and worst of all a poisonous doubt that grew the more she brooded.

Matt sighed, traced her jaw with his thumb. "Guess I can't expect you to understand, honey. But you wouldn't want the man I'd be if I stayed."

"The war's gone on for a year without you."

"But I didn't know."

And you don't know I'm carrying your baby, our baby.

"All right," she said tightly, struggling to keep from sobbing out her secret. "Do what you think you should. But don't expect me to think it's wonderful! Don't expect me to pant like a patriotic whore and give you a royal sendoff!" She twisted from his hands, turning her back.

"You little witch!" He brought her over beneath him, holding her wrists, bent his mouth to hers, bruising, seeking. She kept her lips closed over her teeth, rigid, coldly aloof to his kisses. He set finger and thumb in her jaws, forcing them open, driving his tongue into her mouth, parting her legs with his knee, gripping her buttocks in his hand, lifting her to receive him fully. He thrust deep, groaning, drew back, thrust again, wreaked himself on her like a storm till, in spite of the dulled woodenness of her body, she was trembling and shaken.

He called her name in a last surging, lay spent, one arm flung possessively over her.

"I had to have you," he said at last. "Had to have you!"

"Yes." She was astonished at the rage loosed past checking when she spoke. "You always did, didn't you and that's why we're here—why, really, you're going away!"

For a hushed moment he lay as still as if she'd

slipped a fatal blade into his heart. "What do you mean?" he asked slowly.

One part of her wanted to cradle his head to her breast, tell him she was just upset, that she dreaded to lose him, that they were going to have a baby. But her pride, her own half-buried guilt and despair, drove her past love, even past fairness.

"You can't forget I was Harry's wife—that he died because of us!" she accused. "We ran here to the end of the earth, but that wasn't enough! You had to go spend months in Mexico getting your precious herd! And now you've got a good high-sounding reason to leave me again."

He raised himself on an elbow, and she knew he was trying to see her face in the dark. "Do you believe that, Rachel?"

"What else can I think?" she demanded, unshed tears harshening her voice. "Since you got back from Don Celestino's, we've finished the house and you've spent the rest of your time hunting or seeing after the cattle."

"What else could I do?" His tone was angrily incredulous. "My God, we've been making a new start!"

"Have we?"

He caught her shoulders so hard she bit her lip to keep from wincing. *"I* was! Damned if I know what you've thought you were doing if you really mean all this rubbish!"

Rachel didn't answer. Her heart beat with painful labored heaviness. "I want to build an inheritance for our children," he went on slowly. "I want something good and proud and fine to come out of us, and what we did, and all there is to be ashamed of. Do you want what's past to be all that's remembered of us— an adulterous pair who killed and fled, vanished and left nothing?"

She twisted her head as if trying to avoid invisible blows.

"You want to save your family name! You want it to survive in spite of us. You know Tom's children won't amount to much even if he sires some legitimately."

"A man's blood is before and after him."

"And if you raise up children to your name, and make that name proud even here at the end of the country, then you needn't feel so guilty for killing your brother!" She laughed wildly. "Oh, Matt! I thought it was only in the Old Testament that men were commanded to raise up sons to their dead brother, got on that brother's wife!"

Catching her shoulders, Matt pulled her up to face him. "Stop that! I think you're the one who can't forget! Or you wouldn't spin these crazy fancies! Of course I want children, want to leave them something as splendid in its own way as Gloryoak. But I wanted that while I was still in the army."

He drew her to him in spite of her resistance. "Now listen to me. I love you. In spite of everything, even if I had free choice from the whole world, I would want no one else. But I have to go to this war."

She collapsed in his arms and wept. After a while, they made love again. But a part of her was locked away, sealed because he was leaving. She never told him of the child.

Two days later, Matt left for San Antonio. "I may be able to send letters to Fort Davis," he said. "Changa can ride in now and then to check and get news of the war. But don't worry if you don't hear from me. I'm coming back! Use as much of the money as you need. And don't risk your lives for the stock. Whatever we lose, we can get again—except any of you."

He brushed Lupe's hair with his hand, tossed Juanito, kicking rapturously, into the air, and shook Changa's hand. Then he kissed Rachel, held her till she almost lost the stiffness in her spine that had kept her upright these past few days, swung up on his big gray horse, and was off. At the end of the valley, he stopped and waved. Then he rode out of what they'd come to think of as the Meadow. Out of their lives.

Juanito gave a soft whimper. Changa swept him up and took him along to do chores. The two women started back to the house. Rachel sickened, had to stop. Lupe helped her, then brought a cup of water to rinse out her mouth.

"You didn't tell Don Mateo?" Lupe asked.

Rachel shook her head.

"You're a fool!" Lupe burst out. "If you'd told him he would have stayed."

"And hated me for keeping him from his precious duty," Rachel gasped. She had managed not to be sick around Matthew, but now she retched till only bile came.

"I'll bring you some dry corn bread," Lupe said. "That should help. Just rest here in the shade."

The dry bread, chewed slowly, did quiet Rachel's nausea, but her spirit rebelled at going in the house, lying down and resting as her body dictated. In spite of all reason, she felt deserted by Matt, abandoned; and betrayed by her having conceived when the father would not be there.

"Noght to been a wyf, and be with childe . . ."
Though she was tremblingly weak, Rachel felt driven to master her breeding body, defy its tyranny. In spite of Lupe's protest, she got her bridle out of the

lean-to, went along the valley where the horses ranged and whistled for her mare. Lady whickered and trotted up, accepting the bridle as nicely as she had in the days she'd been pampered, groomed and grain-fed. Rachel led her to the house and put on the saddle.

"Don't worry," she told Lupe, who stood in the door with Juanito. "I'll be back by sundown. I—I just have to get away for a while."

From the valley, Rachel took the right hand turning that led to the Rio, the first place they'd lived in this wild country. She let Lady go her own pace, slowly through the rocks, cantering on the flats.

At last, Lady drank at the waters of the Rio. Rachel got down and drank, too. A bird warbled, swallows flew along their mud honeycombs of nests on the Texas side, and the eagle dropped to its nest to feed the smashed carcass of a rabbit to its fledglings.

Here the Comanches, over two hundred of them, had died. But there was no sign now of that autumn battle. Rachel tied Lady to a willow sapling and walked along the low cliff to the warm spring.

Dusty and hot from the ride, she undressed and washed in the water that bubbled up from the rock side of the spring, shaping a basin large enough to bathe in. As she stood to let the sun dry her body, she became aware of a dull burning pain deep in her belly. Not like nausea, not at all. It intensified. Sweat broke out on her. She sank down in the tepid water, shuddering, fighting back screams.

Cramping spasms racked her, tearing loose the tiny new life. She gripped a young tree and held to it, gritting her teeth, till her body was empty of what would have been Matt's child.

For a while, half-senseless, she lay bleeding sick by the spring. Then she cleansed herself. She couldn't leave the bloody mucus to be eaten by coyotes or fed to eaglets, so she found a niche in the cliff, stuffed the matter there, and filled in the hole with river clay.

This was where she and Matthew had begun their life in the Big Bend; it was where their dead fruit belonged. It was where she would like to die someday, with water sparkling over pebbles polished smooth and round, the eagle's nest high on the Mexican bluff and warblers and swallows nesting low. She lay down again and slept.

It was almost sundown when she felt strong enough to climb into the saddle. There was a full moon, and Lady went carefully, as if she sensed the weakness of her mistress. Rachel's mind floated in and out of her body. There was sticky warmth down her legs. She felt as if her life were flowing out, almost wished she had died near the fragment formed of her love for Matt.

When Lady turned into the valley, Rachel lay almost prone on her neck. By the time Lady stopped at the house, Rachel was slipping from the saddle. Changa found her there, gathered her up in his thin muscular boy's arms. Rachel heard him shouting for Lupe, and then she lapsed into a soft dark haze.

Rachel lived in fever dreams for a week, back at Tristesse or Gloryoak or making the journey southwest.

"Will she live?" she heard Changa ask once, cracking his big knuckles.

"Who knows?" Lupe's voice held pity and anger. "To go riding like that—to lose Don Mateo's child!"

"He left her for the army," Changa defended.

"He is still her man."

"Ay," said Changa slowly, and laughed without gladness. "Perhaps after all I'm lucky. You women can play with a monkey and smile at his tricks, but there's no thought of love. Is there?"

"What a burrito!" scorned Lupe. "A boy must heave burning sighs for a little time to dry the mother's milk on his lips! You're our little brother and we're glad you are here. Now stay with Rachel and Juanito, *por favor,* while I hunt for blueberries! She seems to fancy them more than anything."

One morning Rachel woke gaunt but clear-eyed. She didn't speak about her ride to the river or what had happened there. Nor did she speak of Matthew. She went through the house, checking everything, rode out to look at the cows and horses, and came back looking tired but resolved.

"Tomorrow we'll make soap," she said. "And then we'll gather all the blankets and clothes and have a big wash down at the river."

Next morning Changa carried bucket after bucket of water to pour over the ashes that had been saved through the winter. The brown potash water dripped through a small hole into a wooden trough beneath the ash bin, just as it had when Tante Aurore supervised, but there was no egg to test it with, so when a small green peach off one of Don Celestino's trees would stay on top, Rachel pronounced the liquid ready to pour over the grease which Lupe had been rendering in the big iron kettle over an open fire. When the mixture boiled to taffy thickness, they strained it into their largest earthenware jars. Salt was too precious to add for hardening, so they would use this soft soap, which in spite of its strong smell was an improvement over the yucca root they'd used till now.

With one jug of the soap wrapped with soiled clothes and weighted pannier-fashion against dirty serapes on the back of a led mare, the women started for the river early next morning, escorted by Changa armed with Matthew's carbine. He held Juanito in front of him, and the small boy patted the horse's neck, plucked at its mane and drummed it with his bare heels, squealing his pleasure at being up high on such a big animal.

At the hot spring, Changa dug out the basin a bit more, and the women put in the clothing, beating it against the rocks and adding soap. When the clothes were clean, Lupe rinsed them in the river while Juanito played in the shallowest water. Rachel worked on the serapes. At midday Changa called them to a feast of grilled fish and berries. By the time the last serape was rinsed till its native-dyed colors were clear and bright, it was time to start home. Lupe plaited a mat of rushes to put under the wet serapes so the horse's scruffy sweat wouldn't get on them. The dry clothes were bundled on the women's saddles.

They reached home with a Juanito who had drowsed into sleep in Changa's arms, wet blankets to be spread about for drying and a feeling of virtuous luxury at knowing the laundry well and completely done.

It was a good thing the men had left in summer so that there was much to do and little time to regret or brood. From daylight to dark, it was a round of gathering wild berries and fruits, tending patches of melon, corn, squash and beans, peach and pomegranate trees and making ready for winter.

Changa found a deposit of fine black soil, and this they mixed with water and sand and spread on the floors, buffing it to tile hardness. Lupe made plaster paint of red earth and Rachel helped her paint a border two feet high around the bottom of the walls where the whitewash got very dirty.

When Changa rode to Fort Davis in August to find

it abandoned, Rachel went in her room and cried for a while against the pillow where Matt's head had rested by hers. Not to know where he was, whether he was well or a prisoner or dead! Not to know for months, maybe not ever. Supposing he never came back? She wished then, desperately, that she'd been able to carry his baby, that she'd at least had a child to remember him by.

After a long time, feeling neither wife nor widow nor even a woman, she tidied herself and rejoined the others. When Juanito climbed into her lap, she held him close, comforted a little by the warm trusting clasp of his arms, but something cold had settled on her heart and dried up her tears.

They had prepared for winter all that summer, but there was no way to prepare for the winter in her heart.

XV

Though the women still treated him like a boy, Changa was now a well-muscled, virile young man. He was increasingly restless, sometimes irritable, and frequently disappeared on hunting trips that lasted several days. He returned from one of these with a mountain lion's skin wrapped around something that wriggled as he walked in.

"Look, old one!" Changa called to Juanito. "I've brought you a playmate!" He unrolled the tawny skin, which still needed tanning, to show what looked like a small spotted kitten.

Juanito screamed with glee, squatting to grab the pretty creature, but Changa muffled its outsize paws in the hide, and Lupe snatched back her son.

"That's a *leon* cub!" she said. "Changa, are you crazy? Even a real monkey would have more sense than to bring home such a creature!"

"I killed the mother before I saw the cub," Changa

sounded penitent. "This small one spat at me like a real warrior. I couldn't kill it! People *have* made pets of them." He let the kitten go. It eyed them a minute, then began a thorough exploration of the room, batting at Juanito's ball with its dexterous paws, chasing it as it rolled.

Charmed, Rachel trailed a length of rawhide before it. The cub puzzled and pounced, pursuing it till she laughed and let the cord drop. The small lion crouched and began to chew the leather. Juanito clapped and even Lupe had to laugh.

"Mamacita had one once," ventured Changa hopefully. "It made a good watchdog."

"For how long?" demanded Lupe.

"Till it went back to the *monte*," Changa admitted.

Juanito struggled to get down. "You may watch the cat," Lupe told him. "But don't touch him. He's wild."

The adults hovered near in case either cub or four-year-old boy presumed too far. Juanito crouched down several feet from the kitten, which chewed the rawhide, a warning buzz in his throat, vigilant eye cocked on the child. Juanito hugged himself with delight.

"*Leonito!*" he crooned to the beast. Juanito spoke Spanish and English interchangeably, seemingly unaware they were different tongues. "Pretty *gato!* Cat *lindísimo!*"

He rolled his ball to the cub, which watched intently, furling its tail. Changa pushed the ball the other way with his toe. The cub sprang on it, batting it and sniffing.

"Mamacita!" wheedled Juanito, tugging at her skirt. "Can we feed him? Please, can we feed pretty *gatito? Por favor,* Mamacita!"

Lupe turned up her hands, glancing from Rachel to Changa, who watched her hopefully though they let the decision be hers. "You may feed him," she said. "But you mustn't play with him yet. If he's naughty, he must go."

"He won't be naughty!" Juanito promised, dancing along to the cupboard where Lupe gave him some scraps. "He'll be a good *leonito!*"

Leonito grew with the weeks but stayed playful and lost all wariness of humans. Soon he and Juanito were tumbling on the rug made of Leonito's mother's skin, the cub pulling in his claws. When he tired of the game, he slipped outside, disappeared among the rocks. At first when this happened, Juanito would cry, afraid of losing his playmate, but Leonito always returned. As fall changed to winter, he spent hours by the fire. One day he brought home a rabbit. After that, he seldom returned from his roving without fresh-killed prey.

"He means it for us," said Changa delightedly. "Otherwise he'd eat small game and bury bigger kills to feed on later." Certainly the cat made no protest when the humans cautiously appropriated his offerings.

"A lion won't eat carrion unless he's very hungry," said Changa. "And he prefers prey he kills himself, so whatever he brings us will be as clean as what I get." He grinned at the long sinewy golden-tan creature. "Now you're the hunter, eh? There'll soon be no use for me around here!"

The cat stretched and made a deep lazy sound in its throat which deepened as Juanito scratched between his ears.

Spring brought such a good calf increase that the herd numbered over three hundred, and half of them had to be shifted to one of the outer pastures.

"I wish we didn't have to put them out there,"

Changa said. "Thieves or Apaches may run them off without our even knowing it for days." Then he asked a question that had been in all their minds. "Shall I ride to Fort Davis again and see if soldiers are there again, or anyone who might have word of Don Mateo and the war?"

"Find out what you can, Changa," said Rachel after a glance at Lupe who nodded. "I'll send some of the silver in case you can buy cloth or salt."

He was back in six days, gaunt and exhausted. The fort, still deserted by the Confederates, had become a shelter for deserters, outlaws and pariah Indians, who'd plundered everything usable. Changa had spoken with Rico, the Tres Coronas vaquero who wanted to work for Matt and had since left Mexico. Rico had taken up quarters in the commander's house and seemed to lead a gang of bandits who would surely have killed Changa had they guessed he carried silver. Changa pretended to be looking for work and let Rico think the Meadow had been deserted. Rico knew nothing of the war or of Matthew, only that Apaches were marauding throughout the area, and Comanches and Kiowa, undeterred by any soldiers, were raiding the frontier at will.

A quick look around had shown Changa no cloth or salt was to be had, and he'd left the ruined fort straightaway, considering it safer to sleep on the way home. "Next time I'll go to Ojinaga," he said. "I might learn something there."

Leonito was almost full-grown now, over six feet long, weighing more than Changa. He didn't molest the cattle, even at calving time, but the prey he brought was larger now, often part of an antelope or deer, and he stayed out for several days at a time. His moods were shorter with Juanito. He never bit or scratched, but sometimes, at the end of his patience with being mauled by the boy, he sent him sprawling with a cuff of sheathed paw.

The lion was not the only male whose nature was changing. Changa was nervous around the women, and as summer passed and autumn came he usually went hunting even on the worst days, with the lion padding beside him.

"Why don't you sing for us anymore?" Lupe asked one night as they sat by the fire, which hissed and sparked as it touched off resin. The women were sewing skins into garments which they all wore most of the time in cool weather, hoarding their cloth for summer.

"Yes," put in Rachel. "Give us a song, monkey!"

He stared at them a moment, then let long dark lashes fringe his closed eyes as he hummed and at last began a lilting, lonely song.

So you no longer can doubt of my love,
Take this knife, open my heart . . .
Ay! But be careful. Don't hurt yourself, sweet!
You are inside . . .

His voice throbbed, raw, young, aching. Lupe listened, eyes bright, and it came strongly, rebukingly to Rachel that the Mexican woman had never been wooed, never heard words of love. Unless Quil— And he was gone, too, with no word. Why did men always go, leaving their women? When Changa stopped singing, Lupe touched his hand.

"Sing more, little brother! You have a delightful voice."

"Delightful!" Changa sprang to his feet. He sounded as if he were strangling. "I'm not your little brother!" Snatching up his coat, he ran outside, followed by the lion, though it was snowing and wind battered the walls.

Lupe stared in shock at Rachel. "He—he snaps like a wolf! I'm almost afraid of him. I wish Don Mateo would come home! And Quil!"

"It's late," said Rachel, banking the fire and putting out the spluttering fat-burning lamp. "We'd better go to sleep."

Something in her echoed the raw sex hunger of the young man but not so much that she would plunge out into the blast and storm. *Matt—Matt! When are you coming home?*

Though Changa was often short with the women, he stayed Juanito's idol. The sturdy black-haired youngster tagged after him everywhere. Changa made a small rawhide rope and taught Juanito to lasso everything in sight.

He only snared Leonito once. The cat snarled, chewed through the rope, and stayed away for a week so that a chastened Juanito added the lion to his mother and Rachel, who must not be captured, either, though when in a good mood Changa didn't mind.

As spring of '64 came on, the cows rubbed off their winter coats against trees and rocks, bulls challenged each other, new calves dropped, and the yearlings sometimes kept with their mothers' herds and sometimes ranged off with other youngsters. There had been a drought and not so many calves were born, but the need to thin the herd was getting critical.

"I should go to Tres Coronas," Changa said one morning after he'd stayed out most of the night. "Perhaps the Don will buy some cattle. At the very least I might get a friend or two to help us watch the herds that must graze outside the valley."

"Why not wait a few months?" Lupe urged. "Surely Don Mateo will be back soon—"

"Have you thought that he might not be back at

all?" demanded Changa savagely. "It's been almost two years! If he died, who'd bring us the message, even if they could find this place? Thieves haven't found it, or Indians, so it is, without dispute, hard to locate!"

"You're wicked to have such a thought!" Lupe breathed, eyes blazing. In spite of the hard life, she was more beautiful than ever, fully ripened, her hair glossy, skin glowing a rich copper.

"That's right!" snapped Changa, knotting his hands as if he could scarcely keep them off her. "I'm wicked! Yet I stayed with you while the brave men went away!"

"Changa," calmed Rachel. "Go to Tres Coronas. Your mother will be glad to see you, and perhaps you can sell some of our herd to the Don. Get salt, too, if he has it, and any cloth he'll trade."

Surely some pretty girl there would ease his torment, take his mind off what he mustn't have for all their sakes. He was a boy. Lupe needed a man.

And so do I, thought Rachel, tautening her thighs to ease a sudden pulsing. *So do I. Matt, where are you? Will you never come?*

Changa was back two weeks later with salt, cotton and a gift of chocolate from Don Celestino. "He sends his regards," said Changa importantly, in good humor after his trip. "In midsummer, a dozen men will drive all the cattle we want to sell to Tres Coronas. He suggests you take payment in sheep, but he'll gladly pay silver."

Rachel smiled. "You've done well, Monkey! Matt may be home by then, but if he's not I think we'll try raising sheep! They need less land than cattle and would be easier for us to manage."

That night Leonito dragged a heavy kill to the door.

A deer? Rachel looked down, choking, first at a slaughtered calf, then into the lion's fearless golden eyes, the face as familiar and loved as a pet's.

"Changa!" she called. "Changa!"

He came, saw, sucked in his breath. Without a word, he went for his carbine, sent a bullet crashing into the beautiful head, the wild brain tamed just enough to bring destruction on itself.

Shutting the door, pale around the lips, Changa said to Juanito, who came running up, "It was a wild lion. Don't go out there."

Changa dragged the lion away that night. Perhaps Juanito believed him, but he never asked where Leonito had gone.

After killing Leonito, Changa grew moodier than ever and went several times to Ojinaga, miles up the river on the Mexican side, to return days after stinking of tequila.

"You're worse than a javelina!" Lupe scolded one day when he came in unshaven, reeking of sweat and drink.

"But you need your wild pig!" Changa rejoined.

"This isn't a good life for you," Rachel told him sadly as she brought him a cup of dandelion root coffee. "You need a change, Monkey. When Don Celestino sends for the cattle, you'd better help drive them back and stay at Tres Coronas, at least for a while."

"You can't send me away!" He threw back his head and looked like Juanito on the rare occasions when Lupe punished him. "I must stay and help you!"

"Not if you're so restless you spend half your time carousing in Ojinaga," Rachel said. "We can manage. You mustn't throw yourself away as you are doing."

"There are many thieves around Ojinaga," Lupe added. "If you go often enough, some of them are bound to follow you one day. That would be a poor way to protect us." She ruffled his hair. "Get a wife, Monkey. Then come back to us."

He looked at them sullenly, ate in silence, and took Juanito off to gather wild fruits. He returned in a better humor. Rachel suspected he was trying to prove he could live equably in their proximity. For several days he was nearly his old self.

Late one afternoon he ran into the house where the women were getting supper. "Take Juanito and hide in the cliffs!" he cried. "Men are riding up the valley —and I fear they will not be good ones! That Rico was in Ojinaga the last time I went. He got me drunk. I may have said anything!"

"But—"

"Hide!" he commanded, hustling them toward the door. "Whatever happens, stay hidden till they're gone or I call you out!"

Lupe snatched up a knife. She and Rachel ran out the back entrance, keeping rocks and brush between them and the valley, hauling a protesting Juanito between them. Getting behind a tumble of fallen rock, they gazed in fascinated horror at the dozen horsemen who were galloping now, shouting as they swept past the house and toward the herds.

Then some cattle began to run, broke into a stampede. Changa spurred beside them, driving them forward. He was making a desperate attempt to panic the cattle into trampling down the raiders.

It almost worked. Three horsemen went down, screaming, under the rush of hoofs, but the others managed to veer to the sides and skirt the horned avalanche.

Changa aimed his carbine. Another rider tumbled. But there were other shots. Changa fell, dragged by the stirrup before his horse ran free, joining the pell-mell.

There was nothing the women could do except keep a tight grip on Juanito, who twisted and wriggled, trying to run to his fallen friend. Several of the men hung back to look inside the house, poke into the lean-to. Rachel thought she recognized Rico's red-blond hair and panther way of moving. He rode up to Changa's twisted body, swung down and hauled the limp thin figure up, giving it a shake. Changa's head lolled. He must have looked as dead close up as he did from the rocks, for Rico swore in disgust, let the vaquero slide to the ground, and began to kick him.

"Stop it!" Juanito shrilled, scrambling loose. Evading the frantic women, he ran out of the rocks toward Changa. "Don't hurt Changa, you *maldito!*"

Rico stared, then roared with laughter. As Juanito panted up, the renegade caught him, held him off the ground, gave the writhing, battling child a hard cuff on the head.

"Who'll ransom this little demon?" Rico called. "I give you one minute before I slit his throat!"

Rachel gasped as a knife blade glinted, but Lupe was already climbing out of the rocks, shoving her knife to Rachel. "Keep this!" she ordered. "And stay here! They may be content with me."

"Here comes the mamacita," approved Rico to the eight ruffians gathering around him. "But there is the woman of Don Mateo. Doña Rachel. Come out, *madama,* or I skin the child."

Rachel's knees shook. She felt rigid with terror. But she hid the knife under her skirts and started forward.

Changa. Crumpled and bleeding, dead as Leonito, wasted in the pride of his youth. Little monkey brother. No more hissing like a snake, sighing after women.

Two men had seized Lupe, but they somehow didn't reach for Rachel as she walked straight up to Rico and took Juanito from him.

"Take the cattle and go," she told the man who watched her with widening yellow eyes and a grin that exposed strong white teeth. In his way, he was handsome, and he knew it. He wore black, and his vest and hat were trimmed with silver conchos. "Don Celestino is coming soon. If you don't go at once he will make you very sorry."

Rico's grin broadened. "How will he know whom to look for unless we leave wagging tongues? I've dreamed of you a long time, Doña Rachel. If you please me half as well as you have in my sleep, I may keep you a long time."

Rachel held Juanito close. "If—if I go with you, will you leave the boy and his mother in peace?"

"No. My men need entertainment and I've no wish, yet, to share you."

There was the knife. But the eight lounging raiders would overpower her if she tried to use it now. Offer the silver? They would take it and do what they planned anyway. The knife was a last chance, a thing to use when with one man or for killing oneself. But she preferred to kill Rico.

He barked an order to his men. Five of them, grumbling a bit, mounted and rode after the cattle, began rounding up the scattered herd. Rico took Juanito from Rachel, tossed him to a black-bearded, red-faced man who wore an old army uniform.

"Now, Doña Rachel!" Rico took her arm as gallantly as if proposing some courtly delight. "We shall go to your house. I'm eager to learn if reality exceeds my dream." His hot eyes raked over her. He let his hard muscular hand slide down her throat.

This can't be happening, Rachel thought. It can't be.

But Rico was leading her into the house, starting toward the open door through which he could see her bed.

"Hold onto the cub," he told the uniformed man. "You can have your turn when Chuey's finished."

Lupe whirled suddenly, buried her teeth in her captor's wrist. He yelled and hit her so hard she slumped to the floor. While Juanito screamed, Chuey dragged Lupe into her room.

"Keep the brat still," Rico snapped. "I want a free mind to enjoy this woman!"

The black-bearded thief simply put his big hands around Juanito's throat and strangled him into silence.

"Don't!" Rachel cried. "Don't kill him!"

"Put a hand over his mouth if he squeaks," said Rico. "The women will serve us better if he lives."

Rico swept Rachel into the bedroom, closing the heavy door. He stood there in silence, eyes glowing.

"Now, Doña Rachel! How will you have me? Like a lover or a looter?"

"Would there be a difference?"

"For us both, *madama*." He laughed softly. "For me, both styles have charm. You, I think, would prefer the gentler way." His tone coarsened. *"Con prisa!* Decide!"

The knife. But she must save it till he would die without alerting the guard.

"Be my lover, Rico." The words stuck in her throat. She hoped that sounded passionate. "I've been long without a man."

"Yes, so that young fool Changa said. Undress for me, *madama*. But first pull off my boots."

Sheer unquestioning male vanity. It might save her

yet. As he lounged back on the bed, she pulled off his boots with their cruel silver-rowelled spurs, then began to unbutton her dress, pulled it off her shoulders and braced her legs to hold it till she released the petticoat swathing the knife. Mustn't let it clank against anything. As she stepped clear of her skirts, she turned the folds hiding the knife close to the top of the heap.

The chemise followed. Rico murmured at the sight of her breasts, leaned out to fondle them as if to assure himself they were real. Rachel smiled though her lips were stiff, tried to move languorously as she slipped off her drawers.

"Valgamé Dios!" he breathed. "You're more than my dreams. Stand there a moment. No, don't cover yourself! Let me look."

She closed her eyes to endure his appraisal, feeling already soiled, violated. When he brought her down beside him, caressing her greedily, hurting her breast, kneading her flanks, the old terror that had followed the rape by Tom threatened to overwhelm her, and when Rico's burning mouth closed over hers, it would have been a relief to grasp the knife and make her effort then.

But there was Juanito. And Lupe. Lupe, whom all the men would use. And then what? The bandits might keep them as slaves for a while, but their lives would hang on caprice, a cup too much of tequila, a freakish temper.

No. When Rachel reached for the knife it must be at Rico's most defenseless moment, when he lay exhausted. So she made herself hold him, writhe as if transported, receive his thrusting, and all the time work toward the side of the bed nearest the blade.

He cried out, gripped her buttocks as he exploded within her. For the first time she thought of impregnation, dizzied with horror at the thought, and with great effort got control of herself. He lay face down, his arm flung carelessly across her.

Now.

Stretching luxuriantly, she made a sound of sexual content, dropped her arm to the heap of garments. She found the blade, the handle, under the cloth. Slowly, having to do it by touch, she worked her fingers inside the petticoat, closed them around the handle.

He opened his eyes as she drove the knife into the side of his muscular neck, yanked it down and sideways with all her strength, slicing his startled cry into a thick gurgling, half-beheading him.

His hands, so strong moments before, fell laxly from her. He convulsed, arched, went limp. She could hear the drip of blood on the floor, soaked through the shuck mattress.

Vileness filled her mouth, but she swallowed it back, steeled herself. If she hurried she might save Lupe from that second man. Wiping the blade on Rico's cast-off shirt, she dressed hurriedly, hid the knife behind her, and opened the door.

Good. The deserter sat impatiently on the bench. He had gagged Juanito with an apron and held him between clamped knees.

Male vanity. Would it work again? Giving the surprised guard what she hoped was a seductive smile, Rachel spoke softly. "That Rico! Just like a firecracker, loud but over in a second! Sound asleep, too. From your looks, you were an officer. You must know how to treat a lady."

"Ma'am—" The uniformed man's eyes bulged. He licked his lips.

"Keep still, Juanito!" Rachel told the boy. "Stay right there! I must—talk with this gentleman."

Hand on the door, she smiled invitingly. The guard

stumbled to his feet and with his hairy face she thought he resembled a shambling bear on its hind legs.

"We can be quiet," she assured him and undid the buttons to expose herself. The man gasped and hurried through the door. Rachel struck, again in the throat, again severing the jugular.

Blood gushed out. He pitched forward, crawled a few feet and lay twitching.

Rachel prayed Juanito hadn't seen too much of that. Running to him, she worked off the gag, whispering as she did so.

"Stay here, *chico!* Don't move. I'm going to help your mama."

Chuey must have had the stamina of a bull, for he was atop Lupe when Rachel opened the door. It creaked.

"Wait your turn!" he bellowed, not turning.

The back, Rachel suspected, was not a good target but he might whirl before she got close enough for a sure spot. Perhaps at the side beneath the ribs, cutting deeply to the front. If she could avoid bone, rip deep enough, it should work. She mustn't fail with this last one.

Soundless, she crept forward. The man was holding Lupe up to him, grinding into her with short rutting jolts. Keeping as much behind him as she could, Rachel plunged the blade into his side, throwing her weight forward and curving to slice toward the belly.

He had lurched back from Lupe at the thrust, but blundered into lending the twist of his waist to Rachel's aim before, shrieking, he caught her wrists, struggling for the knife.

"Little bitch!" Pinkish foam came from his mouth, but he was gaining the knife, dragging it from Rachel's desperate hand. It was darting for her face when Lupe uncoiled, dragging him backward.

He gave a horrible cry, strained for a moment while blood pumped from his vitals, then fell against Lupe.

The two women stared at each other. Splashed with blood, disheveled, they looked, Rachel thought, like Furies. "Juanito's all right," she said bracingly. "But you'd better go to him. Do you think the others will come back?"

"Why, when they can sell the cattle and keep the money?" asked Lupe.

"But later, when the money's gone?"

Lupe shrugged. "It's a long way here and women are not that scarce. If they got most of the cattle they won't be back."

She hurried to her son. Rachel, shaking uncontrollably now that the danger was past, turned to the dead man, realizing for the first time that she had killed him and two more. In a matter of minutes.

She felt no regret, only amazement at the fragility of life, and the practicality that asserted itself at even moments like this. Sheets were too hard to come by to use for shrouds, though she'd have been relieved to wrap Chuey and Rico in the stained bedding and get rid of all at the same time.

And where would they bury the men? Except for the garden patches, the ground was so rocky and hard that Rachel agreed to Lupe's proposal to dump the bandits at the end of a shallow arroyo and cover them with rock. When they had done this, hauling the bodies in a handcart, it was time to bury Changa, who had been watched over by Juanito so that scavengers wouldn't get at him while the women got the corpses out of the house.

For Changa, they dug a bed at the bend of the wash beyond the coyote spring. Somehow they didn't want him out of sight, this little monkey, their brother. When they put him into the ground with his spurs, rope and hat, he looked young as the boy who'd come to them with the cattle and Quil, before the war, before all this strange life they had shared these past years. As they piled rocks on the shallow grave to keep coyotes out, Juanito helped, his face stained with dirt and tears.

When Lupe tried to comfort him, he pulled away. "Changa is gone, and Leonito," he said sternly. "Now I am the man!"

Late that night, after the bloody bedding was soaking and Juanito was asleep, Rachel heard Lupe weeping. Rising softly, she went to her companion.

"Are you—hurt, Lupe?"

Lupe drew herself erect. "That was a he-goat, but I'll recover. It is just that—that—" She began to cry again, a most unsettling thing, for Lupe never complained. Hesitantly, Rachel put her arms around her friend. Lupe reached out to her and sobbed. "Two times I've been with a man. Each time was rape. Is something wrong with me?"

"Such men are beasts!" Rachel soothed. "Quil loved you, Lupe. I thought perhaps—"

"I was afraid," Lupe said wearily. "But if he hadn't gone to the war, I think I was almost ready to trust him."

"He'll come back if he can, Lupe. Then you can be happy. This will just be a bad dream."

"Yes. If he comes back."

Rising, Lupe embraced Rachel and summoned a valiant smile. "At least we have had each other. Thank you, amiga."

And each returned to her solitude.

XVI

A few days later, when it seemed sure the other five raiders wouldn't return, Rachel looked across the table at Lupe and said, "I'm taking the silver Matt got for the first cattle and riding to Tres Coronas. I'll buy sheep from the Don, if he'll deliver them, and I must tell Changa's mother how he died."

"Sheep have good meat, give wool and aren't stolen as often as cattle," mused Lupe. "But Don Mateo doesn't like them."

"You and I can watch a flock, but we're not vaqueros. If Matt goes to war, he can't complain of what we've had to do while he's gone."

"Better to find sheep than nothing at all," agreed Lupe. "Shall I go with you?"

Rachel shook her head. "Stay here with Juanito. It's too long a trip for him." She smiled and recast Lupe's words. "If something happens to me, it'll be better for my husband to find one woman in the house than no woman at all!"

Next morning she tied the silver into a rolled serape and strapped it back of her saddle with food for the journey. She put on the green riding habit she'd tried to keep presentable and quite dazzled Juanito.

"Muy bonita!" cried Juanito admiringly. "Tía Rachel looks beautiful!"

"Aunt Rachel's going to be a shepherd—and you'll help, won't you, Juanito?" She gave him a hug and kiss, which he returned so vigorously that her hat was knocked askew.

"Go with God," said Lupe. "I pray it goes well. Beware of Don Celestino. He is known to be most gallant."

After being raped, the prospect of a flirtatious grandee didn't trouble Rachel much. She laughed and waved and rode away.

Except for trips to the river to do laundry and the flight that had shocked Matt's baby from her womb, it was Rachel's first time out of the valley since entering it almost four years ago, and her first journey alone.

At the hot spring by the river, she loosened Lady's cinch and let the mare graze while she gathered yucca root, washed her hair with it and bathed. From what Matt had told her of the Don, he was a fastidious man. She didn't want to meet him looking more unkempt than necessary. Dressed, but with her hair left loose to dry, she filled a water skin, mounted and crossed the river, shielding her eyes to watch the eagles circling for quarry.

This would be the fifth set of eaglets this pair would have raised since Rachel and Matthew had first seen that huge ungainly nest of sticks high on the bluff. Not much had changed for the eagles, but as for their own lives . . .

Matt had earned a herd, stemmed the flow of
Comanches and gone off to war, begetting a child he'd
never known about. Quil had come to them and
gone, his love for Lupe as fruitless as all their loves
had been. And Lupe had helped make a home, while
Juanito grew from a toddler into a lively young boy
with a deft reata. There was Changa, once gay and
full of tricks; if he'd held any woman, she would have
been an Ojinaga whore, not either of the women he'd
served with his youth and longing while the men rode
off to war. It would be hard to tell Mamacita about
the boy.

Rachel's hair dried quickly. She pinned it up beneath her slouched hat, strained water from the hairy
bag through her teeth, and laughed at a paisano that
shot past her, rudder tail aslant, strong bluish legs
flashing, shrilling its *koo-koo-kook!* This bird, a brisk,
breezy creature similar to an angular, elongated pheas-
ant could kill rattlesnakes.

It was a day for birds. Cactus wrens with brown-
spotted white throats and breasts and white-spotted
brown tails perched amid the prickly pear, making
sounds as musical as a tin pail rolling down a rocky
path. Black-masked gray quail with forward-curving
topknots pecked after insects, uttering querulous little
plaints like a long-married couple. Toward evening
Rachel saw white-winged doves as well as Inca and
mourning doves, and listened to the summer migrants'
long, forlorn cooing as twilight fell.

At an outcropping of stone above a *tinaja* which
held enough water for the horse, she unsaddled Lady
and gave her a nosebag of grain. Settling against her
saddle, Rachel munched dried meat and raisins. She
didn't chance a fire, and was very glad of Lady's
shadow nearby as the desert night closed in. Lying
with half her serape underneath and the other half

over her, Rachel roused once or twice as coyotes howled but then sank in a hollow of sleep that held her deeply until the sun burst dazzlingly above the Sierra del Carmen.

Late that day she began to see scattered herds and *manadas* of one color, like those Matt had praised. She camped bone-weary that night, unable to find water and giving Lady most of what was left in the hide bag.

At noon the next day she followed horses to water, let Lady drink and washed herself of travel stains. Vaqueros were surrounding her as she looked up from combing her hair. They stared at her disbelievingly! Reddening, she faced the mustached leader. "Are you of Tres Coronas?"

Something in her tone and excellent Spanish made him check a bold smile and sweep off his sombrero. "We are, *madama.* May we serve you?"

"I am the wife of Don Matthew Bourne," she said, and thrilled to see how respect straightened those who had been lounging. "I must speak with Don Celestino."

"Ay!" breathed the mustached leader. "I'll take you to him myself, *madama.* Tell me, how goes it with your brave husband, and with my brother Changa, and with Quil?"

Changa's brother? Then this was Luz.

She gave him the news as they rode. He crossed himself at hearing Changa's end, cursed under his breath, and couldn't hold back tears.

"Poor little brother! Tell our mother, *por favor,* I'd be flogged! You don't know who the bandits were except for that *sinvergüenza* Rico?"

Rachel shook her head. "I only know, señor, that Changa was brave. He killed four, we killed three and five drove off the cattle."

"Maybe they can be found," muttered the chief vaquero. "I'll ask Don Celestino's permission."

Luz took Rachel first to his mother, who seemed to wither at the story, but shook off Luz's arms and gazed deeply at Rachel, as if trying to know all she could divine of the man her youngest had become.

"Thank you for coming, *madama*," the older woman said at last. "My son had a worship of your husband." She studied Rachel, adding slowly, "And if he had feeling for you, too, as I guessed during his last visit home, I believe you were kind to him and did not laugh."

She saw Rachel to the door of the adobe hut, and Luz held Rachel's stirrup as she mounted to ride to the great house. As the vaquero helped her down, the heavy door with its three crowns opened. A man who could only be the Don stood there.

An aging eagle, she thought him, magnificent, with silver hair winging back from weathered features, lines at nose, mouth and eyes clear and sharp. He stared at her in puzzlement for a moment, then laughed joyously in recognition. He came to meet her, so swiftly she scarcely noticed he was lame.

"You are Mateo's woman," he said, hands claiming hers. "Why do you come alone? The Monkey said——" He broke off, eyes touching her as if he could not believe she was real. "Come in, rest, Madonna! After you've refreshed yourself there's time for all questions, except one. Have you word of Mateo?"

"No word, Don Celestino. As Changa will have told you, my husband went to war two years ago. Fort Davis is abandoned so we hear nothing."

"Two years!" the Don said. His mouth curved down, and he watched her in a way that left no doubt he saw her as a desirable woman. "A long time. But here's María to show you your room."

A slim, pretty girl, full-bosomed, with a provocative way of walking, took Rachel's things from Luz and led her along the hall that faced the patio, brought basins of warm and cool water, linen towels and a mug of frothy chocolate smelling of cinnamon.

"Madama," said the girl, casting Rachel a shy glance from beneath long lashes. "Don Celestino commands you have anything you require, if it can be found on Tres Coronas. I'm to serve you while you are here."

And whom do you serve when I am not here? Rachel wondered. She asked casually, "Do you remember my husband?"

María flushed, but gave Rachel a merry, almost pert look. *"Por Dios, madama,* of a certainty I remember him! We don't often have visitors like Don Mateo! Permit me to say I hope he comes safe from the war. May I help you bathe?"

"I can manage," Rachel said. "But perhaps you'd shake out the dress in my bundle."

María unpacked Rachel's few belongings while Rachel washed with soap smelling of rose leaves and spice and brushed out her hair. She slipped with María's help into the yellow dress made of cloth Matt had brought from Tres Coronas. Coiling her hair into a coronet, feeling more dressed up and feminine than she had in years, Rachel, escorted by María, entered the presence of Don Celestino. He rose from a high-backed carved armchair to kiss her hands.

Again that charged current flowed strong between them. But he was Matt's friend, old enough to be her father with years to spare. Bewildered at these sensations, Rachel was glad when he broke off his intent stare, seated her at a table gleaming with rainbow-tinted handblown glass and heavy silver blazoned with his triple crowns.

"Tell me of Changa," he requested. "Luz wants to

go after the bandits, but first I should hear all the facts."

María and another woman brought food while Rachel told how Changa had died. Of the ordeal she and Lupe suffered, she said only that they'd managed to conceal a knife and kill their captors in an unguarded moment.

"One blade and two women against Rico and a pair of rogues?" the Don murmured. "You and this Lupe must be very brave and very clever." It was clear he suspected the truth but didn't press since Rachel was clearly distressed. "And Changa! Well, I must permit Luz to try and find those other bandits. They shall die for Changa's sake and yours. They might one day decide to return to your meadow. That must not happen."

"So you wish to raise sheep instead of cattle," he said, as they rose from the table. "We'll talk more about this at dinner, after you're rested."

He seated her in one of the massive chairs by the great fireplace tiled with scenes from the lives of the saints and clapped his hands. María fetched brandy in crystal goblets.

Rachel sipped the delicious peach-flavored drink, relaxing, though her chair was far from comfortable in spite of its crimson velvet cushion. This house was stark, despite its grandeur, stunning in its contradiction of rich, costly dishes on a hand-hewn table, an alabaster Virgin enshrined in a niche of native clay. The house was a mixture of native simplicity, materials and color, given austerely elegant point and style by imports from Spain and the Orient.

Rachel sensed in Don Celestino a similar contrast. His iron will, the habit of command, strong beneath the paternal kindness with which he treated his people, the courtesy he showed to Rachel; his virile though aging body chained to an injured leg; his hand-tucked, flowing-sleeve shirt of finest linen belted into leather trousers trimmed with silver conchos. She would not have been surprised to glimpse a hair shirt beneath the linen—or one of chain mail, either, so perfectly was he the Spaniard, possessive, desiring women, land, proud horses and horned cattle, but knowing throughout his struggle to achieve power and glory that his spirit was encased in a body that was only mortal.

He raised his goblet now and drank to her. "Is the brandy pleasing to you, Madonna?" He used the archaic form of "my lady," but it did not seem affected coming from him.

She sipped the sweet, slow-burning liquor and smiled her approval. "It's very good, Don Celestino. My husband told me of it. Remember you sent peach trees with him."

"Do they thrive?"

"They're starting to bear good fruit, but we've made no brandy."

"That will come." He inclined his head, and in the cool darkness of the room the lines in his face did not show, and his hair shone a silver more alive than any color of youth. "I trust, Madonna, that you, with my friend, Don Mateo, will drink many glasses from the fruit of my trees."

Did he, on purpose, remind himself and her of Matt? He rose abruptly. "Will you rest now? In the cool after sunset we can drive to look at the sheep. Then we will have dinner and my sister will join us. She says, Madonna, that you're welcome to borrow some of her dresses during your stay."

Sister? Rachel remembered now that Matt had mentioned a Doña Anatacia so briefly she'd pictured an elderly widow. If the lady shared at all the magnetism of her brother, age wouldn't make much difference.

"Thank your sister," Rachel said, feeling as if a shadow had fallen across her heart. "But I'd better use my own things."

The Don smiled. "That's the simplest rule," he said, his tone deepening with male amusement. "But one must be disciplined indeed or nearsighted to never be tempted by that which is not his."

The pulse hammered in Rachel's throat. He held her with his eyes. Then he bowed. Before those piercing knowledgeable eyes could confound her again, Rachel escaped.

It wasn't for this, for a man, that she'd come to Tres Coronas, yet here he was.

It was hot, and the sheep that could found shade by the brush or stunted trees while others shaded their heads under one another's bellies, facing the wind so it didn't ruffle their grayish-black greasy fleeces. Bare-bellied and long-legged, some with brown curling horns, they were far from pretty, but their shepherd watched them as closely and fondly as if they had been his children.

"Inocencio leads them to peaceful waters and lets them lie down only where it's safe," Don Celestino explained. "He finds the best graze he can in this thorny land, and protects them with his slingshot and throwing stick. He's a good shepherd, like David before he became King and beset with troubles." Don Celestino turned suddenly to Rachel, probing her with his dark eyes. "Madonna, do you think these ugly sheep are worth such care?"

"They can live in this country. They give fleece and meat. Of course they're worth it!"

She wondered if such a practical assessment would annoy the Don, but his laughter was approving. "Madonna, these sheep don't look it, but they have a proud history. The five thousand Coronado brought into what is now the United States were lost, but those Oñate brought a little later have flourished and inherited all this country, on either side of the Rio. They are *churros,* the common sheep of Spain, though I've smuggled in a little merino blood. The *churro* on his migrations from winter to summer range marked out the roads Hannibal followed as he marched across Spain and around to Italy. *Churros* gave the Romans wool. They can forage and multiply in country that would starve prettier, fatter sheep, and their meat is very good. You're right not to despise them because of their looks. Will you have sheep for your meadow now you've seen them, or would you prefer cattle?"

Rachel gazed at frolicking leggy young, sedate mothers, questing rams. "I'll have as many as eight hundred American dollars' worth of Mexican silver will buy."

The Don spoke to Inocencio, the mute shepherd, who looked sad, but bowed. Wheeling the carriage, Don Celestino said, "He'll pick out a flock of the best ewes and finest bucks. They'll be ready in two days, and I'll send enough men to drive them to your valley. One of the shepherds who has a tongue will go with you and teach you all there is to know about tending sheep. A pair of our best dogs must stay with them, of course."

"You mustn't give me more than I can pay for," Rachel objected.

He looked full at her, smiled as blood came to her cheeks. "That," he said with a note of regret, "would be impossible."

As they drove to the stable, a handsome little boy ran up, clambered on the carriage and occupied the Don's knee as if it were a familiar perch.

"Tío!" he commanded. "Let me drive! I'm a big boy! Please, Tío!"

He was so small, about two years old, Rachel guessed, that his earnest entreaty to handle mettlesome horses inspired admiration as well as laughter. The child had shining black hair and clear olive skin, but his eyes were gray—storm blue-gray that made Rachel gasp. Her husband's eyes stared at her beneath the boy's imperious dark eyebrows until they dismissed her as a person of no particular interest and fastened on the Don.

"Tío!" It was both command and plea. "Roque drive!"

"No," said the Don pleasantly, tossing the boy to the ground and climbing down himself while a stablehand assisted Rachel. "Roque will have at each age the right horse, which is now your gray pony. And Roque must acquire manners. Doña Rachel, this is my nephew. Roque, this lady is the wife of my friend, Don Mateo."

"The Tejano of whom the vaqueros sing?" frowned Roque.

"The same."

Don Celestino scowled at his nephew, and it was like seeing an old eagle tower over a ruffling fluffy eaglet. Roque turned. With a sigh of resignation, he bowed over Rachel's hand.

"*A sus ordenes, señora,*" he rattled glibly, then pounced on his uncle. "May I go with Luz for the *bandidos?* May I, Tío?"

The Don gave him a solid but affectionate smack on the seat of his suede trousers. "You may run tell María to give you some flan and put you to bed." Roque balked, panting. The Don smacked him again, harder. "Men need their rest, old one. Sleep sound and we'll ride in the morning before anyone else is awake."

Roque hugged the Don's leg and hurried for the house with one backward glance of those Norteño eyes.

"He's a beautiful child," Rachel said.

"Yes. We spoil him, but he's my heir, desired for a long time." The Don chuckled but Rachel thought he seemed uneasy. "The young and old have the habit of early rising, one my sister abhors. So Roque and I are morning companions."

"That's nice for both of you," Rachel said, and meant it, though a slow subtle poison seemed to spread through her.

She mustn't jump to conclusions. There were, surely, other men with eyes that peculiar violent gray. But Roque was of an age to have been sired during the months Matt spent at Tres Coronas.

"Does your brother-in-law live here?" Rachel asked.

Startled for a moment, the Don recovered to say smoothly, "It is sad, Madonna, but my sister is a widow."

And was years before this child was born! Rachel set her teeth to keep from blurting out her suspicions. Could *hidalgo* pride accept a bastard as an heir? Rachel couldn't believe the aristocrat beside her would tolerate looseness on the part of his sister. And to speak so warmly of Matt—Rachel's head spun.

Had Matt loved Doña Anatacia and returned to the meadow only out of duty? Rachel's lip quivered. She bit it savagely, blinking back the tears stinging her eyes. She didn't realize the Don was watching her until he stopped by the portal.

"Madonna." He took her hands, made her look at him, into eyes that seemed infinitely wise, somewhat cynical and caressingly kind. "I think you have guessed. I will not insult you by pretending. Best you know how it happened and why, though I trust you will not speak of it to my sister."

"I—I don't want to know! If Matt ever comes home, he can tell me!"

"And you'll wonder if it's as he says and if he, God forbid, doesn't return, his memory will have a bitterness." The Don held her in his powerful grasp and told her the fantastic truth.

"I can't think of any other man from either side of the Rio who would have been acceptable both to me and my sister," he finished.

"It all sounds so calculating! Like—like—"

"Maintaining a blood line is a matter of plan and choice," the Don said.

But my child by Matt never even lived! If he didn't come back, that would always haunt her, that she'd lost her baby while this glorious fortunate boy grew up at Tres Coronas.

"Perhaps now you do not want to meet my sister?" suggested the Don.

Rachel considered. "No, I'd rather see her."

"Otherwise you'd always wonder," he said.

Nodding, Rachel gave him a crooked smile. "I suppose I should feel honored you selected my husband."

"You should," said the Don gravely, but his mouth twitched at the corners. "How old are you, Madonna?"

She actually had to think a moment. In the meadow, waiting for Matt, age didn't seem to matter. "I was twenty-one in April," she said.

He shook his head. "So young! So much before you! In truth I don't know whether to envy you or be thankful I don't have all those years to traverse! But since I am more years your elder than I care to admit, allow me this advice, Raquelita Madonna. You and Mateo are paired like eagles. There can be for each of you, really, no other mate." He cupped her face in his hands. "Mateo will give you children, strong and handsome and beautiful. Do not, I beg you, begrudge the one he gave me."

Rachel steeled herself against the hurt burning inside her. It hadn't been casual lust or a love Matt denied for her, but formalizing mating, a way to get an acceptable heir for this vast hacienda. If she had a child, she could have been more reconciled. As it was, Roque's eyes would turn a knife in her heart each time she saw him. And Anatacia—

"Come," said the Don, taking her arm. "You will want a few minutes before dinner. Remember, Raquelita, when you look at my sister, that her bloom is fading. Roque has brought her joy. And she has no man."

She's had better use of mine than I have, Rachel thought. Excusing herself, she hurried to her room, threw herself on the bed and sobbed with jealousy, hurt, self-pity, anger, waves of one feeling surging over the last, until she was spent, emptied—and red-eyed and swollen-faced, as a look in the silver-framed mirror proved.

Splashing her face with cool water, she combed her hair and decided candlelight would conceal the effects of her outburst. At least she was too exhausted to feel much of anything.

Or so she thought until she saw the queenly woman sitting opposite Don Celestino. The sheerest of mantillas softened the severe purity of her features, and her long pale neck rose from the perfect swell of her bosom.

Rachel ached. Matt had been the lover of this regal woman. He might have left her, but how could he ever forget?

Somehow, though, she managed to respond graciously to the Don's introduction and exchange a few polite remarks before the Don took charge of the conversation.

But Rachel had seen a flicker in the depths of those brilliant dark eyes. She felt them studying her covertly. *She knows that I know.* Anyway, Matt hadn't serviced an ordinary woman. There was a bitter satisfaction in that, along with the stinging envy. Rachel knew without being told that Matt could have husbanded this lady had he wished to renounce his wife north of the Rio.

The Don's attentiveness, though, acted like balm while they enjoyed lamb with rice and rich sauce, boiled milk candy, fruits, cheese, tortillas of blue meal and crisp little cakes full of nuts.

Don Celestino had read widely in French and Latin, and by the end of the meal they were arguing Rousseau and St. Augustine till Anatacia yawned and excused herself.

Rachel and her host sat very late, talking over brandy. By the time he saw her to her door, Rachel felt witty and beautiful, gratifyingly admired by this very masculine man. Matt's siring a child from another woman was a throbbing wound, but there were other feelings in Rachel now which made the hurt easier to bear.

"You see?" The crow's-feet deepened around the Don's keen eyes. "You've met my sister, she's no mystery, and you've thoroughly appalled her with your French and Latin. I would judge you will treat each other with mutual respect and bewilderment."

Rachel gave a heartfelt nod. Ridiculous, but this *hidalgo* who made her feel so much a woman also reminded her of her father, except that Don Celestino was worlds more experienced and, of course, powerful. He gave her a sense of security that Bradford, bless him, had not been able to, for she'd often had to be the provider and always the practical one.

"Good night, Madonna." The Don raised her hands to his face. "Thank you, Raquelita, for the most enjoyable evening I've had since Mateo was here." He paused, added with a twinkle, "May I alter that to nearly the most entrancing hours I've ever spent?"

Before she could answer, he touched her cheek and whirled away, as if he were afraid.

Rachel went to her bed with powerfully mixed feelings. Matt had a son by enchanting Anatacia. But the Don thought that she, Rachel, was intriguing. He was starting her with sheep through which she and Lupe might prosper, and he had sent Luz to track down the remaining bandits. All this was a marvelous change after the hard shifts of the past. How wonderful to be prized and cherished by such a man, if only this once, this little while.

As she undressed, she let her hands smooth her body, feeling the caressing warmth of the Don's eyes before she stretched luxuriantly in the great bed and slept with the warm sense of his protection around her.

Next morning after breakfast, the Don took Rachel by carriage around some of the ranch, showing her the manadas of horses, the special cattle herds, the kingdom he ruled. And though he spoke no word of his desire for her, awareness burned between them.

They ate at a cow camp and didn't get back to the big house until after Anatacia had dined. When Rachel spoke of leaving the next day, the Don said Inocencio required more time to select her sheep. Besides, he, the Don, was loath to see her return to the meadow until Luz brought word the last raiders were dead.

"But that might be weeks—or never!" Rachel objected. "Lupe's there, and Juanito. I can't stay much longer or they'll worry."

"One more day," insisted the Don.

The following morning he showed her his extensive library. That afternoon they took another drive. Apparently Roque had been cajoled into being content with his dawn outings with his uncle. He would wave from wherever he might spy the Don and Rachel but made no attempt to join them.

"How strange it is," Rachel said that evening after Anatacia had brought the boy to say his good nights and disappeared with him. "I could adore him if he were given to me. He's so like Matt! And yet he hurts my heart."

The Don watched her with an odd light in his eyes. "What would you say if I told you that's how I experience you?"

Her hand went to her throat, shielding the pulse that throbbed like a captured bird. "Surely I don't hurt you, Don Celestino!"

"It's a pleasant hurt. One I had never expected to feel again. Can you understand, Raquelita, that at my age it's reassuring to know my blood can quicken and I can ache with longing like a boy for his first love?"

As long as nothing was declared, it could be an exciting, flattering game. Rachel had never dreamed the Don felt more for her than he would for any new and attractive woman. At her sound of distress, he shook his head.

"Don't be sorry, Madonna. You are my last dream. And that's so much happier than having none."

"But—"

"You know I would like to keep you forever," he said roughly, his fingers tightening on the stem of his goblet. "I would try if Mateo were not my friend." He sighed. "Don't look frightened, my sweet. Can I offer violence to my soul? Just know that the memories you've given me these few days will shine in my heart the rest of my life to lighten that final darkness."

Rising, he offered his arm, escorted her in silence to her door, brought her hands to his lips. "Good night, Raquelita," he said, releasing her.

She touched his eyes and his gaunt carved cheeks, sensing the spirit behind his austerity. "Please," she whispered. "I—I want to give you one more memory."

With a groan, he swept her close, taking her mouth. She felt like a living fountain from which he drank, nourishing long parched fibers. But then he put her from him.

"No," he whispered. "You are Mateo's. But I will always remember you offered and that will be my joy."

He turned quickly. She watched him with tears in her eyes and a kind of relief in her heart.

At breakfast it was hard to believe this *hidalgo* had almost lain in her arms. Food stuck in her throat. She felt oppressively sad. For a brief time the Don had cherished and helped her, been her father and friend. Now she must go back to the meadow, hold it till Matt returned, if he ever did. The sooner she left, the better.

After breakfast was over, she went for the silver to pay for the sheep, but the Don looked at her almost angrily.

"I don't want money," he said. "No! I won't for any consideration take it." He checked her protest with a raised imperative hand. "Also, Luz returned this morning. Have no fear of those bandits, Raquelita. They will raid no more ranches."

She had already told Anatacia and Roque good-bye. María brought her belongings and Luz fetched her horse.

Don Celestino helped her mount. She rode away from Tres Coronas with four hundred sheep following, tended by dogs and shepherds, and when she turned a last time to wave, Don Celestino answered her salute, bowed to the waist, and stepped behind his heavy door with its three crowns, out of her sight.

XVII

Juanito was proud of himself. He'd coaxed a gourd-
ful of milk from the old gray longhorn cow, and it
was the first night she'd stayed still without being tied
and bawling as if she were being murdered. He gave
her a slap on the rump as she ambled off with her
calf, dewlaps flapping, her curved horns bowing forward. Juanito had first lured her into the corral by
roping the calf and dragging it inside, two weeks ago.
Then he'd tied her hind legs so she couldn't kick,
rubbed her and talked soothingly, pulling her teats,
though of course she'd been too furious and scared to
let down any milk. After several days of leaving her in
the corral, tying and soothing her, he'd begun tugging
and squeezing on the leathery teats, coaxing out thin
squirts of milk. Tía Rachel and Mamacita enjoyed the
milk and praised him for getting it. They called him
the man of the ranch.

Juanito frowned. He couldn't remember any man

well except Changa, who used to play with him and teach him to rope. There'd been the bandits who'd killed Changa and later the men who drove Tía Rachel's sheep into the valley, dressed in leather with peaked hats. One had given him half a hard brown sugar cone and a lesson in casting the rope. Santiago, the shepherd, was a man, of course, but he was very old and stayed with the sheep, seeming to be more like them than a human. He was kind when Juanito visited him, but it was as if he scarcely remembered how to talk.

Dimly, from so long ago he couldn't be sure if he'd remembered or had built their pictures from hearing his mother and Rachel talk, Juanito recalled two big men, the strength of their arms as they tossed him in the air or hoisted him on to a shoulder, the laughter coming from deep within their chests. One had skin almost the color of wild plums, the other, though sunburned, had paler skin than Juanito's and strange gray eyes. Quil and Matt.

Some day they were supposed to come back. When the war was over. There was no war in the valley, and Juanito didn't understand what one was except that men fought and killed, as the bandits had. Whether he really remembered them or not, Juanito hoped Matt and Quil were not dead. For he, Juanito, was not quite seven years old. He might milk cows and be able to catch almost anything with his reata, bring in firewood and water, and look after the sheep, but he was not truly a man.

As he started toward the house, pleased at the slosh of milk in the gourd, he heard hoofbeats, looked up the valley to the narrow pass and saw a rider. He squinted, poised to run if a string of horsemen came in view, breathed freer when he saw it was only one rider. It wasn't Tía Rachel out for a quick canter.

It was—a man! A broad-shouldered man who waved and shouted a greeting. Careless for once of losing the tediously gained milk, Juanito ran forward.

Quil, discharged after serving with Union forces in Missouri and Arkansas, had no news of Matt, but he could tell the women the war was over. It had ended in April with the South defeated.

"Matt ought to be along soon," he said. "I guess it'll be a long time before everyone gets home."

Rachel put their fear into words. "Perhaps he's—not coming."

"Mother of God!" cried Lupe, whirling on her. "How can you say such a thing?"

"It's what we're all thinking."

Quil grinned at Juanito and drew him close with one long arm. "I'm not! Matt'll be home any day. Now tell me how you got along. Where's that Changa?"

The women exchanged distressed glances. "Forgive me," Rachel muttered, stumbling up. "I—I think I'd better go look at the sheep before it gets dark."

"Sheep?" echoed Quil, looking dazed.

But Rachel's throat was knotted too tight for speaking. She was glad Quil was safe, glad the wretched war was over, but it was harder now to believe Matt lived, that he was returning. Best for her to get away for a while, not darken Quil's homecoming more than it would be by hearing about Changa.

Rachel's eyes stung as she hurried up the meadow in the long June twilight, but she couldn't cry. All that spring she'd been haunted by the eagle on the cliff who'd lost her mate. She'd broken her wing but had managed to get to her nest, calling vainly for the tiercel.

He never came. And the eggs were infertile. Even though an eagle was a threat to new lambs, Rachel

prayed this one would get well, and she crossed the
river several times, scaling the cliff and dropping dead
rabbits down into the nest made of sticks as long as a
man's arm and lined with bark. The three eggs never
hatched, and a few weeks ago when Rachel climbed up,
a ruin of feathers and bone was all that was left of the
birds who'd ruled this place from their high aerie
when Matt and Rachel first came to the river over four
years ago.

The eagle's fate had haunted Rachel though she tried
to shake off the foreboding. But she knew now the
war had ended two months ago. Now that Quil had
made his way back, her fears and terrors threatened
to overpower her, and she had to stifle sobs as the old
shepherd came to meet her, his dogs wagging their tails
in welcome.

With old-world courtesy, Santiago invited her for
coffee. He was still happily proud of the spring clip,
which Don Celestino had bought at a very good price.
The Don had sent his experienced shearing men up to
do that job and bring the wool back to Tres Coronas.
He sent her a letter, also, and when she opened it and
scanned the Latin penned in a strong graceful script,
her heart contracted. The Don, as she had with Matt,
remembered the words of Augustine: *"Sero te amavi,
pulchritudo tam antiqua et tam nova, sero te amavi!"*

Too late came I to love thee— That was all except
for the courtly farewell. *Yo beso sus manos.* I kiss
your hands. But the shearing foreman had told her the
Don wished to know how she and her household fared
and if he could serve her in any way, so she had written a long letter back. It had sounded stiff and formal,
but she hoped he would read into it all the things she
must not say.

Now, as always, watching the sheep settling for the
night gave her a sense of calm. She drank coffee with

Santiago, collecting herself to go back to the house and share properly in Quil's homecoming. She turned as the dogs began barking.

"I came to see the sheep," Quil shouted.

Santiago made a pleased sound and quieted the dogs. He remembered Quil from Tres Coronas and had been glad to hear of his return. After the men had talked a bit of hacienda folk and the war, Santiago moved off with his dogs to patrol the far end of the meadow.

"It's quite a flock," Quil praised. "A good thing you have Santiago and the dogs, but even so, you've kept busy with them, I'll bet!"

"Juanito and Lupe had helped a lot. We only lost a few at lambing to eagles and lions and coyotes."

Quil hesitated. "Matt seems not to like sheep. Do you think we should find another range for them so that when he comes back he can restock the valley with cattle?"

Rachel stiffened. "Sheep are better than cattle! No one's as likely to steal them as cows, and they give meat *and* wool. They can find food where cows would starve."

"That's true, but—"

Rachel cut in. "If Matt comes back, he can start cattle if he likes, but I'll keep these sheep!"

A sheep blatted from a distance. She hurried toward the sound with a free-swinging stride, her slingshot dangling from the rawhide belt looped around her waist. When Quil followed, he found her bending over a young buck who'd broken his leg, and helped her splint it with Spanish dagger and fiber from the same plant.

"You like sheep," he accused half-laughingly. He shrugged his massive shoulders. "Sheep and cattle can run on the range. Don Celestino does it."

"Certainly it can be done," Rachel said. "In any case I can take care of sheep and I'm keeping these!" Her voice frayed. "Oh, Quil! Do you think Matt will come?"

He put his arm around her, letting her sob. "Of course he'll come. Sure he will!" But they both knew there was no way of being sure.

Matt came in August, when the sun had baked everything to the color of clay and dusty green. He rode in late one afternoon on his big gray horse. The rider with him was so lithe and slight he seemed a young boy until one saw his frosty hair. He slowed his black horse, holding back, while Matt rode toward the adobe house and gave a shout.

Lupe ran out, drying her hands from some household chore. Quil, filling kettles at the spring, set them down and loped forward with an answering hail, scooping up Juanito, who was with him.

Matt grasped Quil's hand, swung Juanito to his shoulder, gave Lupe a hug and kiss, but looked past them to the house with his plantings of pomegranates and peaches, trees laden with ripening fruit and patches of corn, beans, melons and squash. Then he scanned the bluffs above the spring and turned his head slowly, searching.

"Rachel!" His voice was clipped with sudden fear.

"I'll get her," Quil said quickly. Matt caught his arm.

"Where is she?"

"Tía Rachel's with the sheep!" Juanito burst out. "She took some medicine for a ram who's got worms."

"Sheep?" Matthew moved past the blocking house, gazed at the upper valley. Sheep were there, not quite beyond his view. He whirled to Quil and Lupe. "What's this?" His eyes swept the meadow from one side to the other, snagged on a few dozen head of cattle ranging near the corral. "Where are the cattle?" he demanded. "Where's Changa?"

"Bandits ran off the cattle over a year ago," said Lupe. "They killed Changa when he tried to stop them." She waved her hand toward the scraggly mixture of longhorns, black and Mexican cattle. "The bandits missed a few of these who've calved since, and a few longhorns have strayed in."

Matt almost whispered. "These—these are all that are left? Out of several hundred?"

"Changa's not left at all," said Quil.

Matt passed the back of his hand over his eyes. "The Monkey! Hard to believe—"

Matt was stricken silent, his jaw muscles clamped tight as his gaze roved this changed home place of his, resting finally on his companion who waited, his knee curved across his saddle horn, smoking.

Nels never pushed, stood back to watch and think his own thoughts.

"Nels!" called Matt.

Unhooking his leg and lifting his reins in one easy action, the gray-haired man rode up to the others. A smile touched the edge of his lips, and he took off his battered gray hat to Lupe, bowing in the saddle, while eyes that seemed black but were the translucent darkness of a clear pool regarded her gravely.

"Nels Layne has been with me since we both joined Terry's Rangers," Matt said. "Nels, climb down and get acquainted with Lupe and Quil while I go see my wife!" He handed Juanito back to Quil, swung upon Storm, and rode for the far end of the valley.

Rachel kept her legs clamped tight around the ram's neck in spite of sick disgust at the worms she scraped from the gash in its head where another ram had horned it.

"Hold still, you crazy devil!" she told the struggling beast as she threw away the pointed stick and daubed the flyblown wound with medicine made from twigs and leaves of the creosote bush. The ram struggled to escape the sting, but Rachel held him grimly and daubed the wound till she was sure the sore was thoroughly treated.

"Just like men!" she said, giving one of the ram's coiling gold-brown horns an admonishing tug. "Fighting, hurting each other—"

She let him go, stepping out of his way and looked up to see Matt. Dropping the creosote, she stared in disbelief, her stained, work-calloused hands going to her throat.

"Rachel!"

"Matthew!"

Neither spoke for a minute, or moved. Rachel felt as if she were dreaming, unable to realize this moment she had once longed for, then gradually despaired of. She started to run forward. But his voice, rough and male, brought her up short.

"I never expected to come home and find you straddling a wormy sheep!"

She stiffened. "Is—is *that* what you have to say, after three years?"

"Sheep!" He waved his hand, indicating and rejecting the flock scattered through the brush. "I can understand your not getting more cattle after the raid—but why in hell did you bring in these stinking lousy sheep?"

"Because they don't get stolen, for one thing," she cried furiously. "They give wool, for another, and they can live here when cattle would starve!"

"Cattle *will* starve after those sheep stink everything up with that stuff oozing out of their hoofs!"

"It comes out of an opening above the hoof and it helps sheep find the flock!"

"And runs off any self-respecting animal!"

The rush of joyous welcome curdled in her till she felt she was shouting at a crude stranger. Rachel vented an icy laugh. How could he? How dare he? Worst of all, how could he stay over there arguing when his eyes were still that stormy gray that could melt her? Then she remembered those eyes watching her from Roque's face and threw back her head.

"Does that include people?" she challenged.

"I—" His face changed.

Coming out of the saddle, he sprang across the gully to her, catching her close. "Oh, hell! Rachel, damn you, how I've thought about this—dreamed about getting back, holding you! What are we doing, fussing about sheep—"

But the thought of Roque on top of Matt's first words filled Rachel with furious hurt and disappointment. Wrenching free from him, she spoke between her teeth.

"Did you dream also of Anatacia?"

"Ana—" His puzzled echo broke off and he crimsoned. "How in hell did you—"

"One need only look at her son," Rachel said with poison sweetness. "*Your* son."

"Damn it, Rachel, that hasn't got anything to do with us!"

"Doesn't it?"

"Since you know about it, you must know Don Celestino needed an heir."

"So you gallantly sacrificed yourself!"

"Oh, hell! Anatacia's a beauty. But I didn't seduce her, her brother knew it and it was just one time!"

"Lucky you! To be thanked for what would ordinarily get a knife or a bullet!"

He didn't say anything but seized her wrists and brought her back against him, arching his body over hers until his mouth found hers. He kissed her ruthlessly until her resistance faded, until she would have fallen if he hadn't held her. But in spite of the slow wild stirring in her blood, the softness in her loins, she demanded as soon as he took his lips from hers, "Is it nothing to you that you have a son?"

"He's Celestino's, Rachel. My sons are the ones we'll have." When she stared up at him in angry defiance, he let his hand travel from her cheek to her breast, as if, she thought, he were claiming territory. "I'm back, Rachel, and you're the woman I've loved in all my waking and my dreams. I'm going to love you tonight. Come home now."

He helped her leap the gully, put her up behind him on the stallion. "Of course," he grinned back at her, "you're going to need a bath. Try not to get that creosote on me, will you?"

She gasped in outrage. He chuckled. And they rode up the valley.

Lupe had a feast waiting. Matt and Rachel washed at the basin sitting on a bench outside, Rachel angrily wishing Matt hadn't found her smelly, dusty, sweaty and doctoring that ram!

But he'd been off three years, hadn't he, fighting like the stupid ram? What right did he have to act as if she'd committed treason? She'd done her best to see he came home to something more than bare range, and her reward was being treated as if she were guilty of some loathsome crime! He wasn't even properly contrite about siring a child on Anatacia!

Simmering, Rachel flung into the main room, and collided with a stranger—a tall man who steadied her with swift strong hands and laughed.

"You must be Rachel."

She nodded, blood rushing to her face, and flushed hotly when tingling shock ran up her wrists and she realized he was still holding her hands.

"Sorry!" He stepped back.

Matt came in then, introduced them, and they all sat down to supper, Juanito, big-eyed, in between Quil and Matt, almost squirming with delight.

Quil and Matt did most of the talking, catching up on where each had been, but now and then Matt's gaze traveled to Rachel. She never met it but twice, and glancing up suddenly, she found Nels Layne watching her with a kind of disbelief in his strange ash-colored eyes.

Instantly he'd make some comment in his easy Southern tones on what the others were saying, but Rachel felt alone with him, as if he sensed the upsetting effect he had on her. The frost-gray hair made him seem ageless. And he watched her with secret marveling pleasure.

After the meal the women cleared away the dishes, and the men talked about the war until each was lost in his separate thoughts. After Rachel and Lupe finished, Matt cradled Juanito, who kept waking with fitful jerks to protest any notion of putting him to bed. He turned to Nels, "Too tired to give us a tune on your banjo?"

Nels laughed and rose like a cat stretching. "If you're not too tired to listen, I'm never too tired to play!"

He got the banjo from the separate room built for Changa and Quil, and tuned up, humming.

> I know where I'm goin' and I know who's
>   goin' with me!
> I know who I love but the Lord knows who
>   I'll marry—

Juanito fell asleep. To see the boy limp and trusting in her husband's arms made Rachel's eyes sting, and she bit her lip as she thought of Roque.

Would she and Matt ever have a child? Could they make a new life together? He'd left her alone for so long, so much had happened. They had barely been recovering from Harry's death when Matt had gone to war. And she wasn't a young yielding girl anymore. She'd defended the meadow, killed men, endured the seasons, and couldn't, now, tamely submit to Matt's will and judgment. It wasn't fair! He had no right to expect it!

Better to listen to Nels as his deep sweet voice moved through songs of struggle, high hopes, homesickness, loss. *Bonnie Blue Flag, Lorena, Dixie.*

"We sang that one, too," said Quil. "We sang a lot of your songs. And at sick-call those of us who could used to holler out:

> Are you all dead? Are you all dead?
> No, thank the Lord, there's a few left yet,
> There's a few left—yet—!

Nels and Matt joined in the chorus. "Here's one for any soldier!" Nels said and launched into a swinging lilt. Soon all three men were singing about "the girl I left behind me."

Nels's gaze rested upon Rachel; their eyes locked before she lowered hers to the banjo. After that tune, the music stopped. Matt stood up, carrying Juanito toward Lupe's room. "It's time we turned in!" he said.

Nels got up, again stretching lithely as if tuning his muscles. He bowed formally to Rachel. "Good night, Mrs. Bourne." He and Quil went out to their bachelor quarters.

Unsettled, caught in a spin of sensations and powerful feelings, Rachel went down to the coyote spring, filled a basin and laved her body with night-chilled water, scrubbing with soap to get rid of the lingering odor of creosote. Whatever happened with Matt, she didn't want him wrinkling his nose at her!

Why did the stranger make her feel this way, shy and eager as a girl, in a way she'd known only briefly once before, in the first days she had loved Matt, before guilt and trouble poisoned the sweetness of their love? Shivering in the night breeze, she dried with a rough cloth, starting for the house.

Matt's tall form filled the door. She halted, frozen in a kind of dread. Why had they quarreled the instant they met? Had the years left a chasm between them they wouldn't be able to bridge?

"Rachel?"

It wouldn't do to sulk. They had their whole lives before them. No good to embitter them with what had happened. Matt was home! That was what mattered! Gathering up her skirt, Rachel ran to her husband.

In the bed she'd used so long alone, Matt possessed her with sudden violence that triggered a memory of the last man who'd taken her in that room, Rico, whom she'd killed. That ugly thought along with Matt's urgency left her feeling wooden, completely separate from him. She lay awake for a long time after he slept, her body tightly clenched. It would be better, of course it would, when they got used to each other again.

At last she slept, later waking to long fingers caressing her, a mouth teasing her breasts until she moaned with eagerness and turned fiercely to him. He wooed her till neither could bear it another second, entered her with one deep thrust, rested within her while she gasped and abandoned herself to him, meeting the mounting tempo of his need, feeling him shudder and cry out as a dazzling fountain spilled over within her.

"You're home," she breathed, sobbing laughter muffling her words. "Oh, Matt, you're really home!"

"I am," he assured her, kissing the tip of her ear. "I mean to stay, too! If I left again you might start raising javelinas!"

She stiffened a bit at that, but it was lovely to be in his arms like this and she drifted into sleep happier than she'd enjoyed since her girlhood before her father died.

XVIII

"I'm going to get some cattle!" Matt announced at breakfast next morning. He grinned at Rachel, who stared back, her fork half to her mouth. "If you have to keep those sheep, honey, we'll run them on another pasture. No use wasting the meadow on them."

"Wasting!" Rachel slammed down her fork. "We clipped several pounds of wool off each of those sheep this spring!"

"Fine." he began. "But—"

"And the sheep are still there to furnish meat, or if they're fit for breeding, more lambs and wool!" She cut in breathlessly. "You can't find a thriftier animal, not for this country!"

His dark brows almost met above his nose. "Damn it, I didn't come here to raise bare-bellies!" Rachel knew she should have bit her tongue and answered softly, but she simply couldn't.

"You haven't stayed here long enough to raise anything!" she retorted. "And if Lupe and I hadn't taken care of the place, there wouldn't be anything left but a couple of derelict buildings!"

His eyes darkened like a thundercloud, but she glared back. Lupe poured more dandelion root coffee. Juanito fidgeted, his lower lip thrusting out, plainly not liking these words between Tía Rachel and one of his new idols. Nels murmured his excuses and went outside. Quil sipped his coffee and said nothing.

Matt sucked in a quick breath. "That money we got for the cattle we sold at Fort Davis! Did you pay it out for those sheep?"

"No!" Rachel flung at him. "But I was ready to!" She stalked into the bedroom, returning with a pouch she tossed down by his plate with a heavy clank. "There's all that money! Your money! Don Celestino gave me the sheep."

"That's like him," said Matt, half-grudging, half-grateful. "A gift from a *hidalgo* to a lady!"

"He knew you didn't like sheep," said Rachel, still standing, furious because tears were forming in her eyes. "He must not have wanted you to feel cheated!"

"Now, honey—" Matt reached awkwardly for her hand, turning it up and patting the work-scarred palm. "It's been hard on you, and I'm sorry! I'll do my damnedest to make it up." His jaw hardened. "But this meadow's for cattle. We'll move the sheep as soon as we can, and when the grass is fit for cows, we'll bring some in."

Rachel kept her face turned away. He just came back like a medieval lord and master and took over! After a moment, Matt dropped her hand. Shrugging, he rose to his tall lean height. "Quil, let's have a look for sheep pasture. Want to come along, Juanito?"

When they were gone, Rachel took the money

pouch back to the bedroom chest, glanced up to find Lupe watching her with frowning, puzzled eyes.

"What's the matter?" Rachel asked defiantly.

Lupe raised her shoulders, let them fall. "It's sad that you and Mateo start with a quarrel."

"Quarrel?" Rachel gave a bitter laugh. "He just walks in and commands! I suppose he thinks he's humoring me not to sell off the sheep straightaway or slaughter them!"

"Maybe he knows the sheep are truly only yours," said Lupe, spacing her words.

Rachel blinked. Could Lupe guess about Don Celestino? But her friend seemed guileless enough as she added, "Truly, Rachel, it's not an ill thing to own such a flock! Let Mateo and Quil get cattle! That will keep them happy and give them something to do. Can you imagine either man tending sheep?"

Startled at this approach, Rachel thought a moment, laughing reluctantly. "It doesn't seem to fit, does it?" She gave Lupe an almost playful hug. "All right! You and I will be *dueñas* of all those sheep and loan our grand cattlemen money when their cows get rustled or can't forage!"

"That's it," Lupe agreed.

Rachel gave her a close scrutiny. "Has Quil said anything yet?"

The warm copper of Lupe's skin colored even deeper. "No. Maybe he's changed."

"Of course he hasn't!" Rachel scolded. "He watches you like a hungry bear does a honey tree! He's just afraid of getting stung."

"I—I'm a little afraid, too," Lupe murmured. "It's best we get used to each other, perhaps, before we think beyond that."

"It won't take long," Rachel laughed.

In a way, she envied the other woman. It would be

so much easier with Matt if they didn't have to make all their adjustments at once.

"There's good sheep range all around," Matt said over the supper table. "But if they feed pretty near the river, they can water there."

"And if they don't drown, maybe someone will steal them back across the Rio where people like mutton," Rachel sniffed. "Don Celestino is a cattleman and a grandee, and he runs sheep!"

Matt ignored her. Lightening his tone, he grinned at Nels. "Better change your mind and stay! You can be a sheepman, a cowman or some of both!"

"It's tempting," said Nels. His dark silver eyes came to Rachel, who was surprised to feel dismay at his next words. "But I promised to meet Jo Shelby down in Mexico."

"Mexico?" echoed Rachel, and there might have been no one else in the room.

"Maximilian, the Emperor of Mexico, has promised Confederates their own colony," explained Nels. "General Jo Shelby never surrendered to the Yanks. He crossed the Rio and hopes to raise a force to win back some of the South, or at least shape a new Confederate state in Mexico."

"Hasn't there been enough war?" demanded Rachel.

Nels raised an eyebrow. "Too much, yet not enough, I guess, for those of us who lost."

"There's been enough for me," cut in Matt. "When Lee surrendered, he sure as hell spoke for me, too." He put a hand on his friend's arm. "Forget Mexico, Nels! Don't waste more life and energy! Stay here and be a pardner. Quil says it's fine with him."

"Or you can be my pardner with the sheep," said Rachel, feeling herself blushing hotly.

Nels smiled at her, slowly shook his head. "You're

all more than kind. But I reckon I have to cross the Rio. I'll help you move your livestock first, though, provided you're going to do it within the next month."

"Oh, we are," said Matthew. "Those bare-bellies shift their range in the morning." He hesitated. "Nels, don't be insulted, but it sure would be a relief if you'd keep an eye on them while Quil and I go to Mexico for cattle. Time we get back, they ought to be settled down and the meadow able to carry cows."

"I'll do my best if Mrs. Bourne and her shepherd will tell me how," said Nels.

Rachel brought bowls of peaches sprinkled with winelike seeds of pomegranate. "That's very kind of you," she told Nels. "I'm—sorry you feel you can't stay."

His hand brushed hers. He watched her with those clear fathomless eyes. "I'm sorry, too," he said softly. "But I'm sure it's best."

The men rode after the sheep being herded out of the meadow by the guardian dogs and Santiago. Rachel, watching from tumbled rocks by the pass, put down her head and wept. It was as if her work, her plans, her efforts were being rejected by her husband. The sheep were still hers, but they wouldn't be where she could see them easily.

When she looked up the valley toward the spreading house where they'd carefully built room joined to room, she almost hated it, rebelling against the years she'd clung to that house made of earth and tried to make it home. The house suited Matthew; her sheep didn't, so he'd moved them out.

Lifting her head, angrily blowing her nose, Rachel looked into bead eyes, a tiny wrinkled throat and face crowned with a pointed diadem.

"He's my best horny toad, Tía Rachel." The horn

toad basked on Juanito's open hands, a tiny spotted dragon. "You can keep him if you won't cry."

She laughed through her tears, patting Juanito's cheek, then stroking his offering with great care. "He might squirt blood at me out of his eyes, 'Nito. Thousand thanks, but *you* keep him." She scrambled up, sweeping the boy along with her.

"Don't cry about the sheep," Juanito urged, trotting beside her, the leather hard soles of his feet whispering on the rocks. "I'll be your shepherd! We'll have the best flocks anywhere in the world!"

Such a strange thing for a little river boy who'd never been more than thirty miles from here to say. Rachel ruffled his coarse black hair. "But you're our vaquero, 'Nito! You like to rope and ride. When the men get cattle, you'll forget the sheep."

"No, I won't!" Juanito squeezed her hand in his till the horned toad wriggled in protest. "I'll help with cows and sheep both!"

Well, who could say he wouldn't, this son of Lupe?

"We'll see," promised Rachel. "Anyway, I'm glad you want to try."

She reflected wryly that it was a lot more than Matt would do.

Quil and Matt would ride on to Tres Coronas after cattle once they'd pastured the sheep. Nels would stay with the flock, helping Santiago get them used to their new place. But Rachel resolved not to give complete charge of her sheep to anyone. She'd ride over every few days to see all was well, and at lambing time, whatever Matt said, she'd stay with the flock. Rachel suspected he'd moved the sheep partly to force her attention away from them, but it wouldn't work that way.

The morning after the sheep were moved, she saddled Lady and rode toward the river. The sheep browsed between the water and first range of barren foothills on reasonable graze broken with willow thickets and rock outcroppings. Some stood with their heads tucked under each other for shade, for it was much hotter at this level than in the raised basin of the meadow.

This would be a good place in the winter, but Rachel decided she must find a higher pasture before next summer and move the flock with the seasons.

When Santiago heard Rachel coming, he came forward, white-haired, his skin like smoked leather. A slingshot hung from the woven sash girdling his coarse homespun shirt and trousers, which were villainously dirty and smelled stronger than sheep since the scent of animal was coupled with that of man.

He bowed to her and turned, spreading his arms toward the sheep, smiling. "They will do well here, Madama."

She talked with him awhile and rode on to discover Nels helping up a fat ewe who'd lain down to rest in a hollow and got too much on one side so when she'd tried to get up, she'd rolled helplessly backward. As the ewe scuttled up and made for the flocks, Nels dusted off his hands and grinned at Rachel.

"Now I see why these things need a keeper! Too dumb to lie down where they can get up again!" He eyed her quizzically. "Well, Mrs. Bourne, are you pleasantly surprised to find me scrambling? I bet you didn't trust me to look after your sheep!"

Rachel blushed. "They're a lot of trouble. I thought I should see if they were settling down here."

"Nonsense! You were afraid I'd be snoozing under a bush while Santiago tried to keep the sheep from wandering off to feed all the coyotes and mountain lions in the Big Bend!" His eyes danced, and he took her reins. "Shut your eyes and I'll show you what else I've been doing."

He seemed to be leading the mare a long time. "May I look now?" Rachel asked.

"Just a minute!"

He stopped Lady. There was the smell of mesquite wood and roasting meat. "Keep your eyes shut till I tell you to look," he ordered. "Here, let me help you down."

Feeling vulnerable because she could not see, Rachel let him lift her to the ground, which he did more slowly than necessary. He was amazingly strong, and as he steadied her a terrible flash of awareness shot through her and she quickly stepped clear.

It wouldn't do to feel this way; it wouldn't do at all.

"Now?" she asked into the taut silence.

"Now."

She looked at the start of a house made from limestone daubed with river clay, built against a small bluff that formed the back wall. Half the west wall was up. Two birds grilled over a small cook fire were in the shelter of the bluff.

"Do you think the door should face the east or south to the river?" asked Nels.

East were the pink, gold and purple of the Sierra del Carmen. But south ran the Rio with the ruined eagle's nest above. "Can you leave the door in the southeast corner?" asked Rachel. "Then it can look both ways."

"I'll try," said Nels. "Santiago would like that."

Of course the house was for the shepherd. Of course Nels was leaving. *Must* leave. If he stayed—Shaken, Rachel turned away.

"What's the matter?"

For a moment she had almost imagined the house

was theirs, that he was building it for her. Rachel shook her head, trying to laugh.

"You shouldn't go to all this work, Mr. Layne. You won't be here long enough to benefit."

A strange light glowed in his eyes. "Perhaps I will. Can you eat with me?"

"Why, yes, but—Santiago—"

"He'll eat later." Nels brought her into the angle of bluff and wall, made her sit on his rolled blankets while he turned the spitted birds, and got out ripe *tunas* he'd stored in a tin cup. Deftly skewering a squab onto a sharpened stick, he passed it to her, and put dried dandelion root coffee to boil in a battered pot that she could easily believe had accompanied him through the war.

"Whitewing dove," he said, taking half the other bird in one bite. "If I'd known you were coming, I'd have gone fishing or put on a pot of those beans you gave me, but I don't fool with much cooking on my lonesome."

The tangy cactus fruit gave zest to the dainty meat. Usually, Rachel wouldn't have eaten the doves, but this wasn't an ordinary meal. It reminded her of the ones she and Matt had shared on their flight from Gloryoak, but she'd been too ridden then with guilt and despair to relish the outdoor food.

And that was long ago. A war ago. Lives ago.

Nels poured the brew into the cups. "Careful," he said as Rachel reached for hers. "Don't burn yourself." Their eyes met with a shock that made each turn away, sip cautiously at the hot drink and look from changing mesas and chasms in the east to the towering rock wall on the other side of the river.

"Don't seem to be any eagles in that nest," remarked Nels.

"No. Something happened to the male, and the female died this spring. I was awfully sad about it, but if she were alive, we couldn't keep the sheep here at lambing time. Baby eagles have to be stuffed, and I don't want the stuffing to be newborn kids."

Nel shook his head and laughed, studying her.

Confused and disquieted, Rachel said, "Why are you amused, Mr. Layne?"

"It just seems crazy. You being here in this place and tending sheep!"

She looked down at her stained hands with their ragged cuticles and nails. She must seem a scarecrow, a parody of the women he'd known. How could she have dreamed Nels was attracted to her?

"I suppose it does seem laughable to you." She put down her cup and rose, her skirts clinging stickily to her legs. "Thanks for the lunch."

"Wait!" He was beside her in a flash. "I only meant— Oh, hell! Instead of slaving, you ought to be taken care of, live in a big house—"

"I lived in a big house! I didn't like it!"

She started past, but he caught her hands. "Rachel." He smiled at her and touched her cheek in a lingering way that made her tremble. "Rachel, maybe you haven't been with the right man."

She couldn't answer. He gave her a little shake. "Do you love Matthew?" he demanded. "Are you happy with him?"

"I— I— Let me go!"

"Tell me you're happy," he said relentlessly.

"Nels—"

He brought her to him, finding her mouth. Sweet fire, delicious weakness, ran through her. His hands trembled at her throat, lowered to her breasts. They came together like mountain currents, separate, at first opposed, then mixing in a whirlpool neither could escape.

That was the way of their passion, an irresistible force merging them together even when only their eyes met, a longing for each other as painful as if they'd each been half of a sundered whole. Hunger, madness, healing, delight. Rachel couldn't believe it when she was away from him, or believe anything else when she was near. For two weeks she met him every day. They made love in the steadily growing house, in the grotto, in the grass by the river where hawks screamed.

Lupe and Juanito were shadows at which Rachel smiled vaguely. Matt seemed like someone remembered from a dream, a man who was by now at the home of his former mistress by whom he'd had a child. Rachel felt real only in Nels' arms. They played and laughed like children, reveling in each other, stroking, caressing, teasing, as if there had never been other hands or eyes or mouths and these discoveries must be explored, tasted, marveled at.

But at the end of the second week, Nels raised himself from her to gaze away to the south. Rachel felt swept by a chill wind and she put her hand on his. He kissed her fingers, then held them firmly.

"Rachel, come with me."

She gasped, staring at him until he let go of her hands. "Is that such a surprise?" His tone was harsh. "We can't go on like this!"

"I—hadn't thought about it—"

"My God, I haven't thought about much else! You're my best friend's wife! I've had plenty of women, but I swear I meant to leave you alone. Then I thought we'd both do better to get it out of our systems. What's happened is I don't think I can get along without you."

"Can't you just—stay here?"

"And steal a few hours with you sometimes when Matthew's not looking?" Nels shook his head. "I can't play that game. I feel like a dog as it is. I'm going to Mexico. If you won't come with me, I don't want to see you again."

"Nels!"

He gripped her shoulders hard. "Do you love Matt?" He held her face in his hands, searching her eyes. "Are you paying Matt back for leaving you so long, for moving your sheep? How do you really feel about him?"

She thought a few minutes, shrugged helplessly. "I don't know! So much has happened to us. I've felt so much with and for Matt that I'm numb!"

"Do you love me?" Those smoke-crystal eyes demanded the truth.

"I must," she cried. "But I can't leave Matt. I don't know how I feel about him, but whatever it is, it isn't finished. I don't think it will be as long as we live."

"But you love me."

She looked up and down the river, at the bluffs and sweep of green dotted with her flocks, the desert and distant foothills beyond which peaks towered, hiding the valley which had become her home. Once she had feared this country; now she couldn't imagine living anywhere else.

"Please stay, Nels."

"No." He got up, buttoning his shirt. "In another week, the sheep will be all right with Santiago, and in a week, I'll leave. You can meet me here, ready to cross the Rio, or I'll be gone and in a few months you'll probably think you dreamed all this."

"Nels, please!"

"Your choice," he said roughly.

He helped her mount Lady. "Remember, I'm leaving a week from this morning. Don't come until then, and only if you're ready to go with me."

"Good-bye," she said.

He shrugged and stepped back. "Good luck to you, Rachel, if we don't meet again."

She couldn't answer, rode swiftly up the valley.

She couldn't leave. She loved Nels in some desperate fashion, but Matt was her husband. He held her in a hundred ways. She couldn't ride to Nels in a week or any time. It was over.

She scarcely ate, slept fitfully in the warm nights, hungering for Nels, scorning the hunger. She'd be glad when he was gone; there'd be no use in thinking of him, remembering his mouth and strange eyes that compelled her soul. Let him go on to his lost causes and fighting!

But she turned Lady into the outside meadow so it couldn't be the work of impulse to catch and saddle her. Days went by, then a week. Rachel was tense, listened for hoofbeats. She couldn't believe it would end like this, without his coming to see her at least once more. But she left Lady in the far pasture, the day passed, and though she sobbed into her pillows that night, she felt a kind of relief as if a spell were lifting, an interlude of madness.

Four days later Juanito came shouting that cattle— many and many!—were entering the pass.

Lupe and Juanito hurried to watch, but Rachel went on getting dinner. She was putting biscuits in the Dutch oven when Matt came in. He stood in the door. Her heart felt like a lump of iron beneath her breasts. This was the man she had chosen. Now Nels was the dream, Nels who'd made her feel alive and beautiful, a woman to be pampered, not abandoned and humiliated.

Matt said nothing, didn't move. Could he know? Alarmed, Rachel set the biscuits on the coals, straightening to look at him.

The misery in his eyes smothered the words on her

lips. "Matt!" she cried, running to him. "Matt, what's wrong?"

"Nels is dead."

"Nels?" she repeated stupidly. "Dead?"

He nodded. "He met us a day south of the Rio, and camped with us that night. Something spooked the cattle. He tried to turn them, and they ran him down."

Why did Matt watch her with such appeal? Why were his hands halfway outstretched? How could she help him? Nels was dead! Feeling as if her vitals had twisted into a tight searing knot, Rachel stared at Matt.

"The cattle!" she said. "Just like Changa!"

"Rachel!"

Her knees wanted to go out from under her. She leaned against the wall. "I hope those cows are worth it to you, Matt!"

"Damn it, he was my friend!"

"And my lover." The words ripped from her lips before she could stop them.

"Your lover?" Matt's eyes blazed in his haggard face. He stepped forward, checked as if drained by a secret wound. His face seemed all bone, a death mask. "Nels? Your—lover?"

To that face, to that agony, she must tell the truth, once she had blundered. "Yes."

She waited for him to strike or choke or curse her, but he did a crueler thing, a harder thing to bear. He watched her with naked, tormented eyes, then turned and left the house.

In a few minutes, she heard him calling to Quil. Coldness settled on Rachel's heart. She couldn't stay here. Even if Matt somehow forgave her, even if she forgave him.

She stared for a moment at the set table, smelled the baking biscuits, the bubbling stew. Then she made

a bundle of her clothing, took some jerky and dried
fruit, and went outside, hidden by the house from the
people down at the corral. She'd have to walk to the
far pasture for Lady, but Santiago should still be
awake when she reached the sheep camp.

Lupe came first. Matt had apparently not told about
Rachel's confession, but Rachel thought Lupe guessed.
"Come home," she said urgently. "We miss you."
Rachel only shook her head and went on trimming
saplings to roof the house Nels had begun.

"This is loco!" Lupe scolded. "You cannot hate the
cows that much!"

Oh. The easiest thing to let the others think. Rachel
turned to her companion of so many years, the lonely
years, and was filled with a great, heavy sadness.

"Lupe, I'm sorry. I love you and Juanito. But I can't
live anymore in the meadow."

"What of Mateo?" Lupe demanded.

"He has his cattle."

"He needs his wife! If you could see him— Surely
you must pity him for Señor Layne's death."

"I do."

"But you won't come back?"

Rachel shook her head, her throat too tight to answer. Lupe surveyed the rock cabin. "Winter will be
here soon. And what if robbers come through, or marauding Indians?"

"They might also strike the valley. In fact, now the
cattle are there, it's a much more tempting target. Anyway, there's Santiago and the dogs."

"Rachel!" groaned Lupe. But she finally had to give
up. "Don't stay here out of stubbornness," she adjured.
"If there's trouble, send for Santiago. I will keep a
home for Mateo, but you also are my friend—even
though you're crazy. And wicked!" Lupe's eyes flashed

as she mounted Quil's horse. "Yes, wicked! For you're hurting Mateo terribly!"

She cantered off, stopping at a distance to give a mournful, pleading wave, and when Rachel only waved back, she turned the horse and rode on.

Quil came next, on the pretext of dropping off supplies for the camp, though it was well-supplied.

"Matt needs you," he said abruptly as she brought coffee and corn bread. "The cattle, everything he does, it's for you."

She didn't answer. Quil gave her a serious look. "Tell you something else, Rachel. You need Matt. You sure do. Now stop hurting the both of you and come back where you belong."

"I belong with my sheep."

He made a sound of disgust deep in his throat. "You belong with your man!"

"Matt's done as he pleased. I guess I can do the same."

Quil left without a second cup of coffee. Rachel was sorry for that but glad both he and Lupe seemed to blame her self-exile on the cattle's displacing her flock.

Juanito came next, all the way on his seven-year-old legs. Rachel fed him and hugged him, and they played in the river, which was still warm. Gravely, he inspected the sheep and said he'd come to stay at lambing time.

"And I'll come see you often," he said as she kissed him good-bye, sending him off so he'd get home before real night. "You—you'll always be my Tía, won't you?"

"Of course I will!" she said, and held his wiry little body close, feeling the first warmth, the first peace, she'd had since hearing Nels was dead.

By the time Matt came, she knew she was with

child. It could be Matt's but she'd certainly been far more often with Nels. When she'd meant to live alone for at least a time, her body decreed she wouldn't. She was sick in the mornings, somewhat frightened, and if Matt had approached her softly there might have been a different outcome.

But he rode right up to where she was bathing in the river, around the bend from the camp, and shouted at her.

"Get on your clothes! You're coming home!"

"I am home!" she yelled back.

"Hell you are!" He sent Storm into the river. "Come on or I'll get you. I've had enough of this crap!"

She stood with the current thrusting at her knees, aware of her naked body, the life begun in it, hidden from Matt's angry gaze.

She said deliberately, watching him closely, "I'm going to have a baby."

His eyes went the color of a lightning-rent sky. It took all her pride and strength to stand erect, endure the way he scanned her. She saw his knuckles were white as he gripped the reins.

"No doubt about it then, is there? You've got to come."

And because he'd hesitated, and because she was afraid, and because he didn't ask the question she could almost see burning into his mind, Rachel shook out her wet hair and turned away from him.

"There's a good chance the baby is Nels'. You wouldn't want a questionable heir for the meadow and those valuable cows!"

He didn't speak for a few minutes. When he did, he sounded so tired she almost repented her taunt. Almost.

"Stop it, Rachel. Come home and have the baby, whosoever it is, and let's get on with our lives."

His dogged acceptance of her baby like some kind of natural catastrophe to be endured and ignored sent waves of guilt and anger through her.

"I shall have the baby, Matt, and *if* it looks like you, then we can talk about what to do."

"You can't mean to do such a crazy thing! Have your baby here with no one to help!" Matt paused for breath, and when she didn't answer, he went on savagely, "If it's Nels' child, do you intend to raise him with your damn sheep?"

"Exactly!"

"Why, you crazy little—"

"The sheep are mine, and I certainly have a right to this land. *My* child will have an inheritance without your grudging it!"

"God damn it," Matt thundered, "I'll call the little bastard mine if he has horns and a forked tail!"

"Oh, no, you won't! You've got one bastard down in Mexico." Her throat hurt, and she fought back furious tears. "I thought that was how you'd feel—and I'm glad you let it slip now instead of later! My child won't be a bastard for you, Matt, even if it turns out to be yours!"

He started toward her, guiding the big horse with his knees, beginning to loop the reins loosely about the horn to free his hands.

"Don't do it," Rachel whispered. "If you take me to the meadow, I'll run away, and I don't think you'll find me."

He stopped, gazing at her in baffled anger. Then he squared his shoulders and started on.

"We could have had a child!" she cried, clenching her fists. "You rode off to war about the time I was sure. I miscarried a few days later here on the river. We should have had our baby *then,* Matt!"

He stared at her a long time. At last, sighing, he picked up the reins. "I won't force you. I guess, since I left you, I have to let you leave me, if that's what you want. But I swear that anytime you come back, I'll call your child my own, and we'll start fresh. Leave the past behind."

"Good-bye," Rachel said. In another moment she'd be weeping, reaching up to him, relaxing in the strength of his arms.

"Send if you need anything," Matt said. "In the spring Lupe will come to help."

Wheeling Storm, he splashed ashore. Rachel watched, a numb heaviness pressing against her heart. *"I'll call the little bastard mine even if he has horns—"* Only the echo of those words kept her, naked, barefoot, from running after him.

XIX

Any other woman would have said the baby was his, tried to make peace and have a safe nest. Damn her stiff neck! Matt could have broken it with pleasure. And yet the way she'd stood, proud and naked, clothed in sun . . .

Maybe she'd come around as she grew heavy, when she'd had time to get over Nels—and wasn't that one hell of a thing? Matt ground his teeth to think of Rachel with his friend. Had she loved him? Was it spite over Anatacia and the war and those sheep getting moved from the valley?

God damn her, why had she done it? Raw, aching, Matt told himself it'd be good for her to shift for herself. But then he had to grant she'd been shifting for herself during the years he'd been gone. And she had lost a baby, a baby he hadn't even known about. That made it harder than ever for her to learn about Roque. He and Anatacia had been in Chihuahua when Matt came for cattle. With perfect courtesy the Don had asked Matt to send a messenger ahead when he planned to visit so the boy would not be at Tres Coronas.

"Roque is my heir, Mateo. I don't want him hero-worshipping you and wanting to live in Texas."

Matt shrugged. He saw the sense of it, but it went against his grain to completely ignore the blood tie. He thought, too, that Don Celestino asked too many questions about Rachel. On the whole, Matt was glad to conclude his buying and start home.

And he had three lost years and rustled herd to make up for! The night he returned from seeing Rachel, so lovely in the river he'd groaned silently with wanting her, he said to Quil, "Tomorrow we'll make steers out of a bunch of young bulls and save them lots of trouble."

"I can go?" begged Juanito.

"You've got to go!" said Matt. "Aren't you our top hand?" The boy wriggled with delight and followed them in to dinner.

"Going to sell these cows to the army post if it opens up?" Quil asked as they rode in late next afternoon, streaked with dust, sweat and blood. Juanito had held his rope on the struggling yearlings while Quil held them down and Matt squatted atop and cut.

Matt got rid of more dust than liquid when he spat. "The war's over, but I'm not ready to feed Yank troopers."

"Just me," grinned Quil.

"You're my partner."

"The post would be the closest market."

"We'll find another! Or, hell, if you want, sell your share of the herd to the army!"

Quil's white teeth flashed. "May do just that! Depends on how good a choice you give me."

"Some partner," grumbled Matt.

The work and being with Quil and Juanito had made him feel a little better, but in the sunset he gazed across the mountains toward the river, braced rigid against the desire in his loins, the terrible void in his life.

At least he knew where she was. At least she was no other man's.

He believed in his heart that when winter settled in, she would surely come, but snow gleamed on the high mountains, then the foothills, hoarfrost shone on the palisades, and there was no sign from her.

But there was work, and he drove himself. To handle the spring cattle work, he'd need at least three or four more men. Don Celestino had promised to recruit able and willing vaqueros and send them to the meadow by the end of winter, so when they weren't changing the cattle's range or burning pines off prickly pear for fodder or digging water wells or hunting, Matt and Quil, with Juanito stoutly helping, worked on adding a long room to the bachelor quarters.

If Lupe minded doing all the woman's work alone, she never said so. She was cheerful at mealtimes and on the long winter evenings when the men worked on horse gear or braided ropes she sat sewing or weaving on the handloom Quil had fashioned.

Her presence was a powerful reminder of Rachel's absence, the only thing lending softness and warmth to their angular male lives. Matt had always been aware of Lupe as a magnificent woman with a strong physical lure, and now the awareness was almost a fever sometimes when he longed for Rachel and needed a woman. Matt was thankful Juanito still shared her room.

One chill twilight, Matthew was hunting north of the meadow, riding into the pass with a mule deer behind his saddle when Storm shied at a shadow near the rocks.

"Who's that?" Matt called, for the shape was not an animal's—nor was it Rachel's, he decided after a heart-wrenching instant of hope. Too small. "Juanito?"

"Yes, Don Mateo."

"What're you doing out here with dark falling? Want to worry your mother?"

"I'll run very fast!" Juanito started up, but Matt scooped him into the saddle.

"Now, you young rascal! Where've you been?"

The boy hung his head, then threw it back and watched Matt with big eyes. "I've been to Tía Rachel!"

Matt felt as if a giant fist had struck him in the belly. He wet his lips, swallowing. "How is she?"

Juanito hesitated. Matt gave him a shake. "What's the matter? Is she sick?"

"No, Don Mateo. She's well."

"Is her house warm?"

"Very warm. There's a fireplace. Her door faces the morning sun and a window gets the evening light."

"Has she got plenty of food?"

"Don Santiago gets rabbits with a throwing stick or his sling. Sometimes they have fish, and Quil took beans and corn enough for the winter."

"Have you been there often?"

Juanito's thin body stiffened, but he spoke clearly. "I visit Tía Rachel each week, Don Mateo. And in the lambing season I've promised to help."

"Oh, have you? What about our cows who calve about the same time?"

"Cows can look after their calves. Ewes are stupid,

Don Mateo. Many must be forced to feed their kids."

"So why raise them?"

"For wool and meat," returned Juanito sagaciously. "Besides, I like to watch little lambs skip and dance and play! And I like the way the rams' big horns twist around their ears." As Matt absorbed this information, Juanito added firmly, "I like cattle, Don Mateo, but I also like sheep. When I grow up, I shall have both."

"Not in this meadow, you won't!" said Matt between laughter and vexation at this boy who was already more expert with the rope than he could ever be.

"Ay, Don Mateo," said Juanito, almost giggling, "somewhere on this river there'll be room for me— and my sheep and cattle!"

He sat in front of Matt, independent and yet trustful, little Comanche-Mexican, whose mother had hid him through a massacre and carried him through the desert to drink at the saving spring an old coyote had dug. He *was* this country.

I'm not the country, Matt thought. *But it's mine. Just as Rachel is.*

Surely by spring she'd know that, too, let him bring her home. Their years of separation, guilt, hurt and anger would heal, and they'd really begin to live.

Through the winter a black bull with a white stripe along the backbone and the great chest of his fighting ancestors, the best sire Don Celestino had sold Matthew, grazed by himself while the younger bulls fed companionably near each other. The steers scattered about, with their own kind or the cows, many of them heavy with calves they began to throw as rain and sun restored the grass, making it tall enough for easy feeding.

Tattered winter hair rubbed off on brush and rocks to show healthy bright coats of all colors. Young bulls explored around the heifers, but none was rash enough to challenge the crusty old lineback patriarch either for his sun-warmed private slope or any heifer he chose.

"There's not enough meat on him," Matt said to Quil as they sat looking over the herd. "I'm going to bring in a heavier sire if I can find one."

"They'll fight."

"May the best bull win," Matt retorted. "Hell, I won't get one of those fat-legged shorthorns that can't forage, but I want to breed up the beefiest thrifty stock there can be."

Quil frowned, shoving his hat back and rubbing the mark it left. "Where you going to sell this beef? There're cows all over Texas, anywhere there's graze. If you won't sell to the army, what will you do?"

"I'll drive them to a market."

"You've got one hell of a long drive comin'!"

"Maybe so. And it wouldn't be worth it with just our stock because of the time and having to hire hands. But if I went through Texas collecting cows other ranches wanted to sell, picking up hands to help as the herd grew, I ought to get a pretty fair lot of cattle up to Kansas where they'd ship to Chicago at a good profit."

"What's the difference selling beef to soldier Yanks or civilian Yanks, except several thousand miles and heaps of trouble?"

"It's the difference between maybe five dollars per head in Texas and fifty dollars up north. Anyhow, I don't know who's eating that Illinois beef, do I?"

"No, you can hope it all goes to an old ladies' home!" said Quil in disgust.

Matt grinned, slapping a hand on his friend's shoulder. "You want to hold your part of the cows out?"

"No," Quil grunted. "As long as we're partners, I'll go with your brainstorms!"

"Your cattle can, but not you, Quil. One of us has to stay here." Matt chuckled. "Next year you can go up the trail."

"I'll bet you next year neither of us goes." Quil looked over the long wide meadow and the herd of mixed black and Mexican cattle. "If we keep breeding up the stock, don't overgraze or overload our water, we ought to make out pretty well in the long run."

"Which I aim to shorten all I can!"

The two looked at each other, one burned brown and starting to gray, the son of plantation gentry, the other ebony warmed with copper, born of a slave and a dispossessed Indian.

"It's been four years since we started," Quil said. "We did lose the war time except for what the women saved, but don't get in a rush, Matt."

"We can't sit here till the world outside gets hungry and comes begging for beef!"

"I might," drawled Quil. But he laughed and Matt grinned back, turning at a distant sound.

"Riders!" Quil said, squinting toward the pass.

"Probably those vaqueros Don Celestino promised," Matt said. But both men loaded their guns before they whirled their horses to go meet the strangers.

Four vaqueros had come from Tres Coronas, eager to try their luck on the Texas side of the Rio, on the ranch of the legendary Norteño, Don Mateo, whose feat against the Comanches was still celebrated in *corridos* sung by campfires and on feast days.

Macedonia and Pancho Cruz were brothers in their mid-twenties, born to their saddles, tough and leather-skinned. Both had fought with Matt against the

Comanches. Paco, brother of Luz and the dead
Changa, looked and acted so much like the Monkey
one could almost believe they were the same person,
and Juanito stuck to him like a burr.

Guapo, the fourth man, seemed to have no other
name except this, describing his bold good looks. He
had reddish-blond hair which was thick and wavy,
green eyes and a peculiarly gentle voice. He was from
Chihuahua, and had not been long at Tres Coronas.

All four men knew their work. They settled quickly
into the completed bunkhouse, mooned after Lupe
and enjoyed her cooking. Although a castrating knife
wasn't used much on Tres Coronas, since Spanish
respect for virility extended to livestock, the men ex-
pertly cut the calves not selected for breeding, and
by the middle of May the hundred head of cattle
Matthew was driving were herded down near the pass,
marked with the brand all the stock now wore, a B
joined to a quill, for the partners' names.

"Not too late to try the army post," Quil remarked
the day they finished the gather.

"Yes, it is," said Matt. "We leave at daylight. I'll
sell below the Nueces for ten dollars, below the Red
for twenty-five dollars and the further I drive, the
higher the price climbs."

"Till you'll sell in Kansas or Missouri for whatever
you can damn well get!"

"Well, at least I'll know I couldn't have done better." They were near the pass, and Matt yielded to the
longing that had been building up during preparation
for the trail drive.

"Tell Lupe not to wait dinner on me," he called,
and turned Storm into the pass.

What would he say to Rachel? What would she say
to him? He tried a dozen things out in his mind, dis-
carding them all. He'd tell her he was going away and

ask her to stay in the meadow where she'd have more protection and company.

Or perhaps he wouldn't talk.

Matthew rode near enough the sheep scattered about the river bottom to see their dripping eyes and noses, their sad countenances. Damn sorry beasts! Only the lambs, some very young, all stiltily long-legged, were gay, leaping up the rocks, jumping down, challenging one another for the highest spots with playful butts of their small heads.

Santiago came over a crag and broke into a run, signaling, but Matt rode on to the small adobe, swung off his horse and strode to the door that faced the Sierra del Carmen and the Rio.

Rachel came to her feet, her belly so swollen he stared in shock, then flushed hotly.

"Are you well?" he asked, his lips stiff.

"I'm fine." Her skin was translucent, and she seemed much too small to carry her burden. But she wouldn't go to the meadow.

"Then I'll send Lupe to you." He felt angry, and helpless.

Rachel said politely, "I hope you make a safe journey and get a good price for your cattle."

"Damn the cattle! Rachel—"

"You don't mean that." She smiled faintly. "Good luck, Matt. When you get to a mail stage stop, could you send some silver to Tante Estelle? I want to pay her back what she loaned us, and I can now from the sheep."

"Sure, I'll do that. When I sell the cattle, I'll pay you back. That's my debt."

"Just so it's paid." She went to a chest, took out a leather pouch that clinked softly, and handed it to him.

There was so much between them, so much he couldn't say. "Take care of yourself," he growled and turned away before he packed her home by force.

That wouldn't work. For it to be any good she had to come of her own will.

Would she ever?

That night he asked Lupe to go to Rachel and stay until the baby came.

Past the Pecos, north along the old Butterfield stage route, stopping off at ranches to pick up cattle, mostly longhorns, as wild as deer, with horns hooking sharply forward with a spread of six, seven, even eight feet.

"I've been killing 'em for hides and tallow," one rawboned rancher told Matt. "If you can sell them for anything over twenty dollars, you're sure welcome to half of it."

He got to the Red River with three hundred head and three more hands, ranch boys spoiling to get away from home. If he swung west and missed the settled lands of the Five Civilized Tribes and other farmers, he'd be in Comanche country. East were outlaw gangs and more settlers along the Missouri and Arkansas borders. But from talk with ranchers and a few travelers, he decided to angle toward Missouri and sell the cattle the first chance he got, or at St. Joseph, if he had to drive that far.

In Indian Territory, Cherokees rode out to demand the toll they were entitled to collect for grazing herds passing through their lands. Matt couldn't pay the ten cents a head they asked, but he gave them four steers instead.

Just inside the Missouri border a sheriff arrested Matt, but when they went into town to see a judge about Matt's right to drive through the area, Matt suggested a friendly drink, and in a little over an hour both judge and sheriff were so blissfully drunk they didn't know or care when Matt left. He caught up with the herd, which his men, with Guapo as temporary trail boss, had started driving back into Indian territory as soon as Matt and the sheriff were out of sight.

After driving west a bit, they headed north into Kansas, crossed the Kaw, and got the herd to St. Joseph.

Guapo couldn't swim, and his horse scrambled out on the Missouri bank without him. Matt and the others went along the river throwing in limbs, the ends of their ropes, anything they thought Guapo might catch hold of. They were about to give up when a red head appeared downstream beneath some willows. In a minute, he walked up the shallow part, streaming water, puffing, but alive.

"How'd you do it?" Paco marveled.

"I walked on the bottom." Guapo spun the rowels of his silver spurs and slapped the water from his pants. "This stuff was heavy enough to weight me on the river bed, so I just held my breath and walked."

"It was the devil tugging at your ankles," Paco laughed.

They reached St. Joseph with two hundred and eighty cows. Matt sold them for shipment to Illinois at forty dollars a head.

After paying off the three young hands and turning over twenty dollars a head to the ranchers who'd trailed cattle with him, Matthew sent Guapo and the other vaqueros home while he went hunting the bulls and cows to put beef on his herd.

After expenses, he'd cleared seven thousand dollars on that drive. He was prepared to spend every dime of his share on the right stock to develop the kind of cows to command a market when scrub cattle weren't worth shooting. He talked to local cattle dealers and left Storm at a livery stable while, prepared with the names of several Durham breeders, he took a train to Kentucky.

He shipped fifteen bulls and seven cows to San Antonio, went back to Missouri for his big gray horse, and collected his Durhams in San Antonio. Compared to longhorns, Spanish or Mexican cattle, the Durhams were amiable creatures, easy to drive so long as they weren't pushed. Matthew hired two young brothers, Cal and Wes Biggs, to help get the purebred stock back to the meadow. They drove the Durhams into the long valley one noon in early fall.

Matthew rode ahead, hoping crazily that Rachel would be at the house. She was well, Lupe told him, and had beautiful twins, a boy and girl born in June. Matt forced her from his thoughts to concentrate on getting his herd settled.

He wasn't about to let tough native cattle walk or gore prize Durhams to death. They'd kept the best cows for breeding, and the pick of these were held in the home meadow, along with the Durham bulls and cows. The other select cows were taken to one of the outside pastures along with the best native bulls.

"We need the toughness of the Spanish, Mexican and longhorn breeds along with the meat of the prize stock," Matt told Quil. "One of these days a railroad will come close enough so cattle won't walk off their beef on the way to market."

"But for now we can't raise more meat than can walk itself," grinned Quil. He gazed at the Durhams, so short-legged and broad compared to the native bunch. "I know it's the way to improve a herd, but I guess I'll always like the ornery old stuff better—the ones that rustle for themselves, go without water, and fight lions and coyotes off their young."

"We'll always have their blood around," said Matt.

"The Big Bend won't ever shelter stock that can't forage and shift for itself to some measure. And even if it could," he added softly, "I wouldn't want it to."

He thought of Rachel and was consumed with longing. That afternoon he rode to the river. He had the excuse of returning the money he'd sent Tante Estelle.

She was nursing one child while the other slept in a cradle. Matt stooped to enter the door and stood awkwardly watching the tiny thing in his wife's arms. Both babies had a fluff of soft dark hair, tiny perfect fingers, long eyelashes and fragile-looking necks.

"This is Jonathan." She smiled at the infant against her smooth full breast who set his fists against her and tugged at the nipple like a puppy. "Melissa's asleep."

The twins didn't look like anyone but her. "They're quite a pair," Matt ventured. They scared him silly. He'd probably drop one or break its bones if he tried to hold it, but weren't they *something*? "Why don't we take them home?"

"I hear you made a good sale and bought some blooded Durhams," she remarked.

"Yes." He couldn't help sounding a little proud. "Mixed with the best of our native cattle, they ought to improve the herd a lot." He dropped a bag of silver on a chest. "This is for what you sent Tante."

And because he was nervous he went on talking about the Durhams until the little girl woke up and Rachel put the boy in his cradle while she soothed his sister with soft loving little sounds that melted Matt's loins, made him hunger for the feel and sweetness of this woman who seemed completely absorbed in her children.

Matt felt useless, unwanted, a big lanky intruder. "Are you ready to come home?" he asked gruffly when it grew clear she wasn't going to have any real words or smiles or looks for him, that her attention was focused on whichever baby seemed to need her at the moment. Hell, *he* might as well have been Santiago!

She glanced at him and if she wasn't surprised, she gave a good imitation. "I *am* home, Matt."

"You're joking! This sheep camp?"

"It's mine."

"So's the meadow. Don't be a fool, Rachel! I've got some dandy stock. In a few years we'll really have something to be proud of!"

"I'm proud of my babies!" She had one in either arm now.

"You're my wife. I can make you come."

Her eyes flashed, and she stared at him over the soft little heads like a cornered mother animal. "You can't make me stay. Unless you chain me up, and then I wouldn't be much use, would I?"

Swearing, he spun away, bumping his head on the door. "When are you going to get rid of this nonsense?" he blazed.

"I think you were gone three years."

"Three years!" Matt shouted. "Listen, what am I supposed to do?"

"Changa went to Ojinaga whores," she said.

Maddened, he swung into the saddle before he lost all control and did things they'd neither ever forget.

He rode to Ojinaga, he did buy a whore and he was still drunk when Quil found him and brought him home.

Lupe and Quil got him sober, but craziness had settled into him. He had to either binge or go to the river and throw that proud bitch of a wife on her back, take her hating since she didn't want him loving. Even crazy, he knew that would be the real finish of them, so he always managed to head for Ojinaga.

Three more times Quil dragged him out of stinking rooms. Three more times Matt's friends worked to get him over a gutful of raw tequila and rawer women. After the last bout, once he could sit up and drink black coffee, Lupe came to him and took his face in her hands.

"Mateo, don't do this again. When you need a woman, I can come to you."

She pressed his head against her full warm breasts, stroking his hair as if he were Juanito. Matt tried to sit erect and rebuke her with silence, but the sweetness of her woman's body triggered some irresistible need, and he clasped his arms around her, crying for the first time in all his life as a man.

Somehow he got through that winter, the second without Rachel. Lupe shared his bed whenever he seemed restless, which made him ashamed, for he was never with her in his heart, only with his body, and Lupe deserved better than that, even had she not been one of the builders of the meadow, the first of them to find the pass into the long valley.

One night when Matt couldn't sleep, he got up, hoping to rouse Lupe without waking Juanito. As he started to open his door, he heard voices.

Lupe and Quil arguing?

Matt stopped and put his ear to the door. "Sure, Matt's my friend!" Quil was saying. "But I love you! Do you have any idea what it does to me when you go to him?"

"Quil!"

"Maybe I ought to get drunk and whore around so you'd feel for me." There was a sound of struggle and when Quil spoke, his voice sounded heavy, drugged.

"You wouldn't marry me, woman. You said you were afraid because of that Comanche. Is it that all the time you've wanted Matt?"

Hot and cold, Matt listened. How blind he'd been! Selfish, a fool! Too bound up in his misery to pay attention to his friends.

"I love you, Quil!" Lupe was sobbing. "But I *was* afraid. And then Mateo—"

Another silence. "Matt'll have to get his own woman back or find another!" Quil growled. "We're going to start out tomorrow to find a priest or a preacher and we aren't coming back until we're married."

Straightening, Matt grinned in the darkness. Good for Quil! When he'd finally laid it on the line, he'd done a bang-up job of it! Glad he wouldn't have to pull any heroics to unite the lovers, Matt went back to bed.

Next morning he acted properly surprised and congratulatory when Quil announced the marriage plans. They went off, leaving Juanito with Matt, found a priest at Ojinaga and were back in four days, man and wife.

For Matt the only woman seemed to be Rachel. He could not lock her from his thoughts. Even swollen with what might be another man's child, even holding the twins, her face so thin the bones looked sharp, she was beautiful and necessary to him in a way no other woman could ever be. Sometimes he almost started over to drag her home, but he knew she'd never forgive that.

The winter passed, and spring, with a fair calf crop. They culled the herd again and Matt left with the vaqueros, intending to pick up cattle on the way north as he'd done so successfully the summer before.

But it was a cholera year. He found that out before he got halfway out of Texas. And he heard that a man named McCoy had established a railhead promising fair prices at Abilene, Kansas, but the first shipment of longhorns had sold poorly in Chicago and the second lot found no buyer at all and had to be shipped to Albany, New York. A depression in the East had thrown thousands out of work, and people just couldn't afford meat.

The two Cruz brothers came down with cholera and died. Shorthanded, with the northern market radically reduced, Matt took a hard-eyed look at the situation and decided to follow the advice of several returning drovers who'd lost their shirts trying to sell across the Red River. When they couldn't sell their cattle, some ranchers had set up slaughtering sheds and pens along the Gulf Coast and were selling hides and tallow. The slaughterers weren't paying much, but it was better than nothing.

Matt didn't want to take the cattle back to the meadow. They'd use grass needed for better stock, and besides they'd been exposed to diseases along the trail.

No market. Can't give 'em away. Well, what could you expect with General U. S. Grant, late of the Union Army, as President?

Next morning they swung east across rolling plains clumped with live oak and cedar, keeping north of the hill country till it sloped into the coastal plains. On the way they passed outfits chasing wild cattle out of the brush, killing them on the spot for their hides. Some of the skinners took branded cattle, too, and Matt kept a closer night guard than ever he had when trailing through Comanche country.

When they first caught a gleam of the Gulf, Matt rode ahead to find a buyer. The first two packeries he came to were small affairs—a slaughter shed and pens amid a jumble of pulleys and vats.

"Hell, no, I don't want more cows," said the owner of one plant, pausing over a carcass with a butcher knife in his hand, brushing off swarming flies. "I'm sellin' salted tongues at ten dollars the barrel and prime beef at nine dollars for two hundred pounds. Goin' broke! When I fill the contract I'm on now, I'm closin' down here and headin' back to the brush where I can make more just skinnin' cows and leavin' the carcasses."

Matt struggled against hot nausea. The smell of offal, rendering meat and drying hides was worse than anything he'd ever smelled on a battlefield. As he started to turn away, the packer paused long enough to call after him.

"Try your luck in Rockport. Some big plants down there cornered the New Orleans market. And say, if you'd like a wagon of choice loin steaks for your outfit you can have 'em just for haulin' them off. Hate to throw such good meat to the damn catfish!"

"Thanks," said Matt. "May take you up on that!" Right then he didn't think he'd ever feel like eating beef again.

He could smell Rockport long before he saw the sullen glint of the bay or could figure out what formed the hill where thousands of birds gorged. As he got closer to this mountain, he could scarcely believe his nose and eyes. It was a huge mound of rotting flesh and bone, a giant heap so alive with predators from maggots to dogs that the loathsome pile shimmered with movement.

Matt rode by as fast as he could, but there was no escaping the smell. Packeries spread along the bay. Boys were catching fish from the teeming swarms devouring waste from the plants which was dumped into the water.

A cattleman knew his animals were for beef, and though he'd fight to protect them, put his own life between them and blizzards, floods, rustlers or lions, his ultimate aim was to supply good strong meat. Matt liked to think his cattle were building bone and muscle and strength in hundreds of people he'd never see.

It sickened him to see beef rotting, turned from nourishment into pollution. Yet what could be done with it? What could he do with his own herd? Turn them loose to scatter in the brush? Many would still wind up in these packeries or be slaughtered for hides. He couldn't take them back to the meadow where there already grazed the maximum number of cattle that could be kept in reasonable shape through the winter.

Matt set his shoulders and stopped at the largest packery. Its pens were full, but three slaughter sheds were in use, and at least his beef might not be tossed into the bay, because hundreds of barrels were being filled with tongues, portions of meat and salt brine. It looked like enough mess beef here to feed every army in the world.

A wagon load of barrels was driven off toward the docks as the shirtless man who'd been taking inventory stuffed his record book into his hip pocket and turned to Matt—with a look of impatience which changed to shock.

"Matt! By God, is it really you?"

It was like glimpsing a familiar face in a wavy mirror, the angles blurring, softening. Tom had always been a little pudgy; now his adolescent fat had hardened into sinewy bulges beneath his ribs which made his shoulders appear bull-like.

Matt stared at this burly man with yellow hair and sideburns, the younger brother Matt hadn't seen since he'd gone off to West Point, though Tom had tried to get him lynched after Harry's death. Tom had raped Rachel, too, but it was all ages ago, a lost war and a world ago, so Matt stared at this younger brother he should feel like killing and felt nothing but dull surprise.

"Well, Tom—" Matt broke off, shrugging. "I don't know what to say."

"I'll say it," retorted the other, taking his shirt off a rail and buttoning it up. "Harry's dead. The war's over. You and I are alive and kicking! Let's have a drink!"

In a saloon permeated with the smell of the packeries, Tom called for glasses and a bottle, tossed down two shots right away, rubbed off his mouth with his arm and grinned at Matt.

"So here we are! Looking for a job?"

"I've got a herd to sell."

The bright blue eyes dug into Matt, revealing a shrewd mind in spite of the jolly exterior. "Reckon I could take up to a couple hundred, but prices are low. Can't raise 'em, even for my brother."

"Just so you don't lower them," Matt said. "How'd you get into this business?"

"Oh, I got into meat packing up at Gloryoak before the war. Kept it going one way and another even under Reconstruction, and when cattle got cheap enough to kill for hides and tallow, it was natural to open a packery down here."

"It must be paying."

"You bet! I slaughtered ten thousand head last year, and their hides made up part of the three hundred thousand hides that went out of Rockport and Corpus. Rawhide's being used on ships now, and that's helped the market. There's always a need for tallow." Tom laughed, clasping his thickly haired hands. "These prices on cattle can't last forever, but while they do, I'm making a killing!" He poured Matt another drink.

"Sorry my good luck's your bad news, Matt. Still, you can have a job with me anytime."

"Thanks, but I've got a ranch to run."

Tom squinted quizzically. "So that's what you're doing. Where are you?"

"West Texas," Matt said, not caring to let Tom know exactly.

Tom raised his eyebrows and touched his lower lip with a slightly pointed tongue. "And Rachel? Does she flourish in your Eden at the end of the earth?"

"I'm surprised you've got the nerve to ask."

Tom chuckled, taking out his pocketknife and toying with the blade. "Funny about nerve. I don't see how a man can cause his brother's death and take his wife and forget it. Was she worth it?"

Matt couldn't speak.

Tom pushed down the blade, thrust it back in his pocket. "How many cattle you got?"

"About two hundred head."

"That'll keep my plant running three-four days. Mixed quality?"

"I sure didn't bring my best breeding stock!"

"Well, if they walked this far, they're worth seven dollars a head."

"Make it ten."

"Hell, I may lose money at seven! Wouldn't give more than five to anyone else."

It was a ruinous price, but a price. Tom waved a hand toward the coast. "Try to do better if you want. You won't hurt my feelings!"

Matt got up. "You can't blame a man for trying!"

One large packer was processing his own scrub cattle and *mesteños* his men rounded up. Two weren't bothering with meat and would pay only hide-and-tallow figures.

That kind of slaughter seemed downright wicked to

Matt. To take animal life to feed human beings was part of things unless you were a Hindu or such, but wasting meat seemed outrageous. This whole coast swam in refuse that should have been food for thousands.

No packery could better Tom's offer, so gritting his teeth, Matt went back to make the deal.

"I thought you would," smiled Tom, ticking off another wagon of salt beef. "But the price is down to six. Drops fifty cents an hour."

"But—"

Tom's eyes were chilling, bluff good nature congealed like the fat on his midriff. "It doesn't pay to buck me, Matt." He glanced at the afternoon sun. "If you wait till sundown, that six dollars a head drops to nothing."

Matt almost wheeled without a word, but that wouldn't put money in his pocket. "Two hundred head at six dollars," he said, and rode off.

When the cattle were penned, Tom counted the money slowly, as if it pleased him to know his brother needed even a poor sum for these creatures whose raising was his life.

"There you are, Matt. Glad to help you out. If you go bust on cattle, I can always find some kind of job for you."

"Reckon if it comes to that I'll find something closer to home," said Matt.

Home would never be back at Gloryoak, but was the heart of the Chisos in the deep bend of the Rio.

"Why don't you have dinner and stay the night with me?" Tom drawled. "Catch up on old times."

"I'd rather start some new ones," Matt said. He didn't offer to shake hands.

Finding Paco and Guapo, he rode away, sick in body and spirit, from the stinking pens and flesh piles.

None of them felt like eating much that night. They still seemed to smell that wretched putrefaction.

Rachel could really brag about her sheep now. Matt was exhausted, but the pitiful sale of his cattle and seeing Tom again had him harrowed up, and he wasn't asleep when he heard a stealthy sound.

Instantly alert, he rolled to one side as something struck his head a glancing blow. He reached for his gun, but a boot stomped down on his hand, and this time whatever clubbed him didn't miss.

He awoke with a sour blood taste in his dry mouth, and a splitting headache. He found himself at the bottom of a sprawl of arms and legs. Disentangling himself, he crawled free of his vaqueros' bodies.

Paco had died fast, a knife across his throat, but Guapo's face was set in a scream. His hands had been chopped off before someone finished him.

Why?

Matt looked dazedly around, limped to his saddlebags. The money was gone. So was his gun, and the horses had been stolen or wandered off. Storm would have to have been stolen or he'd be here. Staring at his dead men, Matt gagged. He had no shovel but he dragged them to a little arroyo and tossed rocks over them.

Poor Mamacita had lost another son. Matt shook his head over Guapo's mutilation. Maybe the robbers thought he knew where there was more money. And they must have thought Matt was dead.

He might still be. There was no water and he was on foot and shaky. Not many houses around here, or travelers, either.

Matt started walking.

XX

Spring had always been the start of a year for Rachel, and living near the sheep made that more than ever true. When giant Spanish daggers burst into massive white bloom across the flats, when tiny wildflowers blossomed, ocotillo blazed red and the creosote's shiny green leaves sparkled against dainty yellow flowers, it was time for lambs to drop.

Even last year, when she had been heavy with the twins, Rachel had helped with lambing. Juanito had stayed with her for that period, and it was astonishing how deftly the boy could grasp a lamb who was having trouble being born and guide it to birth. He knew almost as well as Santiago how to guard the newborn from eagles, coyotes and buzzards, and how to put a ewe in a chute so she would have to let her lamb feed instead of blocking it by turning around.

Ewes often had twins, and Juanito would take one of these and tie the skin of a dead lamb around it.

Thus disguised, the twin was brought to the bereaved mother who sniffed the familiar scent around her dead lamb's tail and usually adopted it. In a few days the deceiving hide could be removed. It was important to take great care not to mix the lambs or herd them so close their odors got confused, since if this happened their mothers would reject them.

For several weeks, until all the lambs were dropped and properly owned by ewes, Rachel, Santiago and Juanito scarcely slept, but then the summer stretched peacefully as the lambs grew and played until the shearing some weeks later. That was when sheep lost their fleeces and looked gaunt and nicked for weeks afterward. Five or six men came in a cart, loaded with supplies, from Tres Coronas. The sheep were penned that night in the corral of cholla and ocotilo. Next morning Santiago and Juanito shooed sheep into a small pen with a platform while each shearer held down his sheep with a knee while forcing up its head with one arm and clipping away in long swift strokes, while the fleece, joined by its massed hairs, fell away like a garment, crusty, oily dark-gray on top with rich creaminess beneath.

As a shearer finished, Juanito ran up with a pot of creosote to daub on any cuts. If there were many nicks, he derided the shearer. Juanito was very careful with this chore. The tiniest untreated cut could harbor a blowfly. When its eggs hatched, a small nick would become a mass of worms feeding on flesh and working deep, so in spite of the impatience of some shearers to get on to the next animal, Juanito made sure each was thoroughly treated before shoving it through a chute leading outside where it huddled with other shorn creatures.

Rachel, at the platform, would fold the fleece and stuff it into one of the big bags by the cart, trampling on it to pack it down. Some shearers could do a hundred sheep in a long day broken by good solid meals of beans, tortillas and mutton.

Within three or four days the job was done. The shearers took the fleece-laden cart back to Tres Coronas, from where, within the week, a man would come with silver in a leather pouch, often bringing in his saddlebags small things Rachel needed.

The twins had been born a few weeks after the shearing last year. With Lupe's help, the delivery hadn't been too difficult, but it had seemed unending because several hours passed between Melissa's birth and Jonathan's. When Jonathan was breathing in the outside world, Lupe placed him against Rachel, who was floating free and exhausted, marveling at her daughter.

"A boy and a girl," Lupe smiled. "They are perfect!"

She hadn't asked questions or argued with Rachel about returning to the meadow, but a few weeks later when she was going herself, she held the twins and gazed at Rachel above their tiny heads.

"Mateo would be so happy to find them in his house when he comes home."

Rachel shook her head. "I can't bring them, Lupe, until I'm sure."

"Sure of what?"

Sure that he really wants them. That he won't wonder who fathered them and come to begrudge their lives. And sure that in spite of everything he still loves me as I love him.

Rachel shrugged. Impossible to say everything she thought, and even that was only a small part of what she felt. She must not go back to Matt until they had both put everything behind them.

She'd been so happy last fall when Matt had ridden

up, stared at her with those eyes that always turned
her weak, full of need for him. But the sight of the
babies had seemed to burn him. He'd acted terrified
she might offer to let him hold them, and instead of
talking about them he'd launched into a long account
of his damned cattle and those Durhams he'd chased
to Kentucky instead of coming right back after the
trail drive to see how she was. No doubt if she'd died
in labor he could have consoled himself by adding a
few more prize cows to his stock!

It had been a lonely winter, but the twins had taken
a lot of time and were endlessly beguiling as they
constantly changed and did new things. Rachel's heart
hurt that it was Juanito or Santiago who watched
Melissa and Jonathan crawl, stand, take their first
steps. Wouldn't Matt have *had* to love them, be proud
of them, if he'd seen them? But he never came. And
this summer he'd gone on another trail drive.

Rachel blinked back tears as she wondered if he'd
ever come again, if he'd accept her children so she
could consider him their father. She didn't know, even
now that they were past their first year, which man
had given them to her, for they looked very much like
her. She took them about her chores in a twin leather
back-cradle Santiago had designed for her, but they
were by now so heavy Rachel was glad they could
walk a little.

The twins often napped on a serape, watched by
one of the sheep dogs, who seemed to regard them as
a strange kind of lamb.

Every evening Rachel put crumbs of food on a flat
stone near the house and held the children while small
birds came to feed, yellow-rumped warblers and their
trilling *ssit!*, all kinds of wrens, including some with
white throats, horned larks, mockingbirds, meadow-

larks and blackbirds. A *paisano* came by their house each morning for scraps, and Jonathan especially adored this long-legged bird with its rudder tail, crested head, and shrill cry of *koo-koo-kook!* He mimicked it and the plaintive call of the mourning dove. Both children waved to the cliff swallows nesting along the banks of the Rio Grande, or waded toward sandpipers on the sandbar.

There were so many birds! The timid Inca dove with its scalelike feathers, the whitewing and blue quail. Sometimes they could glimpse a great blue heron in the river. Best of all, there was a new pair of eagles on the cliff that seemed to glide in joyous power and sheer love of the high blue sky, except when their young kept them ceaselessly on the hunt for food. Owls, too, hunted, and hawks, and once Rachel hid with her body the sight of a shrike impaling a field mouse on the spike of a yucca.

The world of the twins held flowers, bright birds, as well as those who blended with the earth, the dull sheen of a green or black rattler, or pepper-and-salt pattern of a diamondback, with his black-and-white ringed tail, horned toads that buried themselves in sand at night to dig out for morning warmth, deer grazing in the flats, big and small sheep, Lady and the different horses Juanito rode, beavers making dams, coons, skunks, rabbits, field mice, squirrels, herds of javelina, yellow-gray coyotes and their night songs.

At night they watched the Big Dipper make its slow swing around the pole star and listened to the muted distant sounds of furred and feathered night hunters, an occasional alarm from the dogs.

Up to now the twins' lives were full with discovery and their own rapid development, but before long they'd enjoy a father's knee to clamber on, his long legs to trot after.

Matt! Rachel thought one summer afternoon as she played with the twins. *Please come soon! And look at the children; let me know if you can love them.*

Melissa was touching flowers, patting their leaves and petals as if they were skin, while Jonathan fingered dandelion wisps and thistle pods with great intentness, laughing when Rachel blew them away.

The dogs began to bark, facing the pass through the mountains. Juanito? He'd just been here yesterday. Anyway the horseman was a full-grown man, and Rachel didn't recognize the horse.

Matt? There might be some reason he wasn't on Storm. But the rider was thick through the body, lacking Matt's grace. Yet there was something, something disturbingly familiar—Rachel sprang to her feet, told the twins to stay where they were, and hurried toward Santiago, who, quieting the dogs, was moving toward the stranger.

"I don't like being barked at," called the horseman. "Keep those damn dogs quiet or I will." He pulled a rifle out of the scabbard and tilted back his slouch hat, and Rachel knew who he was.

Seven years had given him a gross hardness, had coarsened his form and face, but the blue eyes still had the innocent wideness of a child's, the same unnerving clarity as they went over her, flicked the twins who'd scrambled over to hang onto her skirts.

"So, Rachel." He tilted his head critically. "A bit thin and savage but still worth my trouble. You've always been my trouble, darling. The way I hunted for you when you broke Matt out and got away—well, it was comic with women eager and close to hand. I finally gave you up for dead, but then who should ride up to my packery but Matt!"

"Matt?" Rachel whispered.

"He didn't care to talk about you and wouldn't say

where you were, but one of his vaqueros did after losing his hands."

"You—didn't hurt Matt?"

"Doesn't hurt to die in your sleep. I'd like to have let him know first that I meant to follow his and Harry's examples and take you for my woman, but Matt's pretty tough. Neater to kill him where he lay."

Matt dead? Rachel couldn't believe it. When he came back from the war, even after their bitter quarrels, she'd believed there'd come a time when they could be together. When it happened this time, it had to be forever. That was why she'd been so watchful of him with the twins. But deep in the core of her being, she knew Matt was her man.

"You—you're lying!" she panted.

Tom arched his eyebrows. "Well, I should have brought you his head, my dear. Surely you don't think I'd be crazy enough to come for you with Matt still in the world?"

"You're crazy to think I'll come with you."

He smiled, his merry eyes touching the twins. "Now, Rachel, you'll do anything I say for two very good reasons—Melissa and Jonathan. You can kiss them sweetly and tell this old ruffian to look after them, or they can all be dead in five minutes, even the dogs. And you'll still come with me."

Frozen, she shielded the twins, hating Tom so ferociously she felt consumed. He stroked his rifle.

"Hurry," he said.

Santiago frowned. "What is it, my lady? I do not like this man!"

"He brings news of Don Mateo," Rachel said.

"I understand Mex," warned Tom.

"Please take care of the children until I get back," Rachel said, battling horror, trying not to collapse or break down. If she did, Tom might destroy her children and Santiago with no more qualms than if they'd been game.

"Tell him to saddle your horse," Tom instructed. "I guess that old mare's good for a trip back to Gloryoak. If you want to take anything with you, get it together."

She thought of begging to take the twins but stifled the plea. Best not expose them to his erratic temper. Besides, if they were safe here, and later she could get away—

Mechanically, Rachel gave Santiago instructions and moved toward the stone house followed by Tom. "Don't pick up a knife or try anything like that," he advised. "My horse could easily squash in your babies' heads." He watched her while she got her brush and comb, an extra dress. "Don't have much, do you?" he said. "I'll get a dressmaker to stay at Gloryoak and get you outfitted."

Santiago brought Lady, tied Rachel's small bundle back of her saddle. "I will watch the children," he promised. "I hope you will be back soon, Doña Rachel. Perhaps Don Quil could accompany you?"

"This man is Don Mateo's brother," Rachel explained, bitterly amused at Santiago's obvious relief. "Thousand thanks, my friend. Guard my little ones." She pressed his hand, hugged and kissed the twins and, evading Tom, swung into the saddle, hooking her leg over the horn. Santiago picked up the twins, who began to wail. Rachel had never left them.

"Take them to the river to play!" she called to the old shepherd.

He nodded and bore them off. Diverted by the promise of a water frolic with Santiago, they stopped crying. "In a week they'll have forgotten you," Tom said.

Rachel ignored that. "How did you get past the house in the meadow?"

"I *took* the house." At her shocked look, he grinned boastfully. "From what I got out of the vaquero there was only Matt's black partner and a woman and kid at the ranch. The four guys I had with me were enough to handle that. We rode in this morning before they were up."

Fear for her friends turned Rachel dizzy. Dear God, how could creatures like Tom roam the country, doing what they pleased? Savoring her dread, Tom waited a moment.

"The black's all right unless he got too feisty again and the boys decided to do a little cuttin'. That woman's a looker! Would have had her myself but I was saving it all for you."

"You've got no reason to hurt them!"

"No reason not to, either," He shrugged. "Don't worry. If they—and you—behave, I'll just leave a couple of the boys to watch 'em a few days till we're long gone, and there won't be nothing wrong with them a little time won't cure. But I'll remember where they are. You ever try to get away and you can count on my making a clean sweep of everyone in this valley, starting with your twins." His gaze raked her. "Shall I have you now or wait to tumble you in Matt's bed?"

She'd never endure him long. She'd kill him or herself. But she had to last until they were far away from here and there was a way to make sure he couldn't send thugs to the meadow and river before he died.

"Is Tante Estelle at Gloryoak?" she asked.

"Think she'd help you?" Tom laughed softly. "Well, maybe she would. But she picked up typhus nursing during the war. I kept the silver Matt sent her. And Selah went off to fight for the North, and you can bet he'll never dare show me his face again! Too bad," he mocked. "Out of all those pickaninnies you taught, you could think a few would still be around to give you aid and comfort, but they're not, my dear. Harry's will freed all the slaves who hadn't already bought their liberty, and I turned 'em all off, the whole damn boiling! Bought a new lot of hands and got a good overseer."

"Must be hard for you, Tom, now that you can't own men!"

"Near enough I can."

"I thought most plantations were ruined by the war."

"Most were. But I saw how things were going and made a few useful Yankee friends. Gloryoak had some lean times, but now I've bought Belleforest and another place. I've had to hustle and scheme like hell, but I would reckon I'm the richest man in the county, maybe in all of East Texas."

Did he expect her to care? Rachel said nothing.

As if stung by her silence, Tom rode close, brutally closed his hand about her breast. He laughed at her involuntary cry. "I don't know why you've stayed in my blood, Rachel. Must be a fatal addiction I share with my brothers, though thank God I didn't take after them in other ways."

"I hate you. I always will."

"Good. Then you'll never bore me." He stroked her waist and thigh. "You set me on fire! But I'll wait a couple of hours to take you in Matt's bed. In my own way I'm a sentimentalist."

They were at a narrow stretch of the pass. Tom motioned for Rachel to go in front. She had just passed a side canyon obscured by trees and boulders when there was commotion behind her and a voice called "Tom!"

She knew that voice. Whirling, afraid she was imagining things, Rachel's heart swelled as Matt edged his gray stallion between her and his brother.

"Ride on!" Matt ordered her in the second that Tom raised his rifle.

Matt's gun, already out, barked a second before Tom's shot crashed upward against the cliff, broke off rock that skittered down the pass. Tom straightened, stared as if amazed, then pitched from the saddle. When Matt bent over him, he was dead.

Rachel didn't remember scrambling down from Lady or how she got in Matt's arms. She only knew she was there and he was alive and they were back together, his mouth claiming hers, his arms holding her as if he'd never let her go.

"Lupe and Quil?" she asked breathlessly. They were both shaking as if in a storm.

"They're fine. I'll tell you later."

He carried her up the canyon and made love to her there, purging away years of separation, other passions, other loves, so that they came back fresh to each other, trembling, awed, renewed. Hearing the steady comforting rhythm of his heart, Rachel felt utterly at peace, but he sat up, dropping a kiss on her eyes.

"Stay here until I call, sweetheart. And then we'll go get our twins."

She thought Tom must be buried under a heap of rock a little way up the pass. Matt unsaddled Tom's horse and let it loose but it followed them as they rode toward the river.

"Tom said you were dead!" Rachel burst out.

"I'm sure he thought so," Matt said drily. "It must have taken me a day or so to come around from the blow I got on my head. If I hadn't been protected from the sun by my men's bodies, I probably would have died without ever coming to." He explained how he found Storm and the vaqueros' horses at a watering place cattle had scooped out in a dry streambed. Weaponless, without money or food, he'd been lucky to come upon the farm of a German settler who fed him and gave him supplies for the journey.

"I'm going to give Friedrich one of my best Durham bulls," Matt vowed. "I'm not sure I could have made it without his bread and sausage, at least not soon enough to catch Tom."

"The four men at the house?" Rachel asked.

"I didn't know how many there were, but I'd picked up their tracks and knew Tom wasn't by himself. So I used an old trick. Not very elegant, but I hid in the outhouse. The first man had a knife around his neck, so I took that, which made it simpler to take care of the second who came out. The place was crowded by then, so I worked around to the back of the house and came in a window. I could hear Tom's men in the kitchen. They were making Lupe cook while they told Quil all the good times they had planned before Tom came back with you. The door creaked when I opened it, but Lupe branded one with a hot skillet and Quil, who was tied up, managed to lunge into the other bastard and spoil his aim. Quil finished them off when I cut him loose."

"Lupe's not—hurt?"

"She'll get over it. Juanito didn't see much of what went on. They tied him up and stuck him in the bunkhouse." Rachel shuddered, thinking for a horrible moment of what might have been.

The twins tumbled out of Santiago's hut and the dogs started barking, though they stopped at Rachel's voice.

Santiago followed, crossing himself, laughing as he greeted Matt, begging to know if Rachel was well while the twins stared round-eyed at the tall stranger who dropped to his knees and gathered them in a hug along with their mother.

"I'm your daddy," he said huskily. "And I'm going to take you home!"

There was a shrill whoop from up the pass. In a few minutes, Quil rode toward them, Juanito clinging behind him like a burr while Lupe, not used to riding, was just coming in view.

There by the river the companions met with embraces, laughter and tears. The sun was low by the time questions had been asked and answered, the twins had been sufficiently admired and Matt had made clear that his family was moving to the meadow.

"But for tonight," said Rachel, "won't you be my guests? There are enough mats and blankets for everyone, and Santiago barbecued a lamb last night that broke its neck in a fall."

"Lamb!" groaned Matt.

"It saves killing one of your calves," Rachel pointed out.

"Doggone it, that's right!" Matt conceded. He swept her close while the eagles screamed from the river.